Other Books in The Vintage Library
of Contemporary World Literature

SHAME

SHAME

SALMAN RUSHDIE

AVENTURA

The Vintage Library of Contemporary World Literature

VINTAGE BOOKS   A DIVISION OF RANDOM HOUSE   NEW YORK

First Aventura Edition, September 1984

Copyright © 1983 by Salman Rushdie

All rights reserved under International and
Pan-American Copyright Conventions. Published in
the United States by Random House, Inc., New York.
Originally published in Great Britain by Jonathan Cape
Ltd., London, and in the United States by Alfred A.
Knopf, Inc., in 1983.

Library of Congress Cataloging in Publication Data

Rushdie, Salman.

Shame.

(Aventura)

I. Title.

[PR9499.3.R8S5 1984]   823   84-40223

ISBN 0-394-72665-0 (pbk.)

Manufactured in the United States of America

For Sameen

CONTENTS

SHAME

IV

IN THE FIFTEENTH CENTURY

V

JUDGMENT DAY

Acknowledgments

GENEALOGY

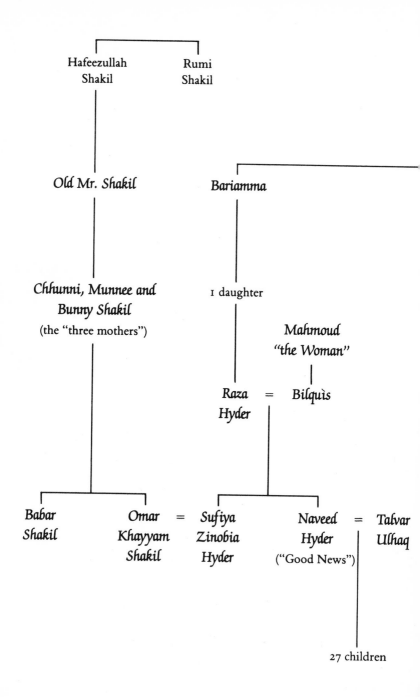

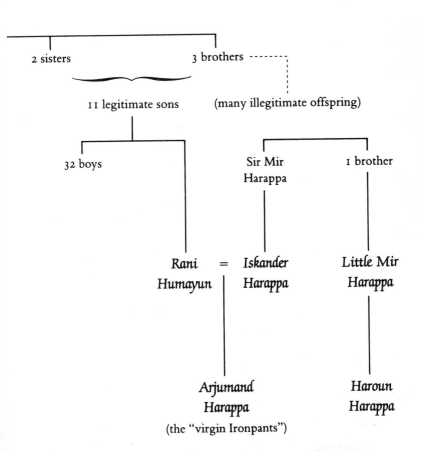

2 sisters   3 brothers - - - - - - - -

11 legitimate sons   (many illegitimate offspring)

32 boys   Sir Mir Harappa   1 brother

Rani Humayun = Iskander Harappa   Little Mir Harappa

Arjumand Harappa
(the "virgin Ironpants")   Haroun Harappa

I

ESCAPES
FROM
THE MOTHER
COUNTRY

1
———

THE
DUMB-WAITER

*I*n the remote border town of Q., which when seen from the
air resembles nothing so much as an ill-proportioned dumb-
bell, there once lived three lovely, and loving, sisters. Their
names . . . but their real names were never used, like the best
household china, which was locked away after the night of their
joint tragedy in a cupboard whose location was eventually forgotten, so that the great thousand-piece service from the Gardner
potteries in Tsarist Russia became a family myth in whose fac-
tuality they almost ceased to believe . . . the three sisters, I should
state without further delay, bore the family name of Shakil, and
were universally known (in descending order of age) as Chhunni,
Munnee and Bunny.

And one day their father died.

Old Mr. Shakil, at the time of his death a widower for eighteen
years, had developed the habit of referring to the town in which
he lived as "a hell hole." During his last delirium he embarked
on a ceaseless and largely incomprehensible monologue amidst
whose turbid peregrinations the household servants could make

out long passages of obscenity, oaths and curses of a ferocity that made the air boil violently around his bed. In this peroration the embittered old recluse rehearsed his lifelong hatred for his home town, now calling down demons to destroy the clutter of low, dun-coloured, "higgling and piggling" edifices around the bazaar, now annihilating with his death-encrusted words the cool white-washed smugness of the Cantonment district. These were the two orbs of the town's dumb-bell shape: old town and Cantt, the former inhabited by the indigenous, colonized population and the latter by the alien colonizers, the Angrez, or British, sahibs. Old Shakil loathed both worlds and had for many years remained immured in his high, fortress-like, gigantic residence, which faced inwards to a well-like and lightless compound yard. The house was positioned beside an open maidan, and it was equidistant from the bazaar and the Cantt. Through one of the building's few outward-facing windows Mr. Shakil on his death-bed was able to stare out at the dome of a large Palladian hotel, which rose out of the intolerable Cantonment streets like a mirage, and inside which were to be found golden cuspidors and tame spider-monkeys in brass-buttoned uniforms and bellhop hats and a full-sized orchestra playing every evening in a stuccoed ballroom amidst an energetic riot of fantastic plants, yellow roses and white mag-nolias and roof-high emerald-green palms—the Hotel Flashman, in short, whose great golden dome was cracked even then but shone nevertheless with the tedious pride of its brief doomed glory; that dome under which the suited-and-booted Angrez of-ficers and white-tied civilians and ringleted ladies with hungry eyes would congregate nightly, assembling here from their bun-galows to dance and to share the illusion of being colourful—whereas in fact they were merely white, or actually grey, owing to the deleterious effect of that stony heat upon their frail cloud-nurtured skins, and also to their habit of drinking dark Burgundies in the noonday insanity of the sun, with a fine disregard for their livers. The old man heard the music of the imperialists issuing from the golden hotel, heavy with the gaiety of despair, and he cursed the hotel of dreams in a loud, clear voice.

"Shut that window," he shouted, "so that I don't have to die listening to that racket," and when the old womanservant Hashmat Bibi had fastened the shutters he relaxed slightly and, summoning up the last reserves of his energy, altered the course of his fatal, delirious flow.

"Come quickly," Hashmat Bibi ran from the room yelling for the old man's daughters, "your fatherji is sending himself to the devil." Mr. Shakil, having dismissed the outside world, had turned the rage of his dying monologue against himself, calling eternal damnation down upon his soul. "God knows what got his goat," Hashmat despaired, "but he is going in an incorrect way."

The widower had raised his children with the help of Parsee wet-nurses, Christian ayahs and an iron morality that was mostly Muslim, although Chhunni used to say that he had been made harder by the sun. The three girls had been kept inside that labyrinthine mansion until his dying day; virtually uneducated, they were imprisoned in the zenana wing, where they amused each other by inventing private languages and fantasizing about what a man might look like when undressed, imagining, during their pre-pubertal years, bizarre genitalia such as holes in the chest into which their own nipples might snugly fit, "because for all we knew in those days," they would remind each other amazedly in later life, "fertilization might have been supposed to happen through the breast." This interminable captivity forged between the three sisters a bond of intimacy that would never completely be broken. They spent their evenings seated at a window behind a lattice-work screen, looking towards the golden dome of the great hotel and swaying to the strains of the enigmatic dance music . . . and there are rumours that they would indolently explore each other's bodies during the languorous drowsiness of the afternoons, and, at night, would weave occult spells to hasten the moment of their father's demise. But evil tongues will say anything, especially about beautiful women who live far away from the denuding eyes of men. What is almost certainly true is that it was during these years, long before the baby scandal, that the three of them, all of whom longed for children with the abstract passion of their virginity, made their secret compact to remain triune, forever bound by the intimacies of their youth, even after the children came: that is to say, they resolved to share the babies. I cannot prove or disprove the foul story that this treaty was written down and signed in the commingled menstrual blood of the isolated trinity, and then burned to ashes, being preserved only in the cloisters of their memories.

But for twenty years, they would have only one child. His name would be Omar Khayyam.

All this happened in the fourteenth century. I'm using the Hegiran calendar, naturally: don't imagine that stories of this type always take place longlong ago. Time cannot be homogenized as easily as milk, and in those parts, until quite recently, the thirteen-hundreds were still in full swing.

When Hashmat Bibi told them that their father had arrived at his final moments, the sisters went to visit him, dressed in their brightest clothes. They found him in the grip of an asphyxiating fist of shame, demanding of God, in gasps of imperious gloominess, that he be consigned for all eternity to some desert outpost of Jahannum, some borderland of hell. Then he fell silent, and Chhunni, the eldest daughter, quickly asked him the only question of any interest to the three young women: "Father, we are going to be very rich now, is that not so?"

"Whores," the dying man cursed them, "don't count on it."

The bottomless sea of wealth on which everyone had supposed the Shakil family fortunes to be sailing proved, on the morning after his foulmouthed death, to be an arid crater. The fierce sun of his financial incompetence (which he had successfully concealed for decades behind his imposing patriarchal façade, his filthy temper and the overweening hauteur which was his most poisonous legacy to his daughters) had dried out all the oceans of cash, so that Chhunni, Munnee and Bunny spent the entire period of mourning settling the debts for which his creditors had never dared to press the old man while he lived, but for payment of which (plus compound interest) they now absolutely refused to wait one moment longer. The girls emerged from their lifelong sequestration wearing expressions of well-bred disgust for these vultures swooping down to feast upon the carcass of their parent's great improvidence; and because they had been raised to think of money as one of the two subjects that it is forbidden to discuss with strangers, they signed away their fortune without even troubling to read the documents which the money-lenders presented. At the end of it all the vast estates around Q., which comprised approximately eighty-five per cent of the only good orchards and rich agricultural lands in that largely infertile region, had been lost in their entirety; the three sisters were left with nothing but the unmanageably infinite mansion stuffed from floor to ceiling with possessions and haunted by the few servants who refused to leave, less out of loyalty than from that terror of the life-prisoner for the outside world. And—as is perhaps the universal custom of aristocratically bred persons—they reacted to the news of their ruin by resolving to throw a party.

In later years, they told each other the story of that notorious gala night with a simple glee that restored to them the illusion of being young. "I had invitations printed in the Cantt," Chhunni Shakil would begin, seated beside her sisters on an old wooden swing-seat. Giggling happily about the old adventure, she continued, "And what invitations! Embossed, with gold lettering, on cards stiff as wood. They were like spits in the eye of fate."

"Also in the closed eyes of our dead father," Munnee added.

"To him it would have seemed like a completely shameless going-on, an abhorrence, the proof of his failure to impose his will on us."

"Just as," Bunny continued, "our ruin proved his failure in another sphere."

At first it seemed to them that the dying shame of their father had been born of his knowledge of the coming bankruptcy. Later, however, they began to consider less prosaic possibilities. "Maybe," Chhunni hypothesized, "he saw on his death-bed a vision of the future."

"Good," her sisters said, "then he will have died as miserably as he made us live."

The news of the emergence into society of the Shakil sisters spread rapidly through the town. And on the much-anticipated evening, the old house was invaded by an army of musical geniuses, whose three-stringed dumbirs, seven-stringed sarandas, reed flutes and drums filled that puritanical mansion with celebratory music for the first time in two decades; regiments of bakers and confectioners and snack-wallahs marched in with arsenals of eats, denuding the shop-counters of the town and filling up the interior of the huge multicoloured shamiana tent that had been erected in the central compound, its mirrorworked fabric reflecting the glory of the arrangements. It became clear, however, that the snobbishness which their father had bred into the sisters' bone-marrow had fatally infected the guest list. Most of the burghers of Q. had already been mortally insulted to find themselves deemed unworthy of the company of the three lustrous ladies, whose gilt-edged invitations were the talk of the town. Now the crimes of omission were compounded by those of commission, because it was seen that the sisters had committed the ultimate solecism: invitations, scorning the doormats of the indigenous worthies, had found their way into the Angrez Cantonment, and into the ballroom of the dancing sahibs. The long-forbidden household remained barred to all but a few locals; but after the cocktail hour at Flashman's, the sisters were visited by a uniformed and ball-gowned crowd of foreigners. The imperialists!—the grey-skinned sahibs and their gloved begums!—raucous-voiced and glittering with condescension, they entered the mirrorworked marquee.

"Alcohol was served." Old mother Chhunni, reminiscing, clapped her hands delightedly at the horror of the memory. But that was the point at which the reminiscing always ceased, and all three ladies became curiously vague; so that I am unable to clear away the improbabilities which have mushroomed around that party during the dark passage of the years.

Can it really have been the case that the few non-white guests—local zamindars and their wives, whose wealth had once been trifling in comparison with the Shakil crores—stood together in a tight clump of rage, gazing balefully at the cavorting sahibs? That all these persons left simultaneously after a very few moments, without having broken bread or eaten salt, abandoning the sisters to the colonial authorities? How likely is it that the three sisters, their eyes shining with antimony and arousal, moved in grave silence from officer to officer, as though they were sizing them up, as if mustachioes were being checked for glossiness and jaws evaluated by the angles of their jutting?—And then (the legend goes) that they, the Shakil girls, clapped their hands in unison and ordered the musicians to start playing Western-style dance music, minuets, waltzes, fox-trots, polkas, gavottes, music that acquired a fatally demonic quality when forced out of the virtuosi's outraged instruments?

All night, they say, the dancing continued. The scandal of such an event would have placed the newly orphaned girls beyond the pale in any case, but there was worse to come. Shortly after the party ended, after the infuriated geniuses had departed and the mountains of uneaten food had been thrown to the pie-dogs—for the sisters in their grandeur would not permit food intended for their peers to be distributed among the poor—it began to be bruited about the bazaars of Q., that one of the three nose-in-the-air girls had been put, on that wild night, into the family way.

O shame, shame, poppy-shame!

But if the sisters Shakil were overwhelmed by any feelings of dishonour, they gave no sign of it. Instead, they dispatched Hashmat Bibi, one of the servants who had refused to leave, into Q., where she commissioned the services of the town's finest handyman, a certain Mistri Yakoob Balloch, and also purchased the largest imported padlock to be found in the God-Willing Ironmongery Store. This padlock was so large and heavy that Hashmat Bibi was obliged to have it carried home on the back of a rented mule, whose owner inquired of the servant woman: "For what your begums want this lock-shock now? Invasion has already occurred." Hashmat replied, crossing her eyes for emphasis: "May your grandsons urinate upon your pauper's grave."

The hired handyman, Mistri Yakoob, was so impressed by the ferocious calm of the antediluvian crone that he worked willingly under her supervision without daring to pass a comment. She had him construct a strange external elevator, or dumb-waiter, large enough to hold three grown adults, by means of which items could be winched by a system of motorized pulleys from the street into the upper storeys of the house, or vice versa. Hashmat Bibi stressed the importance of constructing the whole contraption in such a way that it could be operated without requiring the mansion's inhabitants to show themselves at any window—not so much as a little finger must be capable of being glimpsed. Then she listed the unusual security features which she wished him to install in the bizarre mechanism. "Put here," she ordered him, "a spring release which can be worked from inside the house. When triggered, it should make the whole bottom of the lift fall off justlikethat. Put there, and there, and there, some secret panels which can shoot out eighteen-inch stiletto blades, sharp sharp. My ladies must be defended against intruders."

The dumb-waiter contained, then, many terrible secrets. The Mistri completed his work without once laying eyes on any of the three sisters Shakil, but when he died a few weeks later, clutching his stomach and rolling about in a gully, spitting blood on to the dirt, it got about that those shameless women had had him poisoned to ensure his silence on the subject of his last and most mysterious commission. It is only fair to state, however, that the medical evidence in the case runs strongly against this version of events. Yakoob Balloch, who had been suffering for some time from sporadic pains in the region of the appendix, almost certainly died of natural causes, his death-throes caused not by the spectral poisons of the putatively murderous sisters, but by the genuinely fatal banality of peritonitis. Or some such thing.

The day came when the three remaining male employees of the Shakil sisters were seen pushing shut the enormous front doors of solid teak and brass. Just before those gates of solitude closed upon the sisters, to remain unopened for more than half a century, the little crowd of curious townsfolk outside caught sight of a wheelbarrow on which there gleamed, dully, the outsize lock of their withdrawal. And when the doors were shut, the sounds of the great lock being hauled into place, and of the key being turned, heralded the beginning of the strange confinement of the scandalous ladies and their servants too.

It turned out that on her last trip into town Hashmat Bibi had left a number of sealed envelopes containing detailed instructions at the establishments of the community's leading suppliers of goods and services; so that afterwards, on the appointed days and at the hours specified, the chosen washerwoman, the tailor, the cobbler, as well as the selected vendors of meats, fruits, haberdashery, flowers, stationery, vegetables, pulses, books, flat drinks, fizzy drinks, foreign magazines, newspapers, unguents, perfumes, antimony, strips of eucalyptus bark for tooth-cleaning, spices, starch, soaps, kitchen utensils, picture frames, playing cards and strings for musical instruments, would present themselves at the foot of Mistri Yakoob's last construction. They would emit coded whistles, and the dumb-waiter would descend, humming, to street level bearing written instructions. In this way the Shakil ladies managed to recede entirely and for all time from the world, returning of their own volition into that anchoritic existence whose end they had been so briefly able to celebrate after their father's death; and such was the hauteur of their arrangements that their withdrawal seemed like an act not of contrition but of pride.

There arises a delicate question: how did they pay for it all?

With some embarrassment on their behalf, and purely to show that the present author, who has already been obliged to leave many questions in a state of unanswered ambiguity, is capable of giving clear replies when absolutely necessary, I reveal that Hashmat Bibi had delivered a last sealed envelope to the door of the town's least savoury establishment, wherein the Quranic strictures against usury counted for nothing, whose shelves and storage chests groaned under the weight of the accumulated debris of innumerable decayed histories . . . damn and blast it. To be frank—she went to the pawnshop. And he, the pawnbroker, the ageless, pencil-thin, innocently wide-eyed Chalaak Sahib, would also present himself thereafter at the dumb-waiter (under cover of night, as instructed), to assess the worth of the items he found therein, and to send up into the heart of the silent house cash monies on the nail to a total of eighteen point five per cent approx. of the market value of the irredeemably pawned treasures. The three mothers of the imminent Omar Khayyam Shakil were using the past, their only remaining capital, as a means of purchasing the future.

But who was pregnant?

Chhunni, the eldest, or Munnee-in-the-middle, or "little" Bunny, the baby of the three?—Nobody ever discovered, not even the child that was born. Their closing of ranks was absolute, and effected with the most meticulous attention to detail. Just imagine: they made the servants swear loyalty oaths on the Book. The servants joined them in their self-imposed captivity, and only left the house feet first, wrapped in white sheets, and via, of course, the route constructed by Yakoob Balloch. During the entire term of that pregnancy, no doctor was summoned to the house. And as it proceeded, the sisters, understanding that unkept secrets always manage to escape, under a door, through a keyhole or an open window, until everyone knows everything and nobody knows how . . . the sisters, I repeat, displayed the uniquely passionate solidarity that was their most remarkable characteristic by feigning—in the case of two of them—the entire range of symptoms that the third was obliged to display.

Although some five years separated Chhunni from Bunny, it was at this time that the sisters, by virtue of dressing identically and through the incomprehensible effects of their unusual, chosen life, began to resemble each other so closely that even the servants made mistakes. I have described them as beauties; but they were not the moon-faced, almond-eyed types so beloved of poets in that neck of the woods, but rather strong-chinned, powerfully built, purposefully striding women of an almost oppressively charismatic force. Now the three of them began, simultaneously, to thicken at the waist and in the breast; when one was sick in the morning, the other two began to puke in such perfectly synchronized sympathy that it was impossible to tell which stomach had heaved first. Identically, their wombs ballooned towards the pregnancy's full term. It is naturally possible that all this was achieved with the help of physical contrivances, cushions and padding and even faint-inducing vapours; but it is my unshakable opinion that such an analysis grossly demeans the love that existed between the sisters. In spite of biological improbability, I am prepared to swear that so wholeheartedly did they wish to share the motherhood of their sibling—to transform the public shame of unwedlocked conception into the private triumph of the longed-for group baby—that, in short, twin phantom pregnancies accompanied the real one; while the simultaneity of their behaviour suggests the operation of some form of communal mind.

They slept in the same room. They endured the same cravings—marzipan, jasmine-petals, pine-kernels, mud—at the same times; their metabolic rates altered in parallel. They began to weigh the same, to feel exhausted at the same moment and to awake together, each morning, as if somebody had rung a bell. They felt identical pains; in three wombs, a single baby and its two ghostly mirror-images kicked and turned with the precision of a well-drilled dance troupe . . . suffering identically, the three of them—I will go so far as to say—fully earned the right to be considered joint mothers of the forthcoming child. And when one—I will not even guess at the name—came to her time, nobody else saw whose waters broke; nor whose hand locked a bedroom door from the inside. No outside eyes witnessed the passage of the three labours, two phantom one genuine; or the moment when empty balloons subsided, while between a third pair of thighs, as if in an alleyway, there appeared the illegitimate child; or when hands lifted Omar Khayyam Shakil by the ankles, held him upside-down and thumped him on the back.

Our hero, Omar Khayyam, first drew breath in that improbable mansion which was too large for its rooms to be counted; opened his eyes; and saw, upside-down through an open window, the macabre peaks of the Impossible Mountains on the horizon. One—but which?—of his three mothers had picked him up by the ankles, had pummelled the first breath into his lungs . . . until, still staring at the inverted summits, the baby began to scream.

When Hashmat Bibi heard a key turning in the door and came timidly into the room with food and drink and fresh sheets and sponges and soap and towels, she found the three sisters sitting up together in the capacious bed, the same bed in which their father had died, a huge mahogany four-poster around whose columns carved serpents coiled upwards to the brocade Eden of the canopy. They were all wearing the flushed expression of dilated joy that is the mother's true prerogative; and the baby was passed from breast to breast, and none of the six was dry.

Young Omar Khayyam was gradually made aware that certain irregularities had both preceded and succeeded his birth. We have dealt with the pre-; and as for the suc-:

"I refused completely," his eldest mother Chhunni told him on his seventh birthday, "to whisper the name of God into your ear."

On his eighth birthday, middle-Munnee confided: "There was no question of shaving your head. Such beautiful black-black hair you came with, nobody was cutting it off under my nose, no sir!"

Exactly one year later, his youngest mother adopted a stern expression. "Under no circs," Bunny announced, "would I have permitted the foreskin to be removed. What is this idea? It is not like banana peel."

Omar Khayyam Shakil entered life without benefit of mutilation, barbery or divine approval. There are many who would consider this a handicap.

Born in a death-bed, about which there hung (as well as curtains and mosquito-netting) the ghost-image of a grandfather who, dying, had consigned himself to the peripheries of hell; his first sight the spectacle of a range of topsy-turvy mountains . . . Omar Khayyam Shakil was afflicted, from his earliest days, by a sense of inversion, of a world turned upside-down. And by something worse: the fear that he was living at the edge of the world, so close that he might fall off at any moment. Through an old telescope, from the upper-storey windows of the house, the child Omar Khayyam surveyed the emptiness of the landscape around Q., which convinced him that he must be near the very Rim of Things, and that beyond the Impossible Mountains on the horizon must lie the great nothing into which, in his nightmares, he had begun to tumble with monotonous regularity. The most alarming aspect of these dreams was the sleep-sense that his plunges into the void were somehow appropriate, that he deserved no better . . . he awoke amidst mosquito-netting, sweating freely and even shrieking at the realization that his dreams were informing him of his worthlessness. He did not relish the news.

So it was in those half-formed years that Omar Khayyam took the never-to-be-reversed decision to cut down on his sleeping time, a lifelong endeavour which had brought him, by the end, by the time his wife went up in smoke—but no, ends must not be permitted to precede beginnings and middles, even if recent scientific experiments have shown us that within certain types of closed systems, under intense pressure, time can be persuaded to run backwards, so that effects precede their causes. This is precisely the sort of unhelpful advance of which storytellers must take no notice whatsoever; that way madness lies!—to the point at which a mere forty minutes a night, the famous forty winks, sufficed to refresh him. How young he was when he made the surprisingly adult resolution to escape from the unpalatable reality of dreams into the slightly more acceptable illusions of his everyday, waking life! "Little bat," his three mothers called him tolerantly when they learned of his nocturnal flittings through the inexhaustible chambers of their home, a dark-grey chadar flapping around his shoulders, providing protection against the cold of the winter nights; but as to whether he grew up into caped crusader or cloaked bloodsucker, into Batman or Dracula, I leave it to the reader to decide.

(His wife, the elder daughter of General Raza Hyder, was an insomniac too; but Omar Khayyam's sleeplessness is not to be compared with hers, for while his was willed, she, foolish Sufiya Zinobia, would lie in bed squeezing her eyelids shut between her thumbs and forefingers, as if she could extrude consciousness through her eyelashes, like motes of dust, or tears. And she burned, she fried, in that very room of her husband's birth and his grandfather's death, beside that bed of snakes and Paradise . . . a plague on this disobedient Time! I command this death scene back into the wings at once: shazam!)

By the age of ten young Omar had already begun to feel grateful for the enclosing, protective presence of the mountains on the western and southern skyline. The Impossible Mountains: you will not find that name in your atlases, no matter how large-scale. Geographers have their limitations, however; the young Omar Khayyam, who fell in love with a miraculously shiny brass telescope which he unearthed from the wild abundance of things that clogged his home, was always aware that any silicon creatures or gas monsters inhabiting the stars of the Milky Way which flowed overhead each night would never have recognized their homes by the names in his much-thumbed star charts. "We had our reasons," he said throughout his life, "for the name we gave to our personal mountain range."

The thin-eyed, rock-hard tribals who dwelt in those mountains and who were occasionally to be seen in the streets of Q. (whose softer inhabitants crossed streets to avoid the tribals' mountainous stench and barging, unceremonious shoulders) also called the range "the roof of Paradise." The mountains, in fact the whole region, even Q. itself, suffered from periodic earthquakes; it was a zone of instability, and the tribals believed that the tremors were caused by the emergence of angels through fissures in the rocks. Long before his own brother saw a winged and golden-glowing man watching him from a rooftop, Omar Khayyam Shakil had become aware of the plausible theory that Paradise was located not in the sky but beneath his very feet, so that the earth movements were proof of the angels' interest in scrutinizing world affairs. The shape of the mountain range altered constantly under this angelic pressure. From its crumpled ochre slopes rose an infinite number of stratified pillar-like formations whose geological strata were so sharply defined that the titanic columns seemed to have been erected by colossi skilled in stonemasonry . . . these divine dream-temples, too, rose and fell as the angels came and went.

Hell above, Paradise below: I have lingered on this account of Omar Khayyam's original, unstable wilderness to underline the propositions that he grew up between twin eternities, whose conventional order was, in his experience, precisely inverted; that such headstandings have effects harder to measure than earthquakes, for what inventor has patented a seismograph of the soul?;

and that, for Omar Khayyam, uncircumcised, unwhispered-to, unshaven, their presence heightened his feeling of being a person apart.

But I have been out of doors for quite long enough now, and must get my narrative out of the sun before it is afflicted by mirages or heat-stroke.—Afterwards, at the other end of his life (it seems that the future cannot be restrained, and insists on seeping back into the past), when he got his name into all the papers over the scandals of the headless murders, the customs official's daughter Farah Rodrigues unlocked her lips and released from her custody the story of the day on which the adolescent Omar Khayyam, even then a fat fellow with a missing shirt-button at navel height, had accompanied her to her father's post at the land border forty miles to the west of Q. She sat in an illicit brandy den and spoke to the room in general, in the cackle of splintered glass to which time and the wilderness air had reduced her formerly crystal laugh: "Incredible, I swear," she reminisced, "we just reached there in the jeep and at once a cloud came down and sat on the ground, right along the frontier, like it couldn't get across without a visa, and that Shakil was so scared he passed out, he got vertigo and fainted, even though both his feet had been on solid ground."

Even in the days of his greatest distinction, even when he married Hyder's daughter, even after Raza Hyder became President, Omar Khayyam Shakil was sometimes plagued by that improbable vertigo, by the sense of being a creature of the edge: a peripheral man. Once, during the time of his drinking and carousing friendship with Iskander Harappa, millionaire playboy, radical thinker, Prime Minister and finally miracle-working corpse, Omar Khayyam in his cups described himself to Isky. "You see before you," he confided, "a fellow who is not even the hero of his own life; a man born and raised in the condition of being out of things. Heredity counts, dontyouthinkso?"

"That is an oppressive notion," Iskander Harappa replied.

.   .   .

Omar Khayyam Shakil was raised by no fewer than three mothers, with not a solitary father in sight, a mystery which was later deepened by the birth, when Omar was already twenty years old, of a younger brother who was likewise claimed by all three female parents and whose conception seemed to have been no less immaculate. Equally disturbing, for the growing youth, was his first experience of falling in love, of pursuing with waddling and heated resolution the voluptuously unattainable figure of a certain Farah the Parsee (née Zoroaster), an occupation known to all the local lads, with the solitary exception of his congenitally isolated self, as: "courting Disaster."

Dizzy, peripheral, inverted, infatuated, insomniac, stargazing, fat: what manner of hero is this?

2

A
NECKLACE
OF SHOES

*A*few weeks after Russian troops entered Afghanistan, I returned home, to visit my parents and sisters and to show off my firstborn son. My family lives in "Defence," the Pakistan Defence Services Officers' Co-Operative Housing Society, although it is not a military family. "Defence" is a fashionable part of Karachi; few of the soldiers who were permitted to buy land there at rock-bottom prices could afford to build on it.

But they weren't allowed to sell the empty plots, either. To buy an officer's piece of "Defence," you had to draw up a complex contract. Under the terms of this contract the land remained the property of the vendor, even though you had paid him the full market price and were now spending a small fortune building your own house on it to your own specifications. In theory you were just being a nice guy, a benefactor who had chosen to give the poor officer a home out of your boundless charity. But the contract also obliged the vendor to name a third party who would have plenipotentiary authority over the property once the house was finished. This third party was your nominee, and when the construction workers went home he simply handed the property over to you. Thus two separate acts of goodwill were necessary to the process. "Defence" was almost entirely developed on this nice-guy basis. This spirit of comradeship, of working selflessly together towards a common goal, is worthy of remark.

It was an elegant procedure. The vendor got rich, the intermediary got his fee, you got your house, and nobody broke any laws. So naturally nobody ever questioned how it came about that the city's most highly desirable development zone had been allotted to the defence services in this way. This attitude, too, remains a part of the foundations of "Defence": the air there is full of unasked questions. But their smell is faint, and the flowers in the many maturing gardens, the trees lining the avenues, the perfumes worn by the beautiful soignée ladies of the neighbourhood quite overpower this other, too-abstract odour. Diplomats, international businessmen, the sons of former dictators, singing stars, textile moguls, Test cricketers come and go. There are many new Datsun and Toyota motor cars. And the name "Defence Society," which might sound to some ears like a symbol (representing the mutually advantageous relationship between the country's establishment and its armed forces), holds no such resonance in the city. It is only a name.

One evening, soon after my arrival, I visited an old friend, a poet. I had been looking forward to one of our long conversations, to hearing his views about recent events in Pakistan, and about Afghanistan, of course. His house was full of visitors as usual; nobody seemed interested in talking about anything except the cricket series between Pakistan and India. I sat down at a table with my friend and began an idle game of chess. But I really wanted to get the low-down on things, and at length I brought up the stuff that was on my mind, beginning with a question about the execution of Zulfikar Ali Bhutto. But only half the question got past my lips; the other half joined the ranks of the area's many unasked queries, because I felt an extremely painful kick land on my shins and, without crying out, switched in mid-sentence back to sporting topics. We also discussed the incipient video boom.

People entered, exited, circled, laughed. After about forty minutes my friend said, "It's O.K. now." I asked, "Who was it?" He gave me the name of the informer who had infiltrated this particular group. They treated him civilly, without hinting that they knew why he was there, because otherwise he would vanish, and the next time they might not know who the informer was. Later, I met the spy. He was a nice guy, pleasantly spoken, honest-faced, and no doubt happy that he was hearing nothing worth reporting. A kind of equilibrium had been achieved. Once again, I was struck by how many nice guys there were in Pakistan, by the civility growing in those gardens, perfuming the air.

Since my last visit to Karachi, my friend the poet had spent many months in jail, for social reasons. That is to say, he knew somebody who knew somebody who was the wife of the second cousin by marriage of the step-uncle of somebody who might or might not have shared a flat with someone who was running guns to the guerrillas in Baluchistan. You can get anywhere in Pakistan if you know people, even into jail. My friend still refuses to talk about what happened to him during those months; but other people told me that he was in bad shape for a long time after he got out. They said he had been hung upside-down by the ankles and beaten, as if he were a new-born baby whose lungs had to be coerced into action so that he could squeal. I never asked him if he screamed, or if there were upside-down mountain peaks visible through a window.

Wherever I turn, there is something of which to be ashamed. But shame is like everything else; live with it for long enough and it becomes part of the furniture. In "Defence," you can find shame in every house, burning in an ashtray, hanging framed upon a wall, covering a bed. But nobody notices it any more. And everyone is civilized.

Maybe my friend should be telling this story, or another one, his own; but he doesn't write poetry any more. So here I am instead, inventing what never happened to me; and you will note that my hero has already been ankle-hung, and that his name is the name of a famous poet; but no quatrains ever issued or will issue from his pen.

Outsider! Trespasser! You have no right to this subject! . . . I know: nobody ever arrested me. Nor are they ever likely to. *Poacher! Pirate! We reject your authority. We know you, with your foreign language wrapped around you like a flag: speaking about us in your forked tongue, what can you tell but lies?* I reply with more questions: Is history to be considered the property of the participants solely? In what courts are such claims staked, what boundary commissions map out the territories?

Can only the dead speak?

I tell myself this will be a novel of leavetaking, my last words on the East from which, many years ago, I began to come loose. I do not always believe myself when I say this. It is a part of the world to which, whether I like it or not, I am still joined, if only by elastic bands.

As to Afghanistan: after returning to London, I met a senior British diplomat at a dinner, a career specialist in "my" part of the world. He said it was quite proper, "post-Afghanistan," for the West to support the dictatorship of President Zia ul-Haq. I should not have lost my temper, but I did. It wasn't any use. Then, as we left the table, his wife, a quiet civil lady who had been making pacifying noises, said to me, "Tell me, why don't people in Pakistan get rid of Zia in, you know, the usual way?"

Shame, dear reader, is not the exclusive property of the East.

The country in this story is not Pakistan, or not quite. There are two countries, real and fictional, occupying the same space, or almost the same space. My story, my fictional country exist, like myself, at a slight angle to reality. I have found this off-centring to be necessary; but its value is, of course, open to debate. My view is that I am not writing only about Pakistan.

I have not given the country a name. And Q. is not really Quetta at all. But I don't want to be precious about this: when I arrive at the big city, I shall call it Karachi. And it will contain a "Defence."

Omar Khayyam's position as a poet is curious. He was never very popular in his native Persia; and he exists in the West in a translation that is really a complete reworking of his verses, in many cases very different from the spirit (to say nothing of the content) of the original. I, too, am a translated man. I have been *borne across*. It is generally believed that something is always lost in translation; I cling to the notion—and use, in evidence, the success of Fitzgerald-Khayyam—that something can also be gained.

"The sight of you through my beloved telescope," Omar Khayyam Shakil told Farah Zoroaster the day he declared his love, "gave me the strength to break my mothers' power."

"Voyeur," she replied, "I shit on your words. Your balls dropped too soon and you got the hots, no more to it than that. Don't load your family problems on to me." She was two years his senior, but Omar Khayyam was nevertheless forced to concede that his darling had a dirty mouth . . .

. . . As well as the name of a great poet, the child had been given his mothers' family name. And as if to underline what they meant by calling him after the immortal Khayyam the three sisters gave a name, too, to that underlit corridory edifice that was now all the country they possessed: the house was named "Nishapur." Thus a second Omar grew up in a second place of that name, and every so often, as he grew, would catch a strange look in his three mothers' six eyes, a look that seemed to say, Hurry up, we are waiting for your poems. But (I repeat) no rubaiyat ever issued from his pen.

His childhood had been exceptional by any standards, because what applied to mothers and servants wentwithoutsaying for our peripheral hero as well. Omar Khayyam passed twelve long years, the most crucial years of his development, trapped inside that reclusive mansion, that third world that was neither material nor spiritual, but a sort of concentrated decrepitude made up of the decomposing remnants of those two more familiar types of cosmos, a world in which he would constantly run into—as well as the mothballed, spider-webbed, dust-shrouded profusion of crumbling objects—the lingering, fading miasmas of discarded ideas and forgotten dreams. The finely calculated gesture with which his three mothers had sealed themselves off from the world had created a sweltering, entropical zone in which, despite all the rotting-down of the past, nothing new seemed capable of growth, and from which it became Omar Khayyam's most cherished youthful ambition quickly to escape. Unaware, in that hideously indeterminate frontier universe, of the curvature of space and time, thanks to which he who runs longest and hardest inevitably ends up, gaspingpanting, with wrenched and screaming tendons, at the starting line, he dreamed of exits, feeling that in the claustrophobia of "Nishapur" his very life was at stake. He was, after all, something new in that infertile and time-eroded labyrinth.

Have you heard of those wolf-children, suckled—we must suppose—on the feral multiple breasts of a hairy moon-howling dam? Rescued from the Pack, they bite their saviours vilely in the arm; netted and caged, they are brought stinking of raw meat and faecal matter into the emancipated light of the world, their brains too imperfectly formed to be capable of acquiring more than the most fundamental rudiments of civilization . . . Omar Khayyam, too, fed at too-many mammary glands; and he wandered for some four thousand days in the thing-infested jungle that was "Nishapur," his walled-in wild place, his mother-country; until he succeeded in getting the frontiers opened by making a birthday wish that could not be satisfied by anything lifted up in the machine of Mistri Balloch.

"Drop this jungle-boy business," Farah sneered when Omar tried it on her, "you're no fucking ape-man, sonny jim." And, educationally speaking, she was right; but she had also denied the wildness, the evil within him; and he proved upon her own body that she was wrong.

First things first: for twelve years, he had the run of the house. Little (except freedom) was denied him. A spoiled and vulpine brat; when he howled, his mothers caressed him . . . and after the nightmares began and he started giving up sleep, he plunged deeper and deeper into the seemingly bottomless depths of that decaying realm. Believe me when I tell you that he stumbled down corridors so long untrodden that his sandalled feet sank into the dust right up to his ankles; that he discovered ruined staircases made impassable by longago earthquakes which had caused them to heave up into tooth-sharp mountains and also to fall away to reveal dark abysses of fear . . . in the silence of the night and the first sounds of dawn he explored beyond history into what seemed the positively archaeological antiquity of "Nishapur," discovering in almirahs the wood of whose doors disintegrated beneath his tentative fingers the impossible forms of painted neolithic pottery in the Kotdiji style; or in kitchen quarters whose existence was no longer even suspected he would gaze ignorantly upon bronze implements of utterly fabulous age; or in regions of that colossal palace which had been abandoned longago because of the collapse of their plumbing he would delve into the quake-exposed intricacies of brick drainage systems that had been out of date for centuries.

On one occasion he lost his way completely and ran wildly about like a time-traveller who has lost his magic capsule and fears he will never emerge from the disintegrating history of his race—and came to a dead stop, staring in horror at a room whose outer wall had been partly demolished by great, thick, water-seeking tree-roots. He was perhaps ten years old when he had this first glimpse of the unfettered outside world. He had only to walk through the shattered wall—but the gift had been sprung upon him without sufficient warning, and, taken unawares by the shocking promise of the dawn light streaming through the hole, he turned tail and fled, his terror leading him blindly back to his own comforting, comfortable room. Afterwards, when he had had time to consider things, he tried to retrace his steps, armed with a purloined ball of string; but try as he might, he never again found his way to that place in the maze of his childhood where the minotaur of forbidden sunlight lived.

"Sometimes I found skeletons," he swore to disbelieving Farah, "human as well as animal." And even where bones were absent, the house's long-dead occupants dogged his steps. Not in the way you think!—No howls, no clanking chains!—But disembodied feelings, the choking fumes of ancient hopes, fears, loves; and finally, made wild by the ancestor-heavy, phantom oppressions of these far recesses of the run-down building, Omar Khayyam took his revenge (not long after the episode of the broken wall) on his unnatural surroundings. I wince as I record his vandalism: armed with broomstick and misappropriated hatchet, he rampaged through dusty passages and maggoty bedrooms, smashing glass cabinets, felling oblivion-sprinkled divans, pulverizing wormy libraries; crystal, paintings, rusty helmets, the paper-thin remnants of priceless silken carpets were destroyed beyond all possibility of repair. "Take that," he screeched amidst the corpses of his useless, massacred history, "take that, old stuff!"—and then burst (dropping guilty hatchet and clean-sweeping broom) into illogical tears.

It must be stated that even in those days nobody believed the boy's stories about the far-flung infinities of the house. "Only child," Hashmat Bibi creaked, "always always they live in their poor head." And the three male servants laughed too: "Listening to you, baba, we are thinking this house has grown so huge huge, there mustn't be room for anywhere else in the world!" And three mothers, sitting tolerantly in their favourite swing-seat, stretched out patting hands and sealed the matter: "At least he has a vivid imagination," said Munnee-in-the-middle, and Mother Bunny concurred: "Comes from his poetic name." Worried that he might be sleep-walking, Chhunni-ma detailed a servant to place his sleeping-mat outside Omar Khayyam's room; but by then he had placed the more fantasticated zones of "Nishapur" off-limits for ever. After he descended upon the cohorts of history like a wolf (or wolf-child) on the fold, Omar Khayyam Shakil confined himself to the well-trodden, swept and dusted, used regions of the house.

Something—conceivably remorse—led him to his grandfather's dark-panelled study, a book-lined room which the three sisters had never entered since the old man's death. Here he discovered that Mr. Shakil's air of great learning had been a sham, just like his supposed business acumen; because the books all bore the *ex libris* plates of a certain Colonel Arthur Greenfield, and many of their pages were uncut. It was a gentleman's library, bought *in toto* from the unknown Colonel, and it had remained unused throughout its residence in the Shakil household. Now Omar Khayyam fell upon it with a will.

Here I must praise his autodidactic gifts. For by the time he left "Nishapur" he had learned classical Arabic and Persian; also Latin, French and German; all with the aid of leather-bound dictionaries and the unused texts of his grandfather's deceptive vanity. In what books the young fellow immersed himself! Illuminated manuscripts of the poetry of Ghalib; volumes of letters written by Mughal emperors to their sons; the Burton translation of the *Alf laylah wa laylah*, and the *Travels* of Ibn Battuta, and the Qissa or tales of the legendary adventurer Hatim Tai . . . yes, yes, I see that I must withdraw (as Farah instructed Omar to withdraw) the misleading image of the mowgli, the junglee boy.

The continual passage of items from living quarters via dumbwaiter to pawnshop brought concealed matter to light at regular intervals. Those outsize chambers stuffed brim-full with the material legacy of generations of rapaciously acquisitive forebears were being slowly emptied, so that by the time Omar Khayyam was ten and a half there was enough space to move around without bumping into the furniture at every step. And one day the three mothers sent a servant into the study to remove from their lives an exquisitely carved walnut screen on which was portrayed the mythical circular mountain of Qaf, complete with the thirty birds playing God thereupon. The flight of the bird-parliament revealed to Omar Khayyam a little bookcase stuffed with volumes on the theory and practice of hypnosis: Sanskrit mantras, compendiums of the lore of the Persian Magi, a leathern copy of the *Kalevala* of the Finns, an account of the hypno-exorcisms of Father Gassner of Klosters and a study of the "animal magnetism" theory of Franz Mesmer himself; also (and most usefully) a number of cheaply printed do-it-yourself manuals. Greedily, Omar Khayyam began to devour these books, which alone in the library did not bear the name of the literary Colonel; they were his grandfather's true legacy, and they led him into his lifelong involvement with that arcane science which has so awesome a power for good or ill.

The household servants were as under-occupied as he; his mothers had gradually become very lax about such matters as cleanliness and cuisine. The trio of menservants became, therefore, Omar Khayyam's first, willing subjects. Practising with the aid of a shiny four-anna coin, he put them under, discovering with some pride his talent for the art: effortlessly keeping his voice on a flat, monotonous plane, he lulled them into trances, learning, among other things, that the sexual drives which his mothers appeared to have lost completely since his birth had not been similarly stilled in these men. Entranced, they happily confessed the secrets of their mutual caresses, and blessed the maternal trinity for having so altered the circumstances of their lives that their true desires could be revealed to them. The contented three-way love of the male servants provided a curious balance for the equal, but wholly platonic, love of the three sisters for one another. (But Omar Khayyam continued to grow bitter, despite being surrounded by so many intimacies and affections.)

Hashmat Bibi also agreed to "go under." Omar made her imagine she was floating on a soft pink cloud. "You are sinking deeper," he intoned as she lay upon her mat, "and deeper into the cloud. It is good to be in the cloud; you want to sink lower and lower." These experiments had a tragic side-effect. Soon after his twelfth birthday, his mothers were informed by the three loving men-servants, who stared accusingly at the young master as they spoke, that Hashmat had apparently willed herself into death; at the very end she had been heard muttering, ". . . deeper and deeper into the heart of the rosy cloud." The old lady, having been given glimpses of non-being through the mediating powers of the young hypnotist's voice, had finally relaxed the iron will with which she had clung to life for what she had claimed was more than one hundred and twenty years. The three mothers stopped swinging in their seat and ordered Omar Khayyam to abandon mesmerism. But by then the world had changed. I must go back a little way to describe the alteration.

What was also found in the slowly emptying rooms: a previously mentioned telescope. With which Omar Khayyam spied out of upper-storey windows (those on the ground floor being permanently shuttered and barred): the world seen as a bright disc, a moon for his delight. He watched kite-fights between colourful, tailed *patangs* whose strings were black and dipped in glass to make them razor sharp; he heard the victors' cries—"Boi-oi-oi! Boi-oi!"—come towards him on the gritty breeze; once a green and white kite, its string severed, dropped in through his open window. And when, shortly before his twelfth birthday, there strolled on to this ocular moon the incomprehensibly appealing figure of Farah Zoroaster, at that time no more than fourteen but already possessed of a body that moved with the physical wisdom of a woman, then, in that exact moment, he felt his voice break in his throat, while below his belt other things slid downwards too, to take their appointed places, somewhat ahead of schedule, in hitherto-empty sacs. His longing for the outside was immediately transformed into a dull ache in the groin, a tearing in his loins; what followed was perhaps inevitable.

He was not free. His roving freedom-of-the-house was only the pseudo-liberty of a zoo animal; and his mothers were his loving, caring keepers. His three mothers: who else implanted in his heart the conviction of being a sidelined personality, a watcher from the wings of his own life? He watched them for a dozen years, and, yes, it must be said, he hated them for their closeness, for the way they sat with arms entwined on their swinging, creaking seat, for their tendency to lapse giggling into the private languages of their girlhood, for their way of hugging each other, of putting their three heads together and whispering about whoknowswhat, of finishing one another's sentences. Omar Khayyam, walled up in "Nishapur," had been excluded from human society by his mothers' strange resolve; and this, his mothers' three-in-oneness, redoubled that sense of exclusion, of being, in the midst of objects, out of things.

Twelve years take their toll. At first the high pride which had driven Chhunni, Munnee and Bunny to reject God, their father's memory and their place in society had enabled them to maintain the standards of behaviour which were just about their father's only legacy to them. They would rise, each morning, within seconds of one another, brush their teeth up, down and sideways fifty times each with eucalyptus sticks, and then, identically attired, would oil and comb each other's hair and twine white flowers into the coiled black buns they made of their locks. They addressed the servants, and also each other, by the polite form of the second-person pronoun. The rigidity of their bearing and the precision of their household instructions gave a legitimizing sheen to all their actions, including (which was no doubt the point) the production of an illegitimate child. But slowly, slowly, they slipped.

On the day of Omar Khayyam's departure for the big city, his eldest mother told him a secret that put a date to the beginning of their decline. "We never wanted to stop breast-feeding you," she confessed. "By now you know that it is not usual for a six-

year-old boy to be still on the nipple; but you drank from half a
dozen, one for each year. On your sixth birthday we renounced
this greatest of pleasures, and after that nothing was the same,
we began to forget the point of things."

During the next six years, as breasts dried and shrank, the three
sisters lost that firmness and erectness of body which had accounted
for a good deal of their beauty. They became soft, there were knots
in their hair, they lost interest in the kitchen, the servants got away
with murder. But still they declined at the same rate and in identical fashion; the bonds of their identity remained unbroken.

Remember this: the Shakil sisters had never received a proper
education, except in manners; while their son, by the time his voice
broke, was already something of a self-taught prodigy. He attempted to interest his mothers in his learning; but when he set
out the most elegant proofs of Euclidian theorems or expatiated
eloquently on the Platonic image of the Cave, they rejected the
unfamiliar notions out of hand. "Angrez double-dutch," said
Chhunni-ma, and the three mothers shrugged as one. "Who is
to understand the brains of those crazy types?" asked Munnee-
in-the-middle, in tones of final dismissal. "They read books from
left to right."

The philistinism of his mothers accentuated Omar Khayyam's
feelings, inchoate and half-articulated, of being extraneous, both
because he was a gifted child whose gifts were being returned-
to-sender by his parents, and because, for all his learning, he
guessed that his mothers' point of view was holding him back.
He suffered the sensation of being lost inside a cloud, whose
curtains parted occasionally to offer tantalizing glimpses of the
sky . . . in spite of what he murmured to Hashmat Bibi, cloudi-
ness was not attractive to the boy.

Now then. Omar Khayyam Shakil is almost twelve. He is over-
weight, and his generative organ, newly potent, also possesses a
fold of skin that should have been removed. His mothers are

growing vague about the reasons for their life; while he, in contrast, has overnight become capable of levels of aggression previously foreign to his complaisant fat-boy nature. I offer (have already hinted at) three causes: one, his sighting of fourteen-year-old Farah on the moon of his telescopic lens; two, his awkwardness about his altered speech, which swings out of control between croaks and squeaks while an ugly lump bobs in his throat like a cork; and one must not forget three, namely the time-honoured (or dishonoured) mutations wrought by pubertal biochemistry upon the adolescent male personality . . . ignorant of this conjunction of diabolic forces within their son, the three mothers make the mistake of asking Omar Khayyam what he wants for his birthday.

He surprises them by being sullen: "You'll never give it, what's the point?" Horrified maternal gasps. Six hands fly to three heads and take up hear-no-see-no-speak-no-evil positions. Mother Chhunni (hands over ears): "How can he say this? The boy, what's he talking?" And middling-Munnee, peeping tragically through her fingers: "Somebody has upset our angel, plain to see." And Baby Bunny removes hands from lips to speaknoevil: "Ask! Ask only! What can we refuse? What's so big that we won't do?"

It bursts out of him then: howling, "To let me out of this horrible house," and then, much more quietly, into the aching silence that his words have brought into being, "and to tell my father's name."

"Cheek! Cheek of the chappie!"—this from Munnee his middle mother; then her sisters draw her into an inward-facing huddle, arms round waists in that pose of obscene unity which the watching boy finds so hard to stomach.

"Didn't I tell?"—in grunts and falsettos of anguish—"Then why get it out of me in the first place?"

But now it is possible to observe a change. Quarrelsome syllables fly out of the maternal huddle, because the boy's requests have divided the sisters for the first time in more than a decade.

They are arguing, and the argument is a rusty, difficult business, a dispute between women who are trying to remember the people they once were.

When they emerge from the rubble of their exploded identity they make heroic attempts to pretend to Omar, and to themselves, that nothing serious has happened; but although all three of them stick by the collective decision that has been made, the boy can see that this unanimity is a mask which is being held in place with considerable difficulty.

"These are reasonable requests," Baby Bunny speaks first, "and one, at least, should be granted."

His triumph terrifies him; the cork in his throat jumps, almost as far as his tongue. "Whichwhichwhich?" Fearfully, he asks.

Munnee takes over. "A new satchel will be ordered and will come in the Mistri's machine," she states gravely, "and you will go to school. You need not be too happy," she adds, "because when you leave this house you will be wounded by many sharp names, which people will throw at you, like knives, in the street." Munnee, the fiercest opponent of his freedom, has had her own tongue sharpened on the steel of her defeat.

Finally, his eldest mother says her piece. "Come home without hitting anyone," she instructs, "or we will know that they have lowered your pride and made you feel the forbidden emotion of shame."

"That would be a completely debased effect," middle-Munnee says.

This word: "shame." No, I must write it in its original form, not in this peculiar language tainted by wrong concepts and the accumulated detritus of its owners' unrepented past, this Angrezi in which I am forced to write, and so for ever alter what is written . . .

Sharam, that's the word. For which this paltry "shame" is a wholly inadequate translation. Three letters, *shèn rè mèm* (written, naturally, from right to left); plus *zabar* accents indicating the short vowel sounds. A short word, but one containing encyclopaedias of nuance. It was not only shame that his mothers forbade Omar Khayyam to feel, but also embarrassment, discomfiture, decency, modesty, shyness, the sense of having an ordained place in the world, and other dialects of emotion for which English has no counterparts. No matter how determinedly one flees a country, one is obliged to take along some hand-luggage; and can it be doubted that Omar Khayyam (to concentrate on him), having been barred from feeling shame (vb int.: *sharmàna*) at an early age, continued to be affected by that remarkable ban throughout his later years, yes, long after his escape from his mothers' zone of influence?

Reader: it cannot.

What's the opposite of shame? What's left when *sharam* is subtracted? That's obvious: shamelessness.

Owing to the pride of his parents and the singular circumstances of his life, Omar Khayyam Shakil, at the age of twelve, was wholly unfamiliar with the emotion in which he was now being forbidden to indulge.

"What does it feel like?" he asked—and his mothers, seeing his bewilderment, essayed explanations. "Your face gets hot," said Bunny-the-youngest, "but your heart starts shivering."

"It makes women feel like to cry and die," said Chhunni-ma, "but men, it makes them go wild."

"Except sometimes," his middle mother muttered with prophetic spite, "it happens the other way around."

The division of the three mothers into separate beings became, in the following years, more and more plaintosee. They squabbled over the most alarming trifles, such as who should write the notes that were placed in the dumb-waiter, or whether to take their mid-morning mint tea and biscuits in the drawing room or on the landing. It was as if by sending their son out into the sunlit arenas of the town they had exposed themselves to the very thing they denied him the freedom to experience; as if on the day when the world laid eyes for the first time on their Omar Khayyam the three sisters were finally pierced by the forbidden arrows of *sharam*. Their quarrels died down when he made his second escape; but they were never properly reunited until they decided to repeat the act of motherhood . . .

And there is an even stranger matter to report. It is this: when they were divided by Omar Khayyam's birthday wishes, they had been indistinguishable too long to retain any exact sense of their former selves—and, well, to come right out with it, the result was that they divided up in the wrong way, they got all mixed up, so that Bunny, the youngest, sprouted the premature grey hairs and took on the queenly airs that ought to have been the prerogative of the senior sibling; while big Chhunni seemed to become a torn, uncertain soul, a sister of middles and vacillations; and Munnee developed the histrionic gadfly petulance that is the traditional characteristic of the baby in any generation, and which never ceases to be that baby's right, no matter how old she gets. In the chaos of their regeneration the wrong heads had ended up on the wrong bodies; they became psychological centaurs, fish-women, hybrids; and of course this confused separation of personalities carried with it the implication that they were still not genuinely discrete, because they could only be comprehended if you took them as a whole.

Who would not have wanted to escape from such mothers?— In later years, Omar Khayyam would remember his childhood as a lover, abandoned, remembers his beloved: changeless, incapable of ageing, a memory kept prisoner in a circle of heart's fire. Only he remembered with hatred instead of love; not with flames, but icily, icily. The other Omar wrote great things out of love; our hero's story is poorer, no doubt because it was marinated in bile.

—And it would be easy to argue that he developed pronounced misogynist tendencies at an early age.—That all his subsequent dealings with women were acts of revenge against the memory of his mothers.—But I say in Omar Khayyam's defence: all his life, whatever he did, whoever he became, he did his filial duty and paid their bills. The pawnbroker Chalaak Sahib ceased to pay visits to the dumb-waiter; which indicates the existence of love, love of some sort . . . but he is not grown-up yet. Just now the satchel has arrived via the Mistri's machine; now it hangs over the shoulder of the twelve-year-old escapologist; now he enters the dumb-waiter and the satchel begins its descent back to earth. Omar Khayyam's twelfth birthday brought him freedom instead of cake; also, inside the satchel, blue-lined copybooks, a slate, a washable wooden board and some quill pens with which to practise the sinuous script of his mother tongue, chalks, pencils, a wooden ruler and a box of geometry instruments, protractor, dividers, compass. Plus a small aluminium etherizing box in which to murder frogs. With the weapons of learning hanging over his shoulder, Omar Khayyam left his mothers, who wordlessly (and still in unison) waved good-bye.

Omar Khayyam Shakil never forgot the moment of his emergence from the dumb-waiter into the dust of the no-man's-land around the high mansion of his childhood which stood like a pariah between the Cantonment and the town; or his first sight of the reception committee, one of whose members was carrying a most unexpected sort of garland.

When the wife of Q.'s finest leather-goods merchant received the sisters' order for a school satchel from the peon whom she dispatched to the dumb-waiter once a fortnight in accordance with the Shakils' standing orders, she, Zeenat Kabuli, at once ran round to the house of her best friend, the widow Farida Balloch, who lived with her brother Bilal. The three of them, who had never ceased to believe that Yakoob Balloch's street-death was the direct result of his getting mixed up with the anchoritic sisters, agreed that the flesh-and-blood product of the longago scandal must be about to emerge into plain daylight. They stationed themselves outside the Shakil household to await this event, but not before Zeenat Kabuli had pulled out from the back of her shop a gunny sack filled with old rotting shoes and sandals and slippers of no conceivable value to anyone, annihilated footwear that had been awaiting just such an occasion, and which was now strung together to form the worst of all insults, that is, a necklace of shoes. "The shoe garland," the widow Balloch swore to Zeenat Kabuli, "just see if I don't hang it on that child's neck, personal."

The week-long vigil of Farida, Zeenat and Bilal inevitably attracted attention, so that by the time Omar Khayyam jumped out of the dumb-waiter they had been joined by divers other gawpers and taunters, raggedy urchins and unemployed clerks and washerwomen on their way to the ghats. Also present was the town postman, Muhammad Ibadalla, who bore upon his forehead the *gatta* or permanent bruise which revealed him to be a religious fanatic who pressed brow to prayer-mat on at least five occasions per diem, and probably at the sixth, optional time as well. This Ibadalla had found his job through the malign influence of the beardy serpent who stood beside him in the heat, the local divine, the notorious Maulana Dawood who rode around town on a motor-scooter donated by the Angrez sahibs, threatening the citizens with damnation. It turned out that this Ibadalla had been incensed by the Shakil ladies' decision not to send their letter to the headmaster of the Cantt school via the postal services. It had been included, instead, in the envelope they had sent down in the dumb-waiter to the flower-girl Azra, along with a small extra fee. Ibadalla had been wooing this Azra for some time, but she laughed at him: "I don't care for a type who spends so much time with his backside higher than his head." So the sisters' decision to place their letter in her care struck the postman as a personal insult, a way of undermining his status, and also as further proof of their Godlessness, for had they not allied themselves by this infamous act of correspondence with a slut who

cracked jokes about prayer? "Behold," Ibadalla yelled energetically as Omar Khayyam touched ground, "there stands the Devil's seed."

There now occurred an unfortunate incident. Ibadalla, incensed
by the Azra business, had spoken up first, thus incurring the
displeasure of his patron Maulana Dawood, a loss of divine support which ruined the postman's chance of future promotion and
intensified his hatred of all Shakils; because of course the Maulana
thought it his right to begin the assault on the poor, fat, pre-
maturely pubescent symbol of incarnate sin. In an attempt to
regain the initiative Dawood flung himself to his knees in the dust
at Omar's feet; he ground his forehead ecstatically into the dirt
by Omar's toes, and called out: "O God! O scourging Lord! Bring
down upon this human abomination Thy sizzling fountain of
fire!" Etcetera. This grotesque display greatly irritated the three
who had kept the original vigil. "Whose husband died for a dumb-
waiter?" Farida Balloch hissed to her friend. "That shouting
oldie's? Then who should be speaking now?" Her brother Bilal
did not stop for speech; rope of shoes in hand, he strode forward,
bellowing in that stentorian voice that was almost the equal of
the fabled voice of his namesake, that first, black Bilal, the Proph-
et's muezzin: "Boy! Flesh of infamy! Think yourself lucky I do
no more than this! You think I couldn't squash you flat like one
mosquito?"—And in the background, like raucous echoes, urchins washerwomen clerks were chanting: "Devil's seed!—Fountain of fire!—Whose husband died?—Like one mosquito!"—They
were all closing in, Ibadalla and the Maulana and three vengeful
vigilantes, while Omar stood like a cobra-hypnotized mongoose,
but all around him things were unfreezing, the twelve-year-old,
suspended prejudices of the town were springing back to life . . .
and Bilal could wait no longer, he rushed up to the boy as Dawood
prostrated himself for the seventeenth time; the garland of shoes
was hurled in Omar's direction; and just then the Maulana
straightened up to howl at God, interposing scrawny gizzard

between insulting footwear and its target, and there, next thing anyone knew, was the fateful necklace, hanging around the divine's accidental neck.

Omar Khayyam began to giggle: such can be the effects of fear. And urchins giggled with him; even the widow Balloch had to fight back the laughter until it came out as water from her eyes. In those days, people were not so keen on the servants of God as we are told they have become at present . . . Maulana Dawood rose up with murder in his face. Being no fool, however, he quickly turned this face away from the giant Bilal and reached out his claws for Omar Khayyam—who was saved by the blessed figure, shouldering its way through the mob, of Mr. Eduardo Rodrigues, schoolmaster, who had arrived as arranged to fetch the new pupil to class. And with Rodrigues was a vision of such joy that moonstruck Khayyam at once forgot the danger that had come so close. "This is Farah," Rodrigues told him, "she is two standards senior to you." The vision looked at Omar; then at the shoe-necked Maulana, who in his rage had neglected to remove the garland; then put back its head and roared.

"God, yaar," she said to Omar, her first word a casual blasphemy, "why you didn't sit on at home? This town was already full of fools."

3

MELTING
ICE

Cool, white as a refrigerator, it stood amidst offensively green
lawns: the Cantonment School. In its gardens trees also
flourished, because the Angrez sahibs had diverted large quantities
of the region's sparse water supplies into the hoses with which
the Cantt gardeners strolled around all day. It was clear that those
curious grey beings from a wet northern world could not survive
unless grass and bougainvillaea and tamarind and jackfruit thrived
as well. As for the human saplings nurtured in the School: white
(grey) as well as brown, they ranged from age-three to age-
nineteen. But after the age of eight, the numbers of Angrez children fell away sharply, and the children in the upper standards
were almost uniformly brown. What happened to the fair-skinned
children after their eighth birthdays? Death, vanishment, a sudden
surge of melanin production in their skins?—No, no. For the real
answer it would be necessary to conduct extensive research into
the old ledgers of steamship companies and the diaries of long-
extinct ladies in what the Angrez colonialists always called the
mother country, but what was in fact a land of maiden aunts and

other, more distant female relatives, on whom children could be billeted to save them from the perils of an Oriental upbringing . . . but such research is beyond the resources of the author, who must avert his eyes from such side-issues without further delay.

School is school; everyone knows what goes on there. Omar Khayyam was a fat boy, so he got what fat boys get, taunts, ink-pellets in the back of the neck, nicknames, a few beatings, nothing special. When his schoolfellows found that he had no intention of rising to any gibes about his unusual origins they simply left him alone, contenting themselves with the occasional schoolyard rhyme. This suited him excellently. Unashamed, accustomed to solitude, he began to enjoy his near-invisibility. From his position at the edge of the school's life, he took vicarious pleasure in the activities of those around him, silently celebrating the rise or fall of this or that playground emperor, or the examination failures of particularly unappetizing classfellows: the delights of the spectator.

Once, by chance, he stood in a shadowed corner of the tree-heavy grounds and observed two seniors canoodling energetically behind a flame-of-the-forest. Watching their fondlings, he felt a strangely warm satisfaction, and decided to look for other opportunities of indulging in this new pastime. As he grew older, and was permitted to stay out later, he became skilled in his chosen pursuit; the town yielded up its secrets to his omnipresent eyes. Through inefficient chick-blinds he spied on the couplings of the postman Ibadalla with the widow Balloch, and also, in another place, with her best friend Zeenat Kabuli, so that the notorious occasion on which the postman, the leather-goods merchant and the loud-mouthed Bilal went at one another with knives in a gully and ended up stone dead, all three of them, was no mystery to him; but he was too young to understand why Zeenat and Farida, who should by rights have hated each other like poison once it all came out, shacked up together instead and lived, after that

triple killing, in unbreakable friendship and celibacy for the rest
of their days.

To be frank: what a telescope began at long distance, Omar
Khayyam continued in close-up. Let us not be afraid to mention
the word "voyeur," remembering that it has already been mentioned (in telescopic context) by Farah Zoroaster. But now that
we have named him peeping-tom, we should also say that he was
never caught, unlike that bold fellow in Agra who, they say,
looked over a high wall to spy on the building of the Taj Mahal.
He had his eyes put out, or so the story goes; whereas Omar
Khayyam's peepers were opened wide by his voyeurism, which
revealed to him both the infinitely rich and cryptic texture of
human life and also the bitter-sweet delights of living through
other human beings.

He had one total failure. Needless to say, what mothers had
hidden from him for twelve years, schoolboys unveiled in twelve
minutes: that is, the story of the legendary party at which mustachioed officers had been eyed, sized up, and afterwards . . .
Omar Khayyam Shakil, obeying maternal orders, engaged in no
fisticuffs when taunted with this saga. He existed in a kind of
Eden of the morals, and shrugged the insults off; but after that
he began watching the Angrez gentlemen for signs, examining
them for facial resemblances to himself, waiting to pounce on
some casual or inadvertent expression or gesture that might reveal
the identity of his unknown male progenitor. He had no success.
Perhaps the father was long gone, and living, if still alive, in some
seaside bungalow lapped by tides of nostalgia for the horizons of
his departed glory, fingering the few miserable artifacts—ivory
hunting horns, kukri knives, a photograph of himself at a Ma-
haraja's tiger hunt—which preserved, on the mantels of his de-
clining years, the dying echoes of the past, like seashells that sing
of distant seas . . . but these are fruitless speculations. Unable to
locate his father, the boy selected one for himself out of available
personnel, bestowing the accolade without any reservations upon

Mr. Eduardo Rodrigues the schoolmaster, who was himself a recent arrival in Q., having alighted jauntily from a bus one day some years previously, dressed in whites, with a white fedora on his head and an empty birdcage in his hand.

And one last word about Omar Khayyam's peepings: because of course his three mothers had begun to live vicariously too, they couldn't help themselves, in those days of their weakening resolve they quizzed him eagerly upon his return from Outside about ladies' fashions and all the minutiae of town life, and had he heard anything about *them*; from time to time they covered their faces with their shawls, so that it was evident that they could no longer seal themselves off from the emotion they had anathematized . . . spying on the world through the unreliable eyes of their son (and naturally he did not tell them everything), their own voyeurism-by-proxy had the effect that such things are classically supposed to have: that is, it weakened their moral fibre. Perhaps this is why they were able to contemplate a repetition of their crime.

Mr. Eduardo Rodrigues was as slim and sharp as his enormous collection of pencils, and nobody knew his age. According to the angle at which the light caught his face he could take on the bright-eyed insolent appearance of a teenager or the doleful aspect of a man drowning in half-spent yesterdays. An unexplained southerner, he cut a mysterious figure in the town, having gone directly from the bus depot of his arrival to the Cantonment School, where he had succeeded in talking his way into a teaching post before night fell. "It is necessary to be unusual," was all the explanation he would give, "if one wants to spread the Word."

He lived in a puritanical room as the paying guest of one of the less fortunate Angrez sahibs. On his walls he hung a crucifix, and also glued up a number of cheap pictures, excised from calendars, of a balmy coastal land in which palm trees swayed against impossibly orange sunsets and a Baroque cathedral stood, partially overgrown by creepers, on an ocean inlet crowded with flame-sailed dhows. Omar Khayyam Shakil and Farah Zoroaster, the only students who ever entered this sanctum, saw no signs of anything more personal; it seemed as if Eduardo were hiding his past from the fierce rays of the desert sun, to prevent it from fading. Such was the blinding emptiness of the teacher's quarters that Omar Khayyam did not notice until his third visit the cheap birdcage sitting on top of the room's one cupboard, a cage from which the gold paint had long ago begun to peel, and which was just as empty as it had been on the day of his arrival at the bus depot. "As if," Farah whispered scornfully, "he came up here to catch a bird, and couldn't, the stupid type."

Eduardo and Omar, each in his separate way an outsider in Q., may have been drawn to each other by the half-conscious perception of their likeness; but there were also other forces at work. These forces may all be conveniently collected under a single heading, and this phrase, too, has been mentioned before: it is "courting Disaster."

It had not escaped the notice of the town gossips that Eduardo had arrived, birdcage in hand, fedora on head, a mere two months after the customs officer Zoroaster had been sent up to these parts, minus wife, plus eight-year-old daughter. So it wasn't long before mule-wallahs and ironmongers and scootered divines had worked out that this Zoroaster's previous posting had been in that same zone of creepery cathedrals and coconut beaches whose memory could be smelled on Rodrigues's white suit and in his Portuguese name. Tongues began to wag: "So where is that customs-wallah's wife? Divorced, sent back to her mother, murdered in a rage of the passions? Look at that Farah, she doesn't look like her daddy, not one bit!" But these tongues were also obliged to admit that Farah Zoroaster did not look one bit like the teacher either, so that avenue was reluctantly closed off, especially when it became plain that Rodrigues and Zoroaster were on extremely cordial terms. "So why does a customs officer get shunted out here to this end-of-the-earth job?" Farah had a simple answer. "My stupid father is a type who goes on dreaming after he has woken up. He thinks one day we will return to where we have never been, that damn land of Ahuramazda, and this no-good Irani frontier is the closest we could get. Can you imagine?" she howled. "He *volunteered*."

Gossip is like water. It probes surfaces for their weak places, until it finds the breakthrough point; so it was only a matter of time before the good people of Q. hit upon the most shameful, scandalous explanation of all. "O God, a grown man in love with a little child. Eduardo and Farah—what do you mean it can't happen, happens every day, only a few years back there was that other—yes, that must be it, these Christians are big perverts, God preserve us, he follows his little floozy up here to the backyard of the universe, and who knows what encouragement she gives, because a woman knows how to tell a man if he is wanted or not wanted, of course, even at eight years old, these things are in the blood."

Neither Eduardo nor Farah gave, in their behaviour, the slightest indication that the rumours were rooted in fact. It is true that Eduardo did not marry during the years of Farah's growing towards womanhood; but it is also true that Farah, known as "Disaster," was also called "the ice block" on account of her sub-zero coldness towards her many admirers, a frigidity which extended also to her relations with Eduardo Rodrigues. "But of course they put up a good front, what do you think?"—The gossips were able to point out, triumphantly, that they had been justified by events in the end.

Omar Khayyam Shakil, for all his love of watching-and-listening, pretended to turn a deaf ear to all these stories; such are the effects of love. But they got inside him anyway, they got under his skin and into his blood and worked their way, like little splinters, to his heart; until he, too, proved himself guilty of the alleged Christian perversions of the schoolteacher Rodrigues.

Choose yourself a father and you also choose your inheritance. (But Sufiya Zinobia must wait for a few pages yet.)

I have idled away too many paragraphs in the company of gossips; let's get back onto solid ground: Eduardo Rodrigues, accompanied gossip-feedingly by Farah, collecting Omar Khayyam on his first schoolday, a fact which bore witness to the residual influence of the Shakil name in the town. In the following months, Eduardo discovered the boy's exceptional aptitude for learning, and wrote to his mothers offering his services as a private tutor who could help realize their child's potential. It is a matter of record that his mothers agreed to the schoolteacher's suggestion; also that Eduardo's only other private pupil was Farah Zoroaster, whose father was excused from paying any fee, because Eduardo was a genuinely dedicated teacher; and thirdly, that as the years passed the threesome of Omar, Eduardo and Farah became a common sight in the town.

It was Rodrigues, who had the ability of speaking in capital letters, who steered Omar towards a medical career. "To Succeed in Life," he told the boy amid beach-postcards and empty bird-cage, "one must be Of the Essence. Yes, make yourself Essential, that's the Ticket . . . and who is most Indispensable? Why, the fellow who does the Dispensing! I mean of Advice, Diagnosis, Restricted Drugs. Be a Doctor; it is what I have Seen in You."

What Eduardo saw in Omar (in my opinion): the possibilities of his true, peripheral nature. What's a doctor, after all?—A legitimized voyeur, a stranger whom we permit to poke fingers and even hands into places where we would not permit most people to insert so much as a finger-tip, who gazes on what we take most trouble to hide; a sitter-at-bedsides, an outsider admitted to our most intimate moments (birthdeathetc.), anonymous, a minor character, yet also, paradoxically, central, especially at the crisis . . . yes, yes. Eduardo was a far-sighted teacher, and no mistake. And Omar Khayyam, who had picked Rodrigues for a father, never once considered going against his tutor's wishes. This is how lives are made.

But not only in this way; also by dog-eared books discovered accidentally at home, and by long-suppressed first loves . . . When Omar Khayyam Shakil was sixteen years old, he was flung into a great vortex of fearful joy, because Farah the Parsee, Disaster Zoroaster, invited him one day to come out and see her father's customs post.

". . . and fainted, though both his feet had been on solid ground." We have already been told something of what transpired at the frontier: how a cloud descended, and Omar Khayyam, mistaking it for his childhood nightmare of the void at the end of the earth, passed out. It is possible that this fainting fit gave him the idea for what he did later that day.

Details first: what was the tone of Farah's invitation?—Graceless, curt, I-don't-care-if-you-don't. Its motivation, whence?—From Eduardo, who had urged her privately: "That is one lonely boy, be nice. You bright ones should stick together." (Omar Khayyam was the brighter of the pair; although two years still stood between them, he had caught up to Farah in other ways, and was now in the self-same standard.) How rapidly did Omar Khayyam accept?—Ek dum. Fut-a-fut. At once, or even quicker.

On weekdays, during term, Farah lodged in Q. at the home of a Parsee mechanic and his wife, with whom her father had cultivated a friendship for this very purpose. This mechanic, an unimportant Jamshed who does not even merit a description, drove them out to the frontier on the selected holiday in a jeep he was repairing. And as they neared the border, Farah's spirits rose while Omar's fell . . .

. . . His fear of the Edge mounted, irrationally, as they drove, as he sat behind her in the roofless vehicle while her open, wind-whipped hair flickered in front of him like black fire. Whereas her mood was lightened by the drive, around a spur of the mountains, through a pass in which they were watched by the invisible eyes of suspicious tribals. The emptiness of the frontier pleased Farah, no matter how openly she sneered at her father for having taken this dead-end job. She even began to sing; revealing that she had a melodious voice.

At the frontier: clouds, fainting fit, water sprinkled on face, reawakening, whereamI. Omar Khayyam comes round to find that the cloud has lifted, so that it is possible to see that the frontier is an unimpressive place: no wall, no police, no barbed wire or floodlights, no red-and-white striped barriers, nothing but a row of concrete bollards at hundred-foot intervals, bollards driven into the hard and barren ground. There is a small customs house, and a railhead that has turned brown with rust; on the rails stands a single forgotten goods van, also browned by oblivion. "The trains don't come any more," Farah says. "The international situation does not permit it."

A customs officer depends, for a decent income, on traffic. Goods pass through, he not unreasonably impounds them, their owners see reason, an accommodation is reached, the customs man's family gets new clothes. Nobody minds this arrangement; everyone knows how little public officials are paid. Negotiations are honourably conducted on both sides.

But very little in the way of dutiable items passes through the small brick building that is Mr. Zoroaster's power centre. Under cover of night, tribals stroll back and forth between the countries through bollards and rocks. Who knows what they carry forth and back? This is Zoroaster's tragedy; and, in spite of her scholarship, he has trouble financing his daughter's fine education. How he consoles himself: "Soon, soon the railway line will open . . ." But the rust is accumulating on this belief as well; he gazes across bollards to the ancestral land of Zarathustra and tries to gain solace from its proximity, but there is, these days, a strain in his expression . . . Farah Zoroaster claps her hands and runs in and out between the interminable bollards. "Fun, na?" she yells, "Teep-taap!" Omar Khayyam, for the sake of maintaining her affable mood, agrees that the place is quite tip-top. Zoroaster shrugs without bitterness and retreats into his office with the jeep-driver, warning the young people not to stay out too long in the sun.

Perhaps they stayed out too long, and that was what gave Omar Khayyam the courage to declare his love: "The sight of you through my telescope," etc., but there is no need to repeat his speech, or Farah's coarse reply. Rejected, Omar Khayyam unleashes piteous questions: "Why? Why not? Because I'm fat?" And Farah replies, "Fat would be all right; but there is something ugly about you, you know that?"—"Ugly?"—"Don't ask me what, I dunno. Something. Must be in your personality or somewhere."

Silence between them until late afternoon. Omar meandering in Farah's wake between bollards. He notices that broken pieces of mirrors have been tied to many of the posts with bits of string; as Farah approaches each fragment she sees shards of herself reflected in the glass, and smiles her private smile. Omar Khayyam Shakil understands that his beloved is a being too self-contained to succumb to any conventional assault; she and her mirrors are twins and need no outsiders to make them feel complete . . . and then, in the late afternoon, inspired by too–much–sun or fainting fit, he has his idea. "Have you ever," he asks Farah Zoroaster, "been hypnotized?"—And for the first time in history, she looks at him with interest.

Afterwards, when her womb began to swell; when an outraged headmaster called her into his office and expelled her for calling down shame upon the school; when she was thrown out by her father, who had suddenly found that his empty customs house was too full to accommodate a daughter whose belly revealed her adherence to other, unacceptable customs; when Eduardo Rodrigues had taken her, pulling and fighting against his inexorable, gripping hand, to the Cantt padre and married her by force; when Eduardo, having thus declared himself the guilty party for all to see, was dismissed from his job for conduct unbecoming; when Farah and Eduardo had left for the railway station in a tonga notable for the almost total absence of luggage (although a birdcage, still empty, was present, and malicious tongues said that Eduardo Rodrigues had finally caught two birds instead of one); when they had gone and the town had settled back into ashen nothingness, after the brief blaze of the wicked drama that had been played out in its streets . . . then Omar Khayyam tried, futilely, to find consolation in the fact that, as every hypnotist knows, one of the first reassurances in the hypnotic process, a formula which is repeated many times, runs as follows:

"You will do anything that I ask you to do, but I will ask you to do nothing that you will be unwilling to do."

"She was willing," he told himself. "Then where's the blame? She must have been willing, and everybody knows the risk."

But in spite of nothing-that-you-will-be-unwilling-to-do; in spite, too, of the actions of Eduardo Rodrigues, which had been at once so resolute and so resigned that Omar Khayyam had almost been convinced that the teacher really was the father—why not, after all? A woman who is willing with one will be willing with two!—in spite of everything, I say, Omar Khayyam Shakil was possessed by a demon which made him shake in the middle of breakfast and go hot in the night and cold in the day and sometimes cry out for no reason in the street or while ascending in the dumb-waiter. Its fingers reached outwards from his stomach to clutch, without warning, various interior parts of himself, from adam's-apple to large (and also small) intestine, so that he suffered from moments of near-strangulation and spent long unproductive hours on the pot. It made his limbs mysteriously heavy in the mornings so that sometimes he was unable to get out of bed. It made his tongue dry and his knees knock. It led his teenage feet into cheap brandy shops. Tottering drunkenly home to the rage of his three mothers, he would be heard telling a swaying group of fellow-sufferers: "The only thing about this business is that it has made me understand my mothers at last. This must be what they locked themselves up to avoid, and baba, who would not?" Vomiting out the thin yellow fluid of his shame while the dumb-waiter descended, he swore to his companions, who were falling asleep in the dirt: "Me, too, man. I've got to escape this also."

On the evening when Omar Khayyam, eighteen years old and already fatter than fifty melons, came home to inform Chhunni, Munnee and Bunny that he had won a scholarship at the best medical college in Karachi, the three sisters were only able to hide their grief at his imminent departure by erecting around it a great barrier of objects, the most valuable jewels and paintings in the house, which they scurried to collect from room to room until a pile of ancient beauty stood in front of their old, favourite swing-seat. "Scholarship is all very well," his youngest mother told him, "but we also can give money to our boy when he goes into the world." "What do these doctors think?" Chhunni demanded in a kind of fury. "We are too poor to pay for your education? Let them take their charity to the Devil, your family has money in abundance." "Old money," Munnee concurred. Unable to persuade them that the award was an honour he did not wish to refuse, Omar Khayyam was obliged to leave for the railway station with his pockets bulging with the pawnbroker's banknotes. Around his neck was a garland whose one hundred and one fresh-cut flowers gave off an aroma which quite obliterated the memory-stink of the necklace of shoes which had once so narrowly missed his neck. The perfume of this garland was so intense that he forgot to tell his mothers a last bit of gossip, which was that Zoroaster the customs officer had fallen sick under the spell of the bribeless desert and had taken to standing stark naked on top of concrete bollards while mirror-fragments ripped his feet. Arms outstretched and daughterless, Zoroaster addressed the sun, begging it to come down to earth and engulf the planet in its brilliant cleansing fire. The tribals who bore this tale into the bazaar of Q. were of the opinion that the customs-wallah's fervour was so great that he would undoubtedly succeed, so that it was worth making preparations for the end of the world.

The last person to whom Omar Khayyam spoke before making his escape from the town of shame was a certain Chand Moham-mad, who said afterwards, "That fat guy didn't look so hot when I started talking to him and he looked twice as sick when I fin-ished." This Chand Mohammad was a vendor of ice. As Omar Khayyam, still unable to shake off the terrible debility which had gripped him ever since the incident at the frontier, hauled his obesity into a first-class carriage, Chand ran up and said, "Hot day, sahib. Ice is needed." At first, Shakil, out of breath and gloomy, told him, "Be off and sell other fools your frozen water." But Chand persisted: "Sahib, in the afternoon the Loo wind will blow, and if you do not have my ice at your feet the heat will melt the marrow out of your bones."

Persuaded by this convincing argument, Omar Khayyam pur-chased a long tin tub, four feet long, eighteen inches wide, one foot deep, in which there lay a solid slab of ice, sprinkled with sawdust and sand to prolong its life. Grunting as he heaved it into the carriage, the ice vendor made a joke. "Such is life," he said, "one ice block returns to town and another sets off in the opposite direction."

Omar Khayyam unbuckled his sandals and placed his bare feet on the ice, feeling the healing solace of its coldness. Peeling off too many rupees for Chand Mohammad as he cheered up, he asked idly, "What rubbish are you talking? How can a block of ice return unmelted after the journey? The tin tub, empty, or full of melted water, you must be meaning that."

"O, no, sahib, great lord," the ice-vendor grinned as he pocketed the cash, "this is one ice block that goes everywhere without melting at all."

Colour drained from fat cheeks. Plump feet jumped off ice. Omar Khayyam, looking around fearfully as if he thought she might materialize at any moment, spoke in tones so altered by fury that the ice-vendor backed off, frightened. "Her? When? You are trying to insult . . . ?" He caught the ice-man by his ragged shirt, and the poor wretch had no option but to tell it all, to reveal that on this very train, a few hours back, Mrs. Farah Rodrigues (née Zoroaster) had returned shamelessly to the scene of her infamy and headed straight out to her father's frontier post, "even though he threw her in the street like a bucket of dirty water, sahib, just think."

When Farah came back, she brought neither husband nor child. Nobody ever found out what had become of Eduardo and the baby for which he had sacrificed everything, so of course the stories could circulate without fear of disproof: a miscarriage, an abortion in spite of Rodrigues's Catholic faith, the baby exposed on a rock after birth, the baby stifled in its crib, the baby given to the orphanage or left in the street, while Farah and Eduardo like wild lovers copulated on the postcard beaches or in the aisle of the vegetation-covered house of the Christian God, until they tired of each other, she gave him the boot, he (tired of her lascivious flirtings) gave her the boot, they gave each other simultaneous boots, who cares who it was, she is back so lock up your sons.

Farah Rodrigues in her pride spoke to no one in Q. except to order food and supplies in the shops; until, in her old age, she began to frequent the covert liquor joints, which was where she would reminisce, years later, about Omar Khayyam, after his name got into the papers. On her rare visits to the bazaar she made her purchases without looking anyone in the eye, pausing only to gaze at herself in every available mirror with a frank affection which proved to the town that she regretted nothing. So even when it got about that she had come back to look after her crazy father and to run the customs post, to prevent his dismissal by his Angrez bosses, even then the town's attitude did not soften; who knows what they get up to out there, people said, naked father and whore-child, best place for them is out there in the desert where nobody has to look except God and the Devil, and they know it all already.

And on his train, his feet once more resting on a block of melting ice, Omar Khayyam Shakil was borne away into the future, convinced that he had finally managed to escape, and the cool pleasure of that notion and also of the ice brought a smile to his lips, even while the hot wind blew.

Two years later, his mothers wrote to tell him that he had a brother, whom they had named Babar after the first Emperor of the Mughals who had marched over the Impossible Mountains and conquered wherever he went. After that the three sisters, unified once again by motherhood, were happy and indistinguishable for many years within the walls of "Nishapur."

When Omar Khayyam read the letter, his first reaction was to whistle softly with something very like admiration.

"The old witches," he said aloud, "they managed to do it again."

II

THE
DUELLISTS

4

BEHIND THE SCREEN

This is a novel about Sufiya Zinobia, elder daughter of General Raza Hyder and his wife Bilquìs, about what happened between her father and Chairman Iskander Harappa, formerly Prime Minister, now defunct, and about her surprising marriage to a certain Omar Khayyam Shakil, physician, fat man and for a time the intimate crony of that same Isky Harappa, whose neck had the miraculous power of remaining unbruised, even by a hangman's rope. Or perhaps it would be more accurate, if also more opaque, to say that Sufiya Zinobia is about this novel.

At any rate, it is not possible even to begin to know a person without first gaining some knowledge of her family background; so I must proceed in this way, by explaining how it came about that Bilquìs grew frightened of the hot afternoon wind called the Loo:

On the last morning of his life, her father Mahmoud Kemal, known as Mahmoud the Woman, dressed as usual in a shiny blue two-piece suit shot with brilliant streaks of red, looked approvingly at himself in the ornate mirror which he had removed from the foyer of his theatre on account of its irresistible frame of naked cherubs shooting arrows and blowing golden horns, hugged his eighteen-year-old daughter and announced: "So you see, girl, your father dresses finely, as befits the chief administrative officer of a glorious Empire." And at breakfast, when she began dutifully to spoon khichri on to his plate, he roared in good-natured fury, "Why do you lift your hand, daughter? A princess does not serve." Bilquìs bowed her head and stared out of the bottom left-hand corner of her eyes, whereupon her father applauded loudly. "O, too good, Billoo! What elite acting, I swear!"

It's a fact, strange-but-true, that the city of idolaters in which this scene took place—call it Indraprastha, Puranaqila, even Delhi— had often been ruled by men who believed (like Mahmoud) in Al-Lah, The God. Their artifacts litter the city to this day, ancient observatories and victory towers and of course that great red fortress, Al-Hambra, the red one, which will play an important part in our story. And, what is more, many of these godly rulers had come up from the humblest of origins; every schoolchild knows about the Slave Kings . . . but anyway, the point is that this whole business of ruling-an-Empire was just a family joke, because of course Mahmoud's domain was only the Empire Talkies, a fleapit of a picture theatre in the old quarter of the town.

"The greatness of a picture house," Mahmoud liked to say, "can be deduced from the noisiness of its customers. Go to those deelux palaces in the new city, see their velvet thrones of seats and the mirror tiling all over the vestibules, feel the air-conditioning and you'll understand why the audiences sit as quiet as hell. They are tamed by the splendour of the surroundings, also by the price of the seats. But in the Empire of Mahmoud the paying customers make the very devil of a din, except during the hit song numbers. We are not absolute monarchs, child, don't forget it; especially in these days when the police are turning against us and refuse to come and eject even the biggest badmashes, who make whistlings that split your ears. Never mind. It is a question of freedom of individuals, after all."

Yes: it was a fifth-rate Empire. But to Mahmoud it was quite something, a Slave King's estate, for had he not begun his career out on the suppurating streets as one of those no-account types who push the movie adverts around town on wheelbarrows, shouting, "It is now-showing!" and also, "Plans filling up fast!"—and did he not now sit in a manager's office, complete with cashbox and keys? You see: even family jokes run the risk of being taken seriously, and there lurked in the natures of both father and daughter a literalism, a humourlessness owing to which Bilquìs grew up with an unspoken fantasy of queenhood simmering in the corners of her downcast eyes. "I tell you," she would apostrophize the angelic mirror after her father had left for work, "with me it would be absolute control or zero! These badmashes would not get away with their whistling shistling if it was my affair!" Thus Bilquìs invented a secret self far more imperious than her father the emperor. And in the darkness of his Empire, night after night, she studied the giant, shimmering illusions of princesses who danced before the rackety audience beneath the gold-painted equestrian figure of an armoured medieval knight who bore a pennant on which was inscribed the meaningless word *Excelsior*. Illusions fed illusions, and Bilquìs began to carry herself with the grandeur befitting a dream-empress, taking as compliments the taunts of the street-urchins in the gullies around her home: "Tantara!" they greeted her as she sailed by: "Have mercy, O gracious lady, O Rani of Khansi!" *Khansi-ki-Rani* they named her—queen of coughs, that is to say of expelled air, of sickness and hot wind.

"Be careful," her father warned her, "things are changing in this city; even the most affectionate nicknames are acquiring new and so-dark meanings."

This was the time immediately before the famous moth-eaten partition that chopped up the old country and handed Al-Lah a few insect-nibbled slices of it, some dusty western acres and jungly eastern swamps that the ungodly were happy to do without. (Al-Lah's new country: two chunks of land a thousand miles apart. A county so improbable that it could almost exist.) But let's be unemotional and state merely that feelings were running so high that even going to the pictures had become a political act. The one-godly went to these cinemas and the washers of stone gods to those; movie-fans had been partitioned already, in advance of the tired old land. The stone-godly ran the movie business, that goes without saying, and being vegetarians they made a very famous film: *Gai-Wallah*. Perhaps you've heard of it? An unusual fantasy about a lone, masked hero who roamed the Indo-Gangetic plain liberating herds of beef-cattle from their keepers, saving the sacred, horned, uddered beasts from the slaughterhouse. The stone-gang packed out the cinemas where this movie was shown; the one-godly riposted by rushing to see imported, non-vegetarian Westerns in which cows got massacred and the good guys feasted on steaks. And mobs of irate film buffs attacked the cinemas of their enemies . . . well, it was a time for all types of craziness, that's all.

Mahmoud the Woman lost his Empire because of a single error, which arose out of his fatal personality flaw, namely tolerance. "Time to rise above all this partition foolishness," he informed his mirror one morning, and that same day he booked a double bill into his Talkies: Randolph Scott and *Gai-Wallah* would succeed one another on his screen.

On the opening day of the double bill of his destruction the meaning of his nickname changed for ever. He had been named The Woman by the street urchins because, being a widower, he had been obliged to act as a mother to Bilquìs ever since his wife died when the girl was barely two. But now this affectionate title came to mean something more dangerous, and when children spoke of Mahmoud the Woman they meant Mahmoud the Weakling, the Shameful, the Fool. "Woman," he sighed resignedly to his daughter, "what a term! Is there no end to the burdens this word is capable of bearing? Was there ever such a broad-backed and also such a dirty word?"

How the double bill was settled; both sides, veg and non-veg, boycotted the Empire. For five, six, seven days, films played to an empty house in which peeling plaster and slowly rotating ceiling fans and the intermission gram-vendors gazed down upon rows of undoubtedly rickety and equally certainly unoccupied seats; three-thirty, six-thirty and nine-thirty shows were all the same, not even the special Sunday-morning show could tempt anyone through the swinging doors. "Give it up," Bilquìs urged her father. "What do you want? You miss your wheelbarrow or what?"

But now an unfamiliar stubbornness entered Mahmoud the Woman, and he announced that the double bill would be held over for a Second Sensational Week. His own barrow-boys deserted him; nobody was willing to cry these ambiguous wares through the electric gullies; no voice dared announce, "Plans now open!" or, "Don't wait or it's too late!"

Mahmoud and Bilquìs lived in a high thin house behind the Empire, "straight through the screen," as he said; and on that afternoon when the world ended and began again the emperor's daughter, who was alone with the servant at home, was suddenly choked by the certainty that her father had chosen, with the mad logic of his romanticism, to persist with his crazy scheme until it killed him. Terrified by a sound like the beating wings of an angel, a sound for which she could afterwards find no good explanation but which pounded in her ears until her head ached, she ran out of her house, pausing only to wrap around her shoulders the green dupatta of modesty; which was how she came to be standing, catching her breath, in front of the heavy doors of the cinema behind which her father sat grimly amidst vacant seats watching the show, when the hot firewind of apocalypse began to blow.

The walls of her father's Empire puffed outwards like a hot puri while that wind like the cough of a sick giant burned away her eyebrows (which never grew again), and tore the clothes off her body until she stood infant-naked in the street; but she failed to notice her nudity because the universe was ending, and in the echoing alienness of the deadly wind her burning eyes saw everything come flying out, seats, ticket books, fans and then pieces of her father's shattered corpse and the charred shards of the future. "Suicide!" she cursed Mahmoud the Woman at the top of a voice made shrieky by the bomb. "You chose this!"—and turning and running homewards she saw that the back wall of the cinema had been blown away, and embedded in the topmost storey of her high thin house was the figure of a golden knight on whose pennant she did not need to read the comically unknown word *Excelsior*.

Don't ask who planted the bomb; in those days there were many such planters, many gardeners of violence. Perhaps it was even a one-godly bomb, seeded in the Empire by one of Mahmoud's more fanatical co-religionists, because it seems that the timer reached zero during a particularly suggestive love scene, and we know what the godly think of love, or the illusion of it, especially when admission money must be paid to see it . . . they are Against. They cut it out. Love corrupts.

O Bilquìs. Naked and eyebrowless beneath the golden knight, wrapped in the delirium of the firewind, she saw her youth flying past her, borne away on the wings of the explosion which were still beating in her ears. All migrants leave their past behind, although some try to pack it into bundles and boxes—but on the journey something seeps out of the treasured mementoes and old photographs, until even their owners fail to recognize them, because it is the fate of migrants to be stripped of history, to stand naked amidst the scorn of strangers upon whom they see the rich clothing, the brocades of continuity and the eyebrows of belonging—at any rate, my point is that Bilquìs's past left her even before she left that city; she stood in a gully, denuded by the suicide of her father, and watched it go. In later years it would visit her sometimes, the way a forgotten relative comes to call, but for a long time she was suspicious of history, she was the wife of a hero with a great future, so naturally she pushed the past away, as one rebuffs those poor cousins when they come to borrow money.

She must have walked, or run, unless a miracle occurred and she was lifted by some divine power out of that wind of her desolation. Returning to her senses, she felt the pressure of red stone against her skin; it was night, and the stone was cool upon her back in the dark dry heat. People were surging past her in great herds, a crowd so large and urgent that her first thought was that it was being propelled by some unimaginable explosion: "Another bomb, my God, all these persons blown away by its power!" But it was not a bomb. She understood that she was leaning against the endless wall of the red fortress that dominated the old city, while soldiers shepherded the crowd through its yawning gates; her feet began to move, faster than her brain, and led her into the throng. An instant later she was crushed by the reborn awareness of her nudity, and began to cry out: "Give me a cloth!" until she saw that nobody was listening, nobody even glanced at the body of the singed, but still beautiful, naked girl. Yet she clutched at herself for shame, holding on to herself in that rushing sea as if she were a straw; and felt around her neck the remnants of a length of muslin. The dupatta of modesty had stuck to her body, fixed there by the congealed blood of the many cuts and scratches of whose very existence she had been unaware. Holding the blackened remnants of the garment of womanly honour over her secret places, she entered the dull redness of the fort, and heard the boom of its closing doors.

In Delhi, in the days before partition, the authorities rounded up any Muslims, for their own safety, it was said, and locked them up in the red fortress, away from the wrath of the stone-washers. Whole families were sealed up there, grandmothers, young children, wicked uncles . . . including members of my own family. It's easy to imagine that as my relatives moved through the Red Fort in the parallel universe of history, they might have felt some hint of the fictional presence of Bilquìs Kemal, rushing cut and naked past them like a ghost . . . or vice versa. Yes. Or vice versa.

The tide of human beings carried Bilquìs along as far as the large, low, ornately rectangular pavilion that had once been an emperor's hall of public audience; and in that echoing *diwan*, overwhelmed by the humiliation of her undress, she passed out. In that generation many women, ordinary decent respectable ladies of the type to whom nothing ever happens, to whom nothing is supposed to happen except marriage children death, had this sort of strange story to tell. It was a rich time for stories, if you lived to tell your tale.

Shortly before the scandalous marriage of her younger daughter, Good News Hyder, Bilquìs told the girl the story of her meeting with her husband. "When I woke up," she said, "it was daytime and I was wrapped in an officer's coat. But whose do you think, goof, of course his, your own father Raza's; what to tell you, he saw me lying there, with all my goods on display in the window, you know, and I suppose the bold fellow just liked what there was to see." Good News went *haa!* and *tch tch!*, feigning shock at her mother's sauciness, and Bilquìs said shyly: "Such encounters were not uncommon then." Good News dutifully replied, "Well, Amma, as for his being impressed, I'm not one bit surprised."

Raza arriving in the hall of public audience came to attention before Bilquìs, who was decently coated; he clicked his heels, saluted, grinned. "It is normal during a courtship," he told his future wife, "for clothes to be worn. It is the privilege of a husband eventually to remove . . . but in our case, the reverse procedure will be true. I must dress you, top to toe, as befits a blushing bride." (Good News, full of marriage juices, sighed when she heard this. "His first words! My God, too romantic!")

How he seemed to military-coated Bilquìs: "So tall! So fair-skinned! So proud, like a king!" No photographs were taken of their meeting, but allowances must be made for her state of mind.

Raza Hyder was five-foot-eight: no giant, you'll agree. And as for his skin—it was certainly darker than Bilquìs's adoring eyes were willing to concede. But proud, like a king? That is likely. He was only a Captain then; but it is, nevertheless, a plausible description.

What may also be said fairly of Raza Hyder: that he possessed enough energy to light up a street; that his manners were always impeccable—even when he became President, he met people with such air of humility (which is not irreconcilable with pride) that very few were willing to speak ill of him afterwards, and those that did so would feel, as they spoke, as if they were betraying a friend; and that he bore, upon his forehead, the light but permanent bruise which we have previously noted on the devout forehead of Ibadalla, the postman of Q.: the *gatta* marked Raza for a religious man.

One last detail. It was said of Captain Hyder that he did not sleep for four hundred and twenty hours after the Muslims were gathered in the red fortress, which would explain the black pouches under his eyes. These pouches would grow blacker and baggier as his power increased, until he no longer needed to wear sunglasses the way the other top brass did, because he looked like he had a pair on anyway, all the time, even in bed. The future General Hyder: Razzoo, Raz-Matazz, Old Razor Guts himself! How could Bilquìs have resisted such a one? She was conquered in double-quick time.

During their days in the fort, the pouch-eyed Captain visited Bilquìs regularly, always bringing with him some item of clothing or beautification: blouses, saris, sandals, eyebrow pencils with which to replace the lost hairs, brassières, lipsticks were showered on her. Saturation bombing techniques are designed to force an early surrender . . . when her wardrobe had grown large enough to permit the removal of the military overcoat, she paraded for him in the hall. "Come to think of it," Bilquìs told Good News, "maybe that was when he made that dressing-up remark." Because she remembered how she had replied: lowering her eyes in the elite actressy manner which her father had once praised, she said sadly, "But what husband could I, without hope of dowry, ever find? Certainly not such a generous Captain who outfits strange ladies like queens."

Raza and Bilquìs were betrothed beneath the bitter eyes of the dispossessed multitudes; and afterwards the gifts continued, sweetmeats as well as bangles, soft drinks and square meals as well as henna and rings. Raza established his fiancée behind a screen of stone latticework, and set a young foot-soldier on guard to defend her territory. Isolated behind this screen from the dull, debilitated anger of the mob, Bilquìs dreamed of her wedding day, defended against guilt by that old dream of queenliness which she had invented long ago. "Tch tch," she reproached the glowering refugees, "but this envy is a too terrible thing."

Barbs were flung through the stone lattice: "Ohé, madam! Where do you think he gets your grand-grand clothes? From handicraft emporia? Watch the mud-flats of the river beneath the fortress walls, count the looted naked bodies flung there every night!" Dangerous words, penetrating latticework: scavenger, harlot, whore. But Bilquìs set her jaw against such coarseness and told herself: "How bad-mannered it would be to ask a man from where he brought his gifts! Such cheapness, I will never do it, no." This sentiment, her reply to the gibes of her fellow refugees, never actually passed her lips, but it filled her mouth, making it puff up into a pout.

I do not judge her. In those days, people survived any way they could.

The Army was partitioned like everything else, and Captain Hyder went West to the new, moth-nibbled land of God. There was a marriage ceremony, and then Bilquìs Hyder sat beside her new husband in a troop transport, a new woman, newly-wed, flying to a bright new world.

"What things won't you do there, Raz!" she cried. "What

greatness, no? What fame!" Raza's ears went red under the eyes (hot with amusement) of his companions in that bumping, rackety Dakota; but he looked pleased all the same. And Bilquìs's prophecy came true, after all. She, whose life had blown up, emptying her of history and leaving in its place only that dark dream of majesty, that illusion so powerful that it demanded to enter the sphere of what-was-real—she, rootless Bilquìs, who now longed for stability, for no-more-explosions, had discerned in Raza a boulder-like quality on which she would build her life. He was a man rooted solidly in an indeflectible sense of himself, and that made him seem invincible. "A giant absolutely," she flattered him, whispering in his ear so as not to set off the giggles of the other officers in the cabin, "shining, like the actors on the screen."

I am wondering how best to describe Bilquìs. As a woman who was unclothed by change, but who wrapped herself in certainties; or as a girl who became a queen, but lost the ability possessed by every beggar-woman, that is, the power of bearing sons; or as that lady whose father was a Woman and whose son turned out to be a girl as well; and whose man of men, her Razzoo or Raz-Matazz, was himself obliged, in the end, to put on the humiliating black shroud of womanhood; or perhaps as a being in the secret grip of fate—for did not the umbilical noose that stifled her son find its echo, or twin, in another and more terrible rope? . . . But I find that I must, after all, return to my starting point, because to me she is, and will always be, the Bilquìs who was afraid of the wind.

I'll be fair: nobody likes the Loo, that hot afternoon breath-that-chokes. We pull down our shutters, hang damp cloths over the windows, try to sleep. But as she grew older the wind awakened strange terrors in Bilquìs. Her husband and children noticed how nervous and snappish she became in the afternoons; how she took to pacing about, slamming and locking doors, until Raza Hyder protested against living in a house where you had to ask your wife for a key before you could go to the pot. From her slender wrist there hung, jingling, the ten-ton key-ring of her neurosis. She developed a horror of movement, and placed an embargo on the relocation of even the most trivial of household items. Chairs, ashtrays, flowerpots took root, rendered immobile by the force of her fearful will. "My Hyder likes everything in its place," she would say, but the disease of fixity was hers. And there were days when she had to be kept indoors as a virtual prisoner, because it would have been a shame and a scandal if any outsider had seen her in that state; when the Loo blew she would screech like a *hoosh* or an *afrit* or some such demon, she would shout for the household servants to come and hold down the furniture in case the wind blew it away like the contents of a long-lost Empire, and scream at her daughters (when they were present) to cling tight to something heavy, something fixed, lest the firewind bear them off into the sky.

The Loo is an evil wind.

If this were a realistic novel about Pakistan, I would not be writing about Bilquìs and the wind; I would be talking about my youngest sister. Who is twenty-two, and studying engineering in Karachi; who can't sit on her hair any more, and who (unlike me) is a Pakistani citizen. On my good days, I think of her as Pakistan, and then I feel very fond of the place, and find it easy to forgive its (her) love of Coca-Cola and imported motor cars.

Although I have known Pakistan for a long time, I have never lived there for longer than six months at a stretch. Once I went for just two weeks. Between these sixmonthses and fortnights there have been gaps of varying duration. I have learned Pakistan in slices, the same way as I have learned my growing sister. I first saw her at the age of zero (I, at fourteen, bent over her crib as she screamed into my face); then at three, four, six, seven, ten, fourteen, eighteen and twenty-one. So there have been nine youngest-sisters for me to get to know. I have felt closer to each successive incarnation than to the one before. (This goes for the country, too.)

I think what I'm confessing is that, however I choose to write about over-there, I am forced to reflect that world in fragments of broken mirrors, the way Farah Zoroaster saw her face at the bollarded frontier. I must reconcile myself to the inevitability of the missing bits.

But suppose this were a realistic novel! Just think what else I might have to put in. The business, for instance, of the illegal installation, by the richest inhabitants of "Defence," of covert, subterranean water pumps that steal water from their neighbours' mains—so that you can always tell the people with the most pull by the greenness of their lawns (such clues are not confined to the Cantonment of Q.).—And would I also have to describe the Sind Club in Karachi, where there is still a sign reading "Women and Dogs Not Allowed Beyond This Point"? Or to analyse the subtle logic of an industrial programme that builds nuclear reactors but cannot develop a refrigerator? O dear—and the school text-books which say, "England is not an agricultural country," and the teacher who once docked two marks from my youngest sister's geography essay because it differed at two points from the exact wording of this same text-book . . . how awkward, dear reader, all this could turn out to be.

How much real-life material might become compulsory!— About, for example, the longago Deputy Speaker who was killed in the National Assembly when the furniture was flung at him by elected representatives; or about the film censor who took his red pencil to each frame of the scene in the film *Night of the Generals* in which General Peter O'Toole visits an art gallery, and scratched out all the paintings of naked ladies hanging on the walls, so that audiences were dazzled by the surreal spectacle of General Peter strolling through a gallery of dancing red blobs; or about the TV chief who once told me solemnly that pork was a four-letter word; or about the issue of *Time* magazine (or was it *Newsweek*?) which never got into the country because it carried an article about

President Ayub Khan's alleged Swiss bank account; or about the bandits on the trunk roads who are condemned for doing, as private enterprise, what the government does as public policy; or about genocide in Baluchistan; or about the recent preferential awards of state scholarships, to pay for postgraduate studies abroad, to members of the fanatical Jamaat party; or about the attempt to declare the sari an obscene garment; or about the extra hangings—the first for twenty years—that were ordered purely to legitimize the execution of Mr. Zulfikar Ali Bhutto; or about why Bhutto's hangman has vanished into thin air, just like the many street-urchins who are being stolen every day in broad daylight; or about anti-Semitism, an interesting phenomenon, under whose influence people who have never met a Jew vilify all Jews for the sake of maintaining solidarity with the Arab states which offer Pakistani workers, these days, employment and much-needed foreign exchange; or about smuggling, the boom in heroin exports, military dictators, venal civilians, corrupt civil servants, bought judges, newspapers of whose stories the only thing that can confidently be said is that they are lies; or about the apportioning of the national budget, with special reference to the percentages set aside for defence (huge) and for education (not huge). Imagine my difficulties!

By now, if I had been writing a book of this nature, it would have done me no good to protest that I was writing universally, not only about Pakistan. The book would have been banned, dumped in the rubbish bin, burned. All that effort for nothing! Realism can break a writer's heart.

Fortunately, however, I am only telling a sort of modern fairy-tale, so that's all right; nobody need get upset, or take anything I say too seriously. No drastic action need be taken, either.

What a relief!

And now I must stop saying what I am not writing about, because there's nothing so special about that; every story one chooses to tell is a kind of censorship, it prevents the telling of other tales . . . I must get back to my fairy-story, because things have been happening while I've been talking too much.

On my way back to the story, I pass Omar Khayyam Shakil, my sidelined hero, who is waiting patiently for me to get to the point at which his future bride, poor Sufiya Zinobia, can enter the narrative, head-first down the birth canal. He won't have to wait long; she's almost on her way.

I shall pause only to note (because it is not inappropriate to mention this here) that during his married life Omar Khayyam was forced to accept without argument Sufiya Zinobia's childlike fondness for moving the furniture around. Intensely aroused by these forbidden deeds, she rearranged tables, chairs, lamps, whenever nobody was watching, like a favourite secret game, which she played with a frighteningly stubborn gravity. Omar Khayyam found protests rising to his lips, but he bit them back, knowing that to say anything would be useless: "Honestly, wife," he wanted to exclaim, "God knows what you'll change with all this shifting shifting."

5

THE WRONG
MIRACLE

Bilquìs is lying wide awake in the dark of a cavernous bed-room, her hands crossed upon her breasts. When she sleeps alone her hands habitually find their way into this position, even though her in-laws disapprove. She can't help it, this hugging of herself to herself, as though she were afraid of losing some-thing.

All around her in the darkness are the dim outlines of other beds, old charpoys with thin mattresses, on which other women lie under single white sheets: a grand total of forty females clus-tered around the majestically tiny form of the matriarch Bari-amma, who snores lustily. Bilquìs already knows enough about this chamber to be sure that most of the shapes tossing vaguely in the dark are no more asleep than she. Even Bariamma's snores might be a deception. The women are waiting for the men to come.

The turning door-knob rattles like a drum. At once there is a change in the quality of the night. A delicious wickedness is in the air. A cool breeze stirs, as if the entry of the first man has succeeded in dispelling some of the intense treacly heat of the hot season, enabling the ceiling fans to move a little more efficiently through the soupy atmosphere. Forty women, one of them Bilquìs, stir damply under their sheets . . . more men enter. They are tiptoeing along the midnight avenues of the dormitory and the women have become very still, except for Bariamma. The matriarch is snoring more energetically than ever. Her snores are sirens, sounding the all-clear and giving necessary courage to the men.

The girl in the bed next to Bilquìs, Rani Humayun, who is unmarried and therefore expects no visit tonight, whispers across the blackness: "Here come the forty thieves."

And now there are tiny noises in the dark: charpoy ropes yielding fractionally beneath the extra weight of a second body, the rustle of clothing, the heavier exhalations of the invading husbands. Gradually the darkness acquires a kind of rhythm, which accelerates, peaks, subsides. Then there is a multiple padding towards the door, several times the drum-roll of the turning doorknob and at last silence, because Bariamma, now that it is polite to do so, has quite ceased to snore.

Rani Humayun, who has landed one of the prize catches of the marriage season and will shortly leave this dormitory to wed the fair-skinned, foreign-educated, sensually full-lipped young millionaire Iskander Harappa, and who is, like Bilquìs, eighteen years old, has befriended her cousin Raza's new bride. Bilquìs enjoys (while pretending to be scandalized) Rani's malicious ruminations on the subject of the household sleeping arrangements. "Imagine, in that darkness," Rani giggles while the two of them grind the daily spices, "who would know if her real husband had come to her? And who could complain? I tell you, Billoo, these married men and ladies are having a pretty good time in this joint family set-up. I swear, maybe uncles with nieces, brothers with their brothers' wives, we'll never know who the children's daddies really are!" Bilquìs blushes gracefully and covers Rani's mouth with a coriander-scented hand. "Stop, darling, what a dirtyfilthy mind!"

But Rani is inexorable. "No, Bilquìs, I tell you, you are new here but I have grown up in this place, and by the hairs of our Bariamma's head I vow that this arrangement which is supposed to be made for decency etcetera is just the excuse for the biggest orgy on earth."

Bilquìs does not point out (how rude it would be to do so) that the minuscule, almost dwarfish Bariamma is not only toothless and blind but no longer has a single hair on her ancient head, either. The matriarch wears a wig.

Where are we, and when?—In a large family house in the old quarter of the coastal city which, having no option, I must call Karachi. Raza Hyder, an orphan like his wife, has brought her (immediately after descending from the Dakota of their flight into the West) into the bosom of his maternal relations; Bariamma is his grandmother on his late mother's side. "You must stay here," he told Bilquìs, "until things settle down and we can see what is what and what is not." So these days Hyder is in temporary quarters at the Army base while his bride lies amid sleep-feigning in-laws, knowing that no man will visit her in the night.—And yes, I see that I have brought my tale into a second infinite mansion, which the reader will perhaps already be comparing to a faraway house in the border town of Q.; but what a complete contrast it affords! For this is no sealed-off redoubt; it bursts, positively bursts with family members and related personnel.

"They still live in the old village way," Raza warned Bilquìs before depositing her in that house in which it was believed that the mere fact of being married did not absolve a woman of the shame and dishonour that results from the knowledge that she sleeps regularly with a man; which was why Bariamma had devised, without once discussing it, the idea of the forty thieves. And of course all the women deny that anything of that nature ever took place, so that when pregnancies occurred they did so as if by magic, as if all conceptions were immaculate and all births virgin. The idea of parthenogenesis had been accepted in this house in order to keep out certain other, unpleasantly physical notions.

Bilquìs, the girl with the dream of queenhood, thought but did not say: "O God. Ignoramuses from somewhere. Backward types, village idiots, unsophisticated completely, and I am stuck with them." Aloud, she told Raza meekly: "Much to be said for the old traditions." Raza nodded seriously in simple agreement; her heart sank further after that.

In the empire of Bariamma, Bilquìs, the newest arrival, the junior member, was of course not treated like a queen.

"See if we don't have sons," Raza told Bilquìs. "In my mother's family boys grow on trees."

Lost in the forest of new relatives, wandering in the blood-jungle of the matriarchal home, Bilquìs consulted the family Quran in search of these family trees, and found them there, in their traditional place, monkey-puzzle groves of genealogy inscribed in the back of the holy book. She discovered that since the generation of Bariamma, who had two sisters, Raza's maternal great-aunts, both widowed, as well as three brothers—a landlord, a wastrel and a mental-case fool—since that sexually balanced generation, only two girls had been born in the entire family. One of these was Raza's deceased mother; the other, Rani Humayun, who could not wait to escape from that house which was never left by its sons, who imported their wives to live and breed in battery conditions, like shaver chickens. On his mother's side, Raza had a total of eleven legitimate uncles and, it was believed, at least nine illegitimate ones, the brood of the wastrel, philandering great-uncle. Besides Rani, he could point to a grand total of thirty-two male cousins born in wedlock. (The putative offspring of the bastard uncles did not rate a mention in the Quran.) Of this enormous stock of relatives, a sizeable percentage was in residence under Bariamma's short but omnipotent shadow; wastrel and fool were unmarried, but when the landlord came to stay his wife occupied one of the beds in Bariamma's zenana wing. At the time of which I am speaking, landlord and wife were present; also eight of the eleven legitimate uncles, plus wives; and (Bilquìs had difficulty with her counting) around twenty-nine male cousins, and Rani Humayun. Twenty-six cousinly wives stuffed the wicked bedchamber, and Bilquìs herself made forty, once the three sisters of the oldest generation were included.

Bilquìs Hyder's head whirled. Trapped in a language which contained a quite specific name for each conceivable relative, so that the bewildered newcomer was unable to hide behind such generic appellations as "uncle," "cousin," "aunt," but was continually caught out in all her insulting ignorance, Bilquìs's tongue was silenced by the in-law mob. She virtually never spoke except when alone with Rani or Raza; and thus acquired the triple reputation of sweet-innocent-child, doormat and fool. Because Raza was often away for days at a time, depriving her of the protection and flattery the other women got from their husbands on a daily basis, she also attained the status of poor-thing, which her lack of eyebrows (that no amount of pencilled artistry could disguise) did nothing to diminish. Thanks to this she was given slightly more than her fair share of household duties and also slightly more than her fair share of the rough edge of Bariamma's tongue. But she was also admired, grudgingly, because the family had a high opinion of Raza, the women admitted that he was a good man who did not beat his wife. This definition of goodness alarmed Bilquìs, to whom it had never occurred that she might be beaten, and she raised the subject with Rani. "Oh yes," her cousin-in-law replied, "how they all hit! Tharaap! Tharaap! Sometimes it does your heart good to watch. But one must also watch out. A good man can go bad, like meat, if you do not keep him cool."

As the officially designated poor-thing, Bilquìs was also obliged to sit each evening at Bariamma's feet while the blind old lady recounted the family tales. These were lurid affairs, featuring divorces, bankruptcies, droughts, cheating friends, child mortality, diseases of the breast, men cut down in their prime, failed hopes, lost beauty, women who grew obscenely fat, smuggling deals, opium-taking poets, pining virgins, curses, typhoid, bandits, homosexuality, sterility, frigidity, rape, the high price of food, gamblers, drunks, murderers, suicides and God. Bariamma's mildly droning recital of the catalogue of family horrors had the effect of somehow defusing them, making them safe, embalming them in the mummifying fluid of her own incontrovertible respectability. The telling of the tales proved the family's ability to survive them, to retain, in spite of everything, its grip on its honour and its unswerving moral code. "To be of the family," Bariamma told Bilquìs, "you must know our things, and tell us yours." So Bilquìs was forced, one evening (Raza was present but made no attempt to protect her), to recount the end of Mahmoud the Woman and her nudity in the Delhi streets. "Never mind," Bariamma pronounced approvingly, when Bilquìs was shaking with the shame of her revelations, "at least you managed to keep your dupatta on."

After that Bilquìs often heard her story being retold, wherever one or two of the family were gathered, in the hot lizardy corners of the courtyard or on the starlit roofs of the summer nights, in the nurseries to frighten the children and even in the boudoir of jewel-heavy, hennaed Rani on the morning of her wedding; because stories, such stories, were the glue that held the clan together, binding the generations in webs of whispered secrets. Her story altered, at first, in the retellings, but finally it settled down, and after that nobody, neither teller nor listener, would tolerate any deviation from the hallowed, sacred text. This was when Bilquìs knew that she had become a member of the family; in the sanctification of her tale lay initiation, kinship, blood. "The recounting of histories," Raza told his wife, "is for us a rite of blood."

But neither Raza nor Bilquìs could have known that their story had scarcely begun, that it would be the juiciest and goriest of all the juicygory sagas, and that, in time to come, it would always begin with the following sentence (which, in the family's opinion, contained all the right resonances for the opening of such a narrative):

"It was the day on which the only son of the future President Raza Hyder was going to be reincarnated."

"Yes, yes," the audience would cheer, "tell us that one, that's the best."

In that hot season, the two newly partitioned nations announced the commencement of hostilities on the Kashmiri frontier. You can't beat a northern war in the hot season; officers, footsoldiers, cooks all rejoiced as they headed for the coolness of the hills. "Yara, this is luck, na?" "Shit, sisterfucker, at least this year I won't die in that damn heat." O backslapping camaraderie of the meteorologically fortunate! Jawans went to war with the devil-may-care abandon of holidaymakers. There were, inevitably, deaths; but the organizers of the war had catered for these as well. Those who fell in battle were flown directly, first-class, to the perfumed gardens of Paradise, to be waited on for all eternity by four gorgeous Houris, untouched by man or djinn. "Which of your Lord's blessings," the Quran inquires, "would you deny?"

Army morale was high; but Rani Humayun was most put out, because it would have been unpatriotic to hold a wedding reception in wartime. The function had been postponed, and she stamped her feet. Raza Hyder, however, stepped contentedly into the camouflaged jeep of his flight from the boiling insanity of the summer city, and just then his wife whispered into his ear that she was expecting another sort of happy event. (Taking a leaf out of Bariamma's book, I have turned a blind eye and snored loudly while Raza Hyder visited the dormitory of the forty women and made this miracle possible.)

Raza let fly a yell so swollen by triumph that Bariamma, seated indoors on her takht, became convinced in the confusion of her sweating blindness that her grandson had already received news of some famous victory, so that when such news did in fact come through, weeks later, she replied simply: "Did you just find that out? I knew it one month back." (This was in the days before the people learned that their side almost always lost, so that the national leaders, rising brilliantly to the challenge, perfected no fewer than one thousand and one ways of salvaging honour from defeat.)

"He's coming!" Raza deafened his wife, causing earthen pitchers to topple from the heads of womenservants and frightening the geese. "What did I tell you, Mrs.?" He set his cap more jauntily on his head, slapped his wife too firmly on the stomach, joined the palms of his hands together and made diving gestures. "Whoosh!" he shouted. "Voom, wife! Here he comes!" And he roared off into the north, promising to win a great victory in honour of his forthcoming son, and leaving behind him a Bilquìs who, being washed for the first time by the solipsistic fluids of motherhood, had neglected to notice the tears in her husband's eyes, the tears turning his black eye-pouches into velvet bags, the tears which were among the earliest pointers that the future strong-man of the nation was of the type that cried too easily . . . in private with the frustrated Rani Humayun, Bilquìs crowed proudly: "Never mind this war foolishness; the important news is that I am making a boy to marry your unborn daughter."

An extract from the family's saga of Raza and Bilquìs, given in the formulaic words which it would be a gross sacrilege to alter:

"When we heard that our Razzoo had pulled off an attacking coup so daring that there was no option but to call it a triumph, we started off by refusing to believe our ears,—for already in those days even the sharpest ears had developed the fault of becoming wholly unreliable when they were attuned to the radio news bulletins;—on such occasions everybody heard things that could not possibly have been the case.—But then we nodded our heads, understanding that a man whose wife is about to bear him a son is capable of anything. Yes, it was the unborn boy who was responsible for this, the only victory in the history of our armed forces,—which formed the basis of Raza's reputation for invincibility, a reputation which quickly became invincible itself,—so that not even the long humiliating years of his decline proved capable of destroying it.—He returned a hero, having seized for our holy new land a mountain valley so high and inaccessible that even goats had difficulty in breathing up there; so intrepid he was, so tremendous, that all true patriots had to gasp—and you must not believe that propaganda which says that the enemy did not bother to defend the place;—the fighting was fierce as ice—and with twenty men only he took the valley! That little band of giants, that daredevil crew, and Old Razor Guts at their head—who could have denied them? Who could have stood in their path?

"For all peoples, there are places that mean too much. 'Aansu!' we wept with pride; with true patriotism we sobbed, 'Only imagine—he has taken the Aansu-ki-Wadi!' It's true: the capture of that fabled 'valley of tears' made us all weep as uncontrollably as, in later years, its conqueror became famous for doing.—But after a while it was clear that nobody knew what to do with that place where your spit froze before it hit the ground; except Iskander Harappa, of course;—who, dry-eyed as ever, went off to the Tribal Agencies Department and purchased more or less the whole caboodle, dirt-cheap, snow-cheap, for cash money on the nail,—and a few years later there were ski-lodges up there, and scheduled air flights, and European goings-on at night that made the local tribals faint for shame.—But did Raz, our great hero, see anything of that foreign exchange?" (Here the teller invariably smites her forehead with the palm of her hand.) "No, how would he, that great Army dumbo? Isky always got there first. But" (and now the narrator adopts the most cryptic, menacing tone of which she is capable) "it is being there last that counts."

At this point I must interrupt the legend. The duel between Raza Hyder (promoted to Major for his Aansu exploit) and Iskander Harappa, which began, but certainly did not end in Aansu, will have to wait yet awhile; because now that Old Razor Guts is back in town, and it is peacetime again, the wedding is about to be celebrated which will make the mortal adversaries into cousins-in-law: into *family*.

Rani Humayun, eyes downcast, watches in a mirror-ring her bridegroom approaching her; borne shoulder-high by a turbaned retinue of friends, he sits on a golden plate. Later, after she had fainted under the weight of her jewellery; been revived by the pregnant Bilquìs who then passed out herself; had money thrown in her lap by every member of her family in turn; watched through her veil as her ancient lecherous great-uncle pinched the bottoms of her new husband's female relations, knowing that his grey hairs would prevent them from complaining; and finally lifted the veil beside her while a hand raised her own, and looked long and hard into the face of Iskander Harappa, whose overpowering sexual appeal owed much to the unlined softness of his twenty-five-year-old cheeks—around which curled long hair that was already, and freakishly, the colour of pure silver, and thinning on top to reveal the golden dome of his skull—and between which, also curled, she discovered lips whose patrician cruelty was alleviated by their sensual thickness, the lips, she thought, of a black *hubshee*, an idea which gave her a peculiarly sinful frisson of delight . . . later, after she had ridden with him to a bedchamber opulent with ancient swords and imported French tapestries and Russian novels, after she had descended full of terror from a white stallion whose sex was quite patently standing to attention, after she had heard the doors of her marriage closing behind her in this other home whose grandeur made Bariamma's place look like a village hovel—then, oiled and naked on a bed before which the man who had just turned her into a grown woman stood staring indolently down upon her beauty, she, Rani Harappa, made her first genuinely wifely remark.

"Who was that fellow," she asked, "the fat one, whose horse sat down under him when your procession arrived? I think it must be that bad chap, that doctor or something, that everybody in town is calling such a bad influence on you."

Iskander Harappa turned his back on her and lit a cigar. "Get one thing clear," she heard him say, "you don't pick and choose my friends."

But Rani, seized by helpless laughter under the influence of the remembered image of the proud horse that gave up and subsided, legs splayed to the four points of the compass, under the colossal weight of Omar Khayyam Shakil—and also basking in the soft heat of their recent lovemaking—made mollifying sounds: "I only meant, Isky, what a shameless type he must be, to carry all that tummy about and all."

Omar Khayyam at thirty: five years the senior of Iskander Harappa and more than a decade older than Isky's bride, re-enters our little tale as a character with a high reputation as a doctor and a low reputation as a human being, a degenerate of whom it is often said that he appears to be entirely without shame, "fellow doesn't know the meaning of the word," as if some essential part of his education has been overlooked; or perhaps he has deliberately chosen to expunge the word from his vocabulary, lest its explosive presence there amid the memories of his past and present actions shatter him like an old pot. Rani Harappa has correctly identified her enemy, and now remembers, shuddering, and for the hundred and first time since it happened, the moment during her wedding celebrations when a bearer brought Iskander Harappa a telephone message informing him that the Prime Minister had been assassinated. When Iskander Harappa stood, called for silence and relayed the message to the appalled guests, an awkward hush persisted for fully thirty seconds, and then the voice of Omar Khayyam Shakil, on which everyone could hear the splashing of alcohol, cried out, "That bastard! If he's dead he's dead. Why does he want to come here and spoil the party?"

Back then everything was smaller than it is today; even Raza Hyder was only a Major. But he was like the city itself, going places, growing fast, but in a stupid way, so that the bigger they both got, the uglier they became. I must tell you what things were like in those early days after the partition: the city's old inhabitants, who had become accustomed to living in a land older than time, and were therefore being slowly eroded by the implacably revenant tides of the past, had been given a bad shock by independence, by being told to think of themselves, as well as the country itself, as new.

Well, their imaginations simply weren't up to the job, you can understand that; so it was the ones who really were new, the distant cousins and half-acquaintances and total strangers who poured in from the east to settle in the Land of God, who took over and got things going. The newness of those days felt pretty unstable; it was a dislocated, rootless sort of thing. All over the city (which was, of course, the capital then) builders were cheating on the cement in the foundations of new houses, people—and not only Prime Ministers—got shot from time to time, throats got themselves slit in gullies, bandits became billionaires, but all this was expected. History was old and rusted, it was a machine nobody had plugged in for thousands of years, and here all of a sudden it was being asked for maximum output. Nobody was surprised that there were accidents . . . well, there were a few voices saying, If this is the country we dedicated to our God, what kind of God is it that permits—but these voices were silenced before they had finished their questions, kicked on the shins under tables, for their own sakes, because there are things that cannot be said. No, it's more than that: there are things that cannot be permitted to be true.

At any rate: Raza Hyder had already shown, in the taking of Aansu, the advantages of the energy-giving influx of immigrants, of novel beings; but energy or no energy, he was unable to prevent his first-born son from being strangled to death in the womb.

Once again (in the opinion of his maternal grandmother) he cried too easily. Just when he should have been demonstrating the stiffness of his upper lip he began to bawl his eyes out, even in public. Tears were seen sliding off the wax on his bulbous mustache, and his black eye-pouches glistened once more like little pools of oil. His wife, Bilquìs, however, did not let fall a single tear.

"Hey, Raz," she consoled her husband in words iced with the brittle certainty of her desperation, "Razzoo, chin up. We'll get him back the next time."

"Old Razor Guts, my toe," Bariamma scoffed to all and sundry. "You know he invented that name for himself and forced his troops to call him so, by order? Old Leaky Water Reservoir, more like."

An umbilical cord wound itself around a baby's neck and was transformed into a hangman's noose (in which other nooses are prefigured), into the breath-stopping silken rumal of a Thug; and an infant came into the world handicapped by the irreversible misfortune of being dead before he was born. "Who knows why God will do such things?" Bariamma, mercilessly, told her grandson. "But we submit, we must submit. And not take out baby-tears before women."

However: being stone dead was a handicap which the boy managed, with commendable gallantry, to surmount. Within a matter of months, or was it only weeks, the tragically cadaverous infant had "topped" in school and at college, had fought bravely in war, had married the wealthiest beauty in town and risen to a high position in the government. He was dashing, popular, handsome, and the fact of his being a corpse now seemed of no more consequence than would a slight limp or a minor speech impediment.

Of course I know perfectly well that the boy had in reality perished before he even had time to be given a name. His subsequent feats were performed entirely within the distracted imaginations of Raza and Bilquìs, where they acquired an air of such solid actuality that they began to insist on being provided with a living human being who would carry them out and make them real. Possessed by the fictive triumphs of their stillborn son, Raza and Bilquìs went at one another with a will, heaving silently in the blind-eyed dormitory of the family wives, having convinced themselves that a second pregnancy would be an act of replacement, that God (for Raza was, as we know, devout) had consented to send them a free substitute for the damaged goods they had received in the first delivery, as though He were the manager of a reputable mail-order firm. Bariamma, who found out everything, clicked her tongue noisily over this reincarnation nonsense, aware that it was something they had imported, like a germ, from that land of idolaters they had left; but curiously she was never harsh with them, understanding that the mind will find strange means of coping with grief. So she must bear her share of responsibility for what followed, she should not have neglected her duty just because it was painful, she should have ditched that rebirth notion while she could, but it took root so fast, and then it was too late, not a matter for discussion any more.

Many years later, when Iskander Harappa stood in the dock of the courtroom in which he was on trial for his life, his face as grey as the imported suit he wore, which had been tailored for him when he weighed twice as much, he taunted Raza with the memory of this reincarnation obsession. "This leader who prays six times a day, and on national television too!" Isky said in a voice whose siren melodies had been untuned by jail. "I recall when I had to remind him that the idea of avatars was a heresy. Of course he never listened, but then Raza Hyder has made a custom of not listening to friendly advice." And outside the courtroom, the bolder members of Harappa's disintegrating entourage were heard to mutter that General Hyder had been raised in the enemy state across the border, after all, and there was evidence of a Hindu great-grandmother on his father's side, so those ungodly philosophies had long ago infected his blood.

And it is true that Iskander and Rani both tried to argue with the Hyders, but Bilquìs's lips just got stretched tight as a drum by her obstinacy. At that time Rani Harappa was expecting, she had managed it like a shot, and Bilquìs was already making it a matter of principle not to do what her old dormitory buddy advised, one reason for which may have been that she, Bilquìs, in spite of all the nocturnal goings-on, was finding it very difficult to conceive.

When Rani gave birth to a daughter, her failure to produce a male child offered Bilquìs a little consolation, but not much, because another dream had bitten the dust, the fantasy of a marriage between their firstborn children. Now, of course, the newborn Miss Arjumand Harappa was older than any future male Hyder could ever be, so the match was out of the question. Rani had, in fact, delivered her side of the deal; her efficiency deepened Bilquìs's well-like gloom.

And under Bariamma's roof little sneers and comments began to be aimed at this unnatural female who could produce nothing but dead babies; the family was proud of its fecundity. One night, after Bilquìs had retired to bed, having washed the eyebrows off her face and regained her appearance of a startled rabbit, she was staring jealously at the empty bed which had once been occupied by Rani Harappa when, from her other flank, a particularly vicious cousin named Duniyazad Begum hissed night-dark insults: "The disgrace of your barrenness, Madam, is not yours alone. Don't you know that shame is collective? The shame of any one of us sits on us all and bends our backs. See what you're doing to your husband's people, how you repay the ones who took you in when you came penniless and a fugitive from that godless country over there."

Bariamma had switched the lights out—the master-switch hung

on a cord above her bed—and her snoring dominated the blackness of the zenana chamber. But Bilquìs did not lie still in her bed; she arose and fell upon Duniyazad Begum, who had been awaiting her eagerly, and the two of them, hands entangled in hair, knees driving into yielding fleshy zones, tumbled softly to the floor. The fight was conducted soundlessly, such was the power of the matriarch over the night; but the news spread through the room on ripples of darkness and the women sat up in their beds and watched. When the men came they, too, became mute spectators of this mortal combat, during which Duniyazad lost several handfuls of hair from her luxuriant armpits and Bilquìs broke a tooth on her adversary's clawing fingers; until Raza Hyder entered the dormitory and pulled them apart. It was at this point that Bariamma ceased to snore and switched on the light, releasing into the illuminated air all the noise, all the cheers and screams, that had been held back by the darkness. As women rushed to prop up the bald, blind matriarch with gaotakia bolsters, Bilquìs, trembling in her husband's arms, refused to go on living under that roof of her calumniation. "Husband, you know it," she pulled about herself the tattered shreds of her queenly childhood, "I was raised in a higher fashion than this; and if my children do not come it is because I cannot make them here, in this zoo, like they all do, like animals or what."

"Yes, yes, we know how you think yourself toogood for us." Bariamma, subsiding into gaotakias with a hissing noise, as of a deflating balloon, had the last word. "Then you take her away, Raza, boy," she said in her hornet's whine of a voice. "You, Billoo Begum, begone. When you leave this house your shame leaves with you, and our dear Duniya, whom you attacked for speaking the truth, will sleep more easily. Come on, *mohajir*! Immigrant! Pack up double-quick and be off to what gutter you choose."

I, too, know something of this immigrant business. I am an emigrant from one country (India) and a newcomer in two (England, where I live, and Pakistan, to which my family moved against my will). And I have a theory that the resentments we *mohajirs* engender have something to do with our conquest of the force of gravity. We have performed the act of which all men anciently dream, the thing for which they envy the birds; that is to say, we have flown.

I am comparing gravity with belonging. Both phenomena observably exist: my feet stay on the ground, and I have never been angrier than I was on the day my father told me he had sold my childhood home in Bombay. But neither is understood. We know the force of gravity, but not its origins; and to explain why we become attached to our birthplaces we pretend that we are trees and speak of roots. Look under your feet. You will not find gnarled growths sprouting through the soles. Roots, I sometimes think, are a conservative myth, designed to keep us in our places.

The anti-myths of gravity and of belonging bear the same name: flight. *Migrations, n., moving, for instance in flight, from one place to another.* To fly and to flee: both are ways of seeking freedom . . . an odd thing about gravity, incidentally, is that while it remains uncomprehended everybody seems to find it easy to comprehend the notion of its theoretical counter-force: anti-gravity. But anti-belonging is not accepted by modern science . . . suppose ICI or Ciba-Geigy or Pfizer or Roche or even, I guess, NASA came up with an anti-gravity pill. The world's airlines would go broke overnight, of course. Pill-poppers would come unstuck from the ground and float upwards until they sank into the clouds. It would be necessary to devise special waterproof flying garments. And when the effects of the pill wore off one would simply sink gently down to earth again, but in a different place, because of prevailing windspeeds and planetary rotation. Personalized international travel could be made possible by manufacturing pills of different strengths for different lengths of journey. Some kind of directional booster-engine would have to be constructed, perhaps in back-pack form. Mass production could bring this within the reach of every household. You see the connection between gravity and "roots": the pill would make migrants of us all. We would float upwards, use our boosters to get ourselves to the right latitude, and let the rotating planet do the rest.

When individuals come unstuck from their native land, they are called migrants. When nations do the same thing (Bangladesh), the act is called secession. What is the best thing about migrant peoples and seceded nations? I think it is their hopefulness. Look into the eyes of such folk in old photographs. Hope blazes undimmed through the fading sepia tints. And what's the worst thing? It is the emptiness of one's luggage. I'm speaking of invisible suitcases, not the physical, perhaps cardboard, variety containing a few meaning-drained mementoes: we have come unstuck from more than land. We have floated upwards from history, from memory, from Time.

I may be such a person. Pakistan may be such a country.

It is well known that the term "Pakistan," an acronym, was originally thought up in England by a group of Muslim intellectuals. P for the Punjabis, A for the Afghans, K for the Kashmiris, S for Sind and the "tan," they say, for Baluchistan. (No mention of the East Wing, you notice; Bangladesh never got its name in the title, and so, eventually, it took the hint and seceded from the secessionists. Imagine what such a double secession does to people!)—So it was a word born in exile which then went East, was borne-across or trans-lated, and imposed itself on history; a returning migrant, settling down on partitioned land, forming a palimpsest on the past. A palimpsest obscures what lies beneath. To build Pakistan it was necessary to cover up Indian history, to deny that Indian centuries lay just beneath the surface of Pakistani Standard Time. The past was rewritten; there was nothing else to be done.

Who commandeered the job of rewriting history?—The immigrants, the *mohajirs*. In what languages?—Urdu and English, both imported tongues, although one travelled less distance than the other. It is possible to see the subsequent history of Pakistan as a duel between two layers of time, the obscured world forcing its way back through what-had-been-imposed. It is the true desire of every artist to impose his or her vision on the world; and Pakistan, the peeling, fragmenting palimpsest, increasingly at war with itself, may be described as a failure of the dreaming mind. Perhaps the pigments used were the wrong ones, impermanent, like Leonardo's; or perhaps the place was just *insufficiently imagined*, a picture full of irreconcilable elements, midriffbaring immigrant saris versus demure, indigenous Sindhi shalwar-jurtas, Urdu versus Punjabi, now versus then: a miracle that went wrong.

As for me: I, too, like all migrants, am a fantasist. I build imaginary countries and try to impose them on the ones that exist. I, too, face the problem of history: what to retain, what to dump, how to hold on to what memory insists on relinquishing, how to deal with change. And to come back to the "roots" idea, I should say that I haven't managed to shake myself free of it completely. Sometimes I do see myself as a tree, even, rather grandly, as the ash Yggdrasil, the mythical world-tree of Norse legend. The ash Yggdrasil has three roots. One falls into the pool of knowledge by Valhalla, where Odin comes to drink. A second is being slowly consumed in the undying fire of Muspellheim, realm of the flame-god Surtur. The third is gradually being gnawed through by a fearsome beast called the Nidhögg. And when fire and monster have destroyed two of the three, the ash will fall, and darkness will descend. The twilight of the gods: a tree's dream of death.

My story's palimpsest-country has, I repeat, no name of its own. The exiled Czech writer Kundera once wrote: "A name means continuity with the past and people without a past are people without a name." But I am dealing with a past that refuses to be suppressed, that is daily doing battle with the present; so it is perhaps unduly harsh of me to deny my fairyland a title.

There's an apocryphal story that Napier, after a successful campaign in what is now the south of Pakistan, sent back to England the guilty, one-word message, "Peccavi." *I have Sind.*

I'm tempted to name my looking-glass Pakistan in honour of this bilingual (and fictional, because never really uttered) pun. Let it be *Peccavistan*.

It was the day on which the only son of the future General Raza Hyder was going to be reincarnated.

Bilquìs had moved out of Bariamma's contraceptive presence into a simple residence for married officers and wives in the compound of the Army base; and not long after her escape she had conceived, just as prophesied. "What did I say?" she triumphed, "Raz, he's coming back, the little angel, just you wait and see." Bilquìs put her new-found fertility down to the fact that she was finally able to make a noise during their lovemaking, "so that the little angel, waiting to be born, can hear what's going on and respond accordingly," she told her husband fondly, and the happiness of the remark prevented him from replying that it was not only angels who were within earshot of her passionate love-moans and ululations, but also every other married officer on the base, including his immediate superior and also some junior chaps, so that he had been obliged to put up with a fair amount of raillery in the mess.

Bilquìs entered labour—the rebirth was imminent—Raza Hyder awaited it, stiffly seated in an anteroom of the military hospital's maternity ward. And after eight hours of howling and heaving and bursting blood-vessels in her cheeks and using the filthy language that is permitted to ladies only during parturition, at last, pop! she managed it, the miracle of life. Raza Hyder's daughter was born at two-fifteen in the afternoon, and born, what's more, as vivaciously alive and kicking as her big brother had been dead.

When the swaddled child was handed to Bilquìs, that lady could not forebear to cry, faintly, "Is that all, my God? So much huffery and puffery to push out only this mouse?"

The heroine of our story, the wrong miracle, Sufiya Zinobia, was as small a baby as anyone had ever seen. (She remained small when she grew up, taking after her near midget paternal great-grandmother, whose name, Bariamma, Big Mother, had always been a sort of family joke.)

A surprisingly small bundle was returned by Bilquìs to the midwife, who bore it out to the anxious father. "A daughter, Major Sahib, and so beautiful, like the day, dontyouthinkso?" In the delivery room, silence flooded from the pores of the exhausted mother; in the anteroom, Raza was quiet, too. Silence: the ancient language of defeat.

Defeat? But this was Old Razor Guts himself, conqueror of glaciers, vanquisher of frosty meadows and ice-fleeced mountain sheep! Was the future strong-man of the nation so easily crushed? Not a bit of it. Did the midwife's bombshell lead to unconditional surrender? Certainly not. Raza began to argue; and the words came in rushes, inexorable as tanks. The walls of the hospital shook and retreated; horses shied, unseating riders, on the nearby polo fields.

"Mistakes are often made!" Raza shouted. "Terrible blunders are not unknown! Why, my own fifth cousin by marriage when he was born . . . ! But me no buts, woman, I demand to see the hospital supervisor!"

And even louder: "Babies do not come clean into this world!"

And blasted from his lips like cannonballs: "Genitalia! Can! Be! Obscured!"

Raza Hyder raging roaring. The midwife stiffened, saluted; this was a military hospital, don't forget, and Raza outranked her, so she admitted yes, what the Major Sahib was saying was possible certainly. And fled. Hope rose in the moist eyes of the father, also in the dilated pupils of Bilquìs, who had heard the noise, of course. And now it was the baby, its very essence in doubt, who fell silent and began to muse.

The supervisor (a Brigadier) entered the quaking room in which the future President was trying to affect biology by a superhuman act of will. His words, weighty, final, outranking Raza's, murdered hope. The stillborn son died again, even his ghost snuffed out by the medico's fatal speech: "No possibility of error. Please to note that the child has been washed. Prior to swaddling procedure. Matter of sex is beyond dispute. Permit me to tender my congratulations." But what father would allow his son, twice-conceived, to be executed thus, without a fight? Raza tore away swaddling cloth; having penetrated to the baby within, he jabbed at its nether zones: "There! I ask you, sir, what is that?"—"We see here the expected configuration, also the not uncommon postnatal swelling, of the female . . ."—"A bump!" Raza shrieked hopelessly. "Is it not, doctor, an absolute and unquestionable *bump*?"

But the Brigadier had left the room.

"And at this point"—I am quoting from the family legend again—"when her parents had to admit the immutability of her gender, to submit, as faith demands, to God; at this very instant the extremely new and soporific being in Raza's arms began— it's true!—to blush."

O rubescent Sufiya Zinobia!

It is possible that the above incident has been a little embellished during its many tellings and retellings; but I shall not be the one to question the veracity of oral tradition. They say the baby blushed at birth.

Then, even then, she was too easily shamed.

6

AFFAIRS OF
HONOUR

There is a saying that the frog who croaks in the shaft of a
well will be frightened by the booming voice of the giant
frog who answers him.

When the great gas fields were discovered in Needle Valley in
the district of Q., the unpatriotic behaviour of the intemperate
local tribals became a matter for national concern. After the team
of drilling engineers, surveyors and gas scientists which had been
sent to Needle to plan the construction of the butane had been
attacked by the tribals, who raped each member of the team
eighteen point six six times on average (of which thirteen point
nine seven assaults were from the rear and only four point six
nine in the mouth) before slitting one hundred per cent of the
expert gullets, the State Chief Minister Aladdin Gichki requested
military assistance. The commander of the forces appointed for
the protection of the invaluable gas resources was none other than
Raza Hyder, hero of the Aansu-ki-Wadi expedition, and already

Raza Hyder, hero of the Aansu-ki-Wadi expedition, and already a full Colonel. It was a popular appointment. "Who better to defend one precious mountain valley," the nation's premier daily paper *War* rhetorically inquired, "than the conqueror of another such jewel?" Old Razor Guts himself made the following statement, to a reporter from the same journal, on the steps of the newly air-conditioned mail train to the West: "These brigands are the frogs in the well, good sir, and, God willing, I intend to be the giant who scares off their pants."

At that time his daughter Sufiya Zinobia was fifteen months old. She, and his wife Bilquìs, accompanied Colonel Hyder on his journey towards the Impossible Mountains. And no sooner had their train pulled out of the station than sounds of "Godless carousing" (Raza's phrase) began to filter into their compartment. Raza asked the guard for the identities of his neighbours. "Very big persons, sir," was the reply, "certain executives and also lady stars of a famous bioscope company." Raza Hyder shrugged. "Then we must put up with the racket, because I will not lower myself by disputing with film types." When she heard this Bilquìs set her lips in a tight and bloodless smile, and her eyes stared ferociously through the mirror on the wall which divided her from the empires of her past.

The carriage was a new model with a corridor running past the compartment doors, and a few hours later Bilquìs was returning from the Ladies when a youth with lips as fat as Iskander Harappa's leaned out of the depraved compartment of the cinema people and made kissing noises at her, whispering whiskied endearments: "I swear, yaar, you can keep your goods from foreign, the home produce is the best, no question." Bilquìs could feel his eyes squeezing her breasts, but for some unaccountable reason she did not mention this insult to her honour when she returned to her husband's side.

Raza Hyder's honour also received an insulting blow on that trip, or, to be precise, at its conclusion, because when they arrived at the Cantt station in Q. they found a crowd of locust proportions awaiting them on the platform, singing hit songs and throwing flowers and waving banners and flags of welcome, and although Bilquìs could see Raza twirling his moustache her smiling lips never moved to warn him of the obvious truth, which was that the welcome was not for the Colonel but for the cheap riff-raff next door. Hyder descended from the train with arms spread wide and a speech guaranteeing the safety of the crucial gas seams dripping from his lips, and was almost knocked over by the rush of autograph hunters and hem-kissers towards the demure lady actresses. (Off balance, he failed to notice a fat-lipped youth wiggling his fingers in farewell in the direction of Bilquìs.) The injury sustained here by his pride explained much of what followed; in the illogical manner of the humiliated, he began taking it out on his wife, who shared a bioscopic background with his adversaries—whereupon his rage at the botched reincarnation of his only son awoke again, and crossed over the newly established bridges between his wife and the cinema fans, until Raza began, unconsciously, to hold his progenitorial difficulties against the shallow moviegoers of Q.

Trouble in a marriage is like monsoon water accumulating on a flat roof. You don't realize it's up there, but it gets heavier and heavier, until one day, with a great crash, the whole roof falls in on your head . . . leaving Sindbad Mengal, the kiss-lipped boy who was the youngest son of the president of the bioscope corporation, and who had arrived to take charge of cinematic activity in that region, making promises of weekly programme changes, new picture palaces, and regular personal appearances by top stars and playback singers, the Hyders packed away their own assurances of triumph and pushed their way out of the station through the rejoicing crowd.

At Flashman's Hotel, they were shown into a honeymoon suite which smelled oppressively of naphthalene balls by an enfeebled bearer who was accompanied by the last of the trained monkeys in bellhop uniform, and who could not, in the depths of his despair, resist touching Raza Hyder on the arm and inquiring,

"Please, great sir, do you know, when are the Angrez sahibs coming back?"

And Rani Harappa?

Wherever she looks are peering faces; wherever she listens, voices, using a vocabulary of such multicoloured obscenity that it dyes her listening ears in rainbow colours. She wakes up one morning soon after her arrival at her new home to find peasant girls rummaging through her clothes drawers, taking out and holding up lacy imported lingerie, examining ruby lipsticks. "What do you think you're doing?"—The two girls, unashamed, turn to stare, still holding garments, cosmetics, combs. "O, Isky's wife, nothing to worry, Isky's ayah said to look." "We polished floors and so she gave permission." "Ohé, Isky's wife, look out on those floors we polished! Slipperier than a monkey's bottom, I swear."—Rani rises to her elbows in bed; her voice fights off sleep. "Get out! Don't you blush to be here? Go on, flee before I." The girls fan themselves as if a fire were blazing in the room. "O, God, too hot!" "Hey, Isky's wife, dip your tongue in water!" She shouts, "Don't be insol . . . ," but they interrupt. "Never mind all that, lady, in this house it's still what Isky's ayah says." The girls move, wiggling cheeky hips, towards the door. And pause in the doorway for a parting shot: "Shit, but Isky gives his wife good clothes, the best of everything, no mistake." "That is true. But if a peacock dances in the jungle, there is nobody to see its tail."

"And tell Isky's—tell the ayah I want to see my daughter," she cries, but the girls have closed the door, and one of them shouts through it, "Why be so high and mighty? The child will come when she's ready."

Rani Harappa no longer weeps, no longer tells her mirror *This can't be happening* or sighs with inaccurate nostalgia for the dormitory of the forty thieves. Plus daughter, minus husband, she is stranded in this backyard of the universe: Mohenjo, the Harappa country estate in Sind, stretching from horizon to horizon, afflicted by a chronic water shortage, populated by laughing scornful monsters, "Frankensteins, absolutely." She no longer imagines that Iskander does not know how she is treated here. "He knows," she says to her mirror. Her beloved husband, her groom on the golden plate. "A woman becomes looser after having a child," she confides to the glass, "and my Isky, he likes things tight." Then her hand covers her lips and she runs to door and windows to make sure nobody has heard.

Later, she sits in shalwar and kurta of Italian crêpe-de-chine on the coolest porch, embroidering a shawl, watching a little dust cloud on the horizon. No, how can it be Isky, he is in town with his bosom pal Shakil; I knew trouble, knew it the moment I saw him, the fat pigmeat tub. Probably just one of those little whirlwinds that skip across the scrub.

Mohenjo earth is obstinate. It bakes its people hard as rocks as in the heat. The horses in the stables are made of iron, the cattle have diamond bones. The birds here beak up clods of earth, spit, build nests out of mud; there are few trees, except in the little haunted wood, where even the iron horses bolt . . . an owl, while Rani embroiders, lies sleeping in a burrow in the ground. Only a wingtip can be seen.

"If I was murdered here, the news would never leave the estate." Rani is uncertain whether or not she has spoken aloud. Her thoughts, loosened by solitude, often burst these days through her unconscious lips; and often contradict one another, because the very next notion to form in her mind as she sits on the heavy-eaved verandah is this: "I love the house."

Verandahs run along all four walls; a long covered mosquito-netted walkway joins the house to the kitchen bungalow. It is one of the miracles of the place that chapatis do not cool down on their journey along this wood-floored avenue to the dining hall; nor do soufflés ever fall. And oil paintings and chandeliers and

100

high ceilings and a flat tar-macadamed roof upon which, once, before he abandoned her there, she knelt giggling through a morning skylight at her husband still in bed. Iskander Harappa's family home. "At least I have this piece of him, this soil, his first place. Bilquìs, what a shameless person I must be, to settle for such a small part of my man." And Bilquìs, on the telephone from Q.: "Maybe it's O.K. for you, darling, but I could never put up with it, no sir, anyway my Raza is away at the gas, but spare me your sympathy, dear, when he comes home he may be tired as hell but never so tired, you understand what I mean."

The dust cloud has reached Mir Village now, so it is a visitor and not a whirlwind. She tries to suppress her excitement. The village bears the name of Iskander's father, Sir Mir Harappa, now deceased, once proudly knighted by the Angrez authorities for services rendered. The birdshit is cleaned off his equestrian statue every day. Sir Mir in stone gazes with equal hauteur upon village hospital and brothel, the epitome of an enlightened zamindar . . . "A visitor." She claps her hands, rings a bell. Nothing. Until at length Isky's ayah, a heavy-boned woman with soft uncalloused hands, brings out a jug of pomegranate water. "No need to make such noise, Isky's wife, your husband's household knows how to entertain." Behind the ayah is old Gulbaba, deaf, half-blind, and behind him a trail of spilled pistachio nuts leading to the half-empty dish in his hands. "O God, your servants, darling," Bilquìs has offered long-distance views, "all those fogey types left over from five hundred years ago. I swear you should take them to the doctor and give the painless injections. What you put up with! Queen by name, you must make yourself queen by fame."

She rocks in her verandah chair, the needle moving unhurriedly, and feels the youth and gaiety being crushed out of her, drop by drop, by the pressure of the passing moments, and then the horsemen ride into the courtyard and she recognizes Iskander's cousin, Little Mir Harappa from the Daro estate that begins just over the northern horizon. In these parts horizons serve as boundary fences.

"Rani Begum," Little Mir shouts from horseback, "no point you blaming me for this. Blame your husband, you should keep him on a tighter rein. Excuse me, but the fellow's a real mother-fucker, he's got me all worked up."

A dozen armed horsemen dismount and begin to loot the house, while Mir wheels and rears his mount and hurls justifications at his cousin's wife, in the throes of a giddy, neighing frenzy that sets his tongue free of all constraints. "What do you know about that bullock's arsehole, madam? Fuck me in the mouth, but I know. That pizzle of a homosexual pig. Ask the villagers how his great father locked up his wife and spent every night in the brothel, how a whore disappeared when her fat stomach couldn't be explained by what she ate, and then the next thing Lady Harappa was holding the baby even though everyone knew she hadn't been screwed in a decade. Like father, like son, my honest opinion, sorry if you don't like it. Sisterfucking bastard spawn of corpse-eating vultures. Does he think he can insult me in public and get away with it? Who is the elder, me or that sucker of shit from the rectums of diseased donkeys? Who is the bigger land-owner, me or him with his six inches of land on which even the lice cannot grow fat? You tell him who is king in these parts. Tell him who can do what he likes round here, and that he should come crawling to kiss my feet like a murdering rapist of his own grandmother and beg for pardon. That nibbler of a crow's left nipple. This day shows him who's the boss."

Looters cut from gilded frames paintings of the school of Rubens; Sheraton chairs have their legs amputated. Antique silver is placed in worn old saddle-bags. Cut-glass decanters splinter on thousand-knot carpets. She, Rani, goes on with her embroidery in the midst of the punitive riot. The old servants, the ayah, Gulbaba, the polishing girls, syces, villagers from Mir Village stand and watch, squat and listen, Little Mir, a proud equestrian figure, the tall hawkish avatar of the statue in the village, does not fall silent until his men are back upon their horses. "A man's honour is in his women," he shouts. "So when he took that whore from me he took my honour, tell him that, the little jumped-up piss drinker. Tell him about the frog in the well, and how the giant frog replied. Tell him to be afraid and to think himself lucky I am a mild-mannered man. I could have regained my honour by depriving him of his. Lady, I could do to you anything, anything, and who would dare say no? Here it is my law, Mir's law, that runs. Salaam aleikum." The dust of the departing horsemen settles on the surface of the untouched pomegranate water, then sinks to form a thick sediment at the bottom of the jug. "I just can't tell him yet," Rani tells Bilquìs on the telephone. "It makes me feel too ashamed."

"O, Rani, you got your problems, darling," Bilquìs sympathizes down the Army telephone line. "What do you mean you don't know? Here I am, stuck away just like you, and even in this zero-town I know what the whole of Karachi is saying. Darling, who hasn't seen how your Isky and that fat doctor run around, belly-dancer shows, international hotel swimming-pools where the naked white women go, why do you think he puts you where you are? Alcohol, gambling, opium, who knows what. Those women in their waterproof fig leaves. Excuse me, darling, but somebody has to tell you. Cock fights, bear fights, snake-and-mongoose fights, that Shakil fixes everything like a pimp or what. And how many women? O baba. Under banquet tables he grabs their thighs. They say the two of them go to the red-light district with movie cameras. Of course it's clear what that Shakil is up to, that nobody from nowhere is getting the high life on a plate, maybe some of those women are willing to be passed on, crumbs from the rich man's table, you understand my meaning. Anyway the point is darling your Isky pinched his cousin's juiciest little French tart from right under his nose, at some big cultural event, I'm sorry to say it but it was all over town, so funny to see Mir standing there while Isky walked off with the floozy. O God I don't know why you don't just cry and cry. Now what's to get worked up about, honestly you should know who is your friend and who is poisoning your name behind your back. You should hear me on the phone, darling, how I defend you, like a tiger, you've got no idea, sweetie, sitting up there and lording it over your antique Gulbabas and all."

She encounters the ayah clucking ruefully in the wreckage of the dining hall. "Went too far," the ayah says. "My Isky, such a naughty boy. Always he got his cousins' goat. Went too far. The little hooligan."

Wherever she looks are peering faces; wherever she listens, voices. She is watched as, blushing with the humiliation of it, she calls Iskander to give him the news. (It has taken her five days to build up her courage.) Iskander Harappa says just three words:

"Life is long."

Raza Hyder led his gas soldiers out to Needle Valley after a week in which their activities had so alarmed the town that State Chief Minister Gichki had ordered Raza to get moving double-quick before the stock of virgins available to the bachelors of Q. dwindled to a point at which the moral stability of the region would be jeopardized. Accompanying the soldiers were numerous architects, engineers and construction workers, all of whom were in a condition of moist-trousered panic, because for security reasons none of them had been informed of the fate of the advance party until they arrived in Q., where they were immediately given magnificently elaborated versions of the tale by every street-corner paan-wallah. The construction personnel sobbed inside locked vans; soldiers on guard jeered: "Cowards! Babies! Women!" Raza in his flagbearing jeep heard none of this. He was unable to turn his thoughts away from the events of the preceding day, when he had been visited at the hotel by an obsequious gnome whose loose garments smelled powerfully of motor-scooter exhaust fumes: Maulana Dawood, the ancient divine, around whose chicken-thin neck had once hung a necklace of shoes.

"Sir, great sir, I look upon your hero's brow and am inspired."

The *gatta*, the bruise of devotion on Raza's forehead, did not go unremarked.

"No, O most wise, it is I who am at once humbled and exalted by your visit." Raza Hyder would have been prepared to continue in this vein for at least eleven minutes, and felt a little disappointed when the holy man nodded and said briskly, "So then, to business. You know about this Gichki of course. Not to be trusted."

"Not?"

"Completely not. Most corrupt individual. But your files will show this."

"Allow me to benefit from the knowledge of the man on the spot . . ."

"Like all our politicos these days. No fear of God and big smuggling rackets. This is boring for you; the Army is well up in such matters."

"Please proceed."

"Foreign devilments, sir. Nothing less. Devil things from abroad."

What Gichki was accused of bringing illicitly into God's pure land: iceboxes, foot-operated sewing machines, American popular music recorded at seventy-eight revolutions per minute, love-story picture books that inflamed the passions of the local virgins, domestic air-conditioning units, coffee percolators, bone china, skirts, German sunglasses, cola concentrates, plastic toys, French cigarettes, contraceptive devices, untaxed motor vehicles, big ends, Axminster carpets, repeating rifles, sinful fragrances, brassières, rayon pants, farm machinery, books, eraser-tipped pencils and tubeless bicycle tyres. The customs officer at the border post was mad and his shameless daughter was willing to turn a blind eye in return for regular gratuities. As a result all these items from Hell could arrive in broad daylight, on the public highway, and find their way into the gypsy markets, even in the capital itself. "Army," Dawood said in a voice that had dropped to a whisper, "must not stop at stamping out tribal wild men. In God's name, sir."

"Sir, put your point."

"Sir, it is this. Prayer is the sword of the faith. By the same token, is not the faithful sword, wielded for God, a form of holy prayer?"

Colonel Hyder's eyes became opaque. He turned away to look out of the window towards an enormous silent house. From an upper window of the house a young boy was training fieldglasses on the hotel. Raza turned back towards the Maulana. "Gichki, you say."

"Here it is Gichki. But everywhere things are the same. Ministers!"

"Yes," Hyder said absently, "they are ministers, that's true."

"Then I have said my piece and take my leave, abasing myself before you for the privilege of this encounter. God is great."

"Be in the hands of God."

Raza headed for the threatened gas fields with the above conversation in his mind's ear; and in his mind's eye the picture of a small boy with binoculars, alone at an upstairs window. A boy who was someone's son: a drop appeared on Old Razor Guts's cheek and was blown off by the wind.

"Gone for three months minimum," Bilquìs sighed into her telephone. "What to do? I am young, I can't sit all day like a water-buffalo in mud. Thank God I can go to the movies." Every night, leaving her child in the care of a locally hired ayah, Bilquìs sat in the brand-new cinema called Mengal Mahal. But Q. was a small town; eyes saw things, even in the dark . . . but I shall return to this theme at a later point, because I can no longer avoid the story of my poor heroine:

Two months after Raza Hyder departed into the wilderness to do battle with the gas-field dacoits, his only child Sufiya Zinobia contracted a case of brain fever that turned her into an idiot. Bilquìs, rending hair and sari with equal passion, was heard to utter a mysterious sentence: "It is a judgment," she cried beside her daughter's bed. Despairing of military and civilian doctors she turned to a local Hakim who prepared an expensive liquid distilled from cactus roots, ivory dust and parrot feathers, which saved the girl's life but which (as the medicine man had warned) had the effect of slowing her down for the rest of her years, because the unfortunate side-effect of a potion so filled with elements of longevity was to retard the progress of time inside the body of anyone to whom it was given. By the day of Raza's return to furlough Sufiya Zinobia had shaken off the fever, but Bilquìs was convinced she could already discern in her not-yet-two-year-old child the effects of that inner deceleration which could never be reversed. "And if there is this effect," she feared, "who knows what else? Who can say?"

In the clutches of a guilt so extreme that even the affliction of her only child seemed insufficient to explain it, a guilt in which, were I possessed of a scandalously wagging tongue, I would say that something Mengalian, something to do with visits to the cinema and fat-mouthed youths, was also present. Bilquìs Hyder spent the night before Raza's return pacing sleeplessly around the honeymoon suite of Flashman's Hotel, and it should perhaps be noted that one of her hands, acting, apparently, of its own volition, continually caressed the region around her navel. At four a.m. she obtained a long-distance line to Rani Harappa in Mohenjo and made the following injudicious remarks:

"Rani, a judgment, what else? He wanted a hero of a son; I give him an idiot female instead. That's the truth, excuse me, I can't help it. Rani, a simpleton, a goof! Nothing upstairs. Straw instead of cabbage between the ears. Empty in the breadbin. To be done? But darling, there is nothing. That birdbrain, that mouse! I must accept it: she is my shame."

When Raza Hyder returned to Q. the boy was standing at the window of the great solitary house once again. One of the local guides, in answer to the Colonel's inquiry, told Raza that the house was owned by three crazy sinful witches who never came outside but who managed to produce children nevertheless. The boy at the window was their second son: witch-fashion, they claimed to share their offspring. "But the story is, sir, that in that house is more wealth than in the treasury of Alexander the Great." Hyder replied with what sounded like contempt: "So. But if a peacock dances in the jungle, who will see its tail?" Still, his eyes never left the boy at the window until the jeep arrived at the hotel, where he found his wife awaiting him with her hair loose and her face washed clean of eyebrows, so that she was the very incarnation of tragedy, and he heard what she had been too ashamed to send word of. The illness of his daughter and the vision of the fieldglass-eyed young boy combined in Hyder's spirits with the bitterness of his ninety days in the desert and sent him storming out of the honeymoon suite bursting with a rage so terrible that for the sake of his personal safety it was necessary to find a release for it as soon as possible. He ordered a staff car to drive him to the residence of Chief Minister Gichki in the Cantonment, and, without waiting on ceremony, he informed the Minister that although construction work at Needle was well advanced the threat from the tribals could never be eliminated unless he, Hyder, were empowered to take draconian punitive measures. "With God's help we are defending the site, but now we must stop this pussyfooting. Sir, you must place the law in my hands. Carte blanche. At certain moments civil law must bend before military necessity. Violence is the language of these savages; but the law obliges us to speak in the discredited womanly tongue of minimum-force. No good, sir. I cannot guarantee results." And when Gichki responded that on no account were the laws of the State to be flouted by the armed forces—"We'll have no barbarisms in those hills, sir! No tortures, no stringings-up by toes, not while I am Chief Minister here!"—then Raza, in discourteously loud tones that escaped through the doors and windows of Gichki's office and terrified the peons outside because they had issued from the lips of one so habitually polite, gave the Chief Minister a warning. "Army is watching these days, Gichki Sahib. All over the country the eyes of honest soldiers see what they see, and we are not pleased, no sir. The people stir, sir. And if they look away from politicians, where will they turn for purity?"

Raza Hyder in his wrath left Gichki—small, bullet-cropped hair, flat Chinese face—formulating his never-to-be-delivered reply; and found Maulana Dawood awaiting him by the staff car. Soldier and divine rode on the back seat, their words shielded from the driver by a sheet of glass. But it seems probable that behind this screen a name passed from divine tongue into martial ear: a name, carrying with it intimations of scandal. Did Maulana Dawood tell Hyder about the meetings of Bilquìs and her Sindbad? I say only that it seems probable. Innocent until proven guilty is an excellent rule.

That night the cinema executive Sindbad Mengal left his office at Mengal Mahal by the back door as usual, emerging into a dark gully behind the cinema screen. He was whistling a sad tune, the melody of a man who cannot meet his beloved even though the moon is full. In spite of the loneliness of the tune he had dressed up to the nines, as was his custom: his bright European garb, bush-shirt and duck pants, was radiant in the gully, and the melancholy moonlight bounced off the oil in his hair. It is likely that he never even noticed that the shadows in the gully had begun to close in on him; the knife, which the moon would have illuminated, was clearly kept sheathed until the last instant. We know this because Sindbad Mengal did not stop whistling until the knife entered his guts, whereupon someone else began to whistle the same tune, just in case anybody was passing by and got curious. A hand covered Sindbad's mouth as the knife went to work. In the next few days Mengal's absence from his office inevitably attracted attention, but it was not until several moviegoers had complained about the deterioration in the cinema's stereophonic sound quality that an engineer inspected the loudspeakers behind the screen and discovered segments of Sindbad Mengal's white shirt and duck pants concealed within them, as well as black Oxford shoes. The knife-sliced garments still contained the appropriate pieces of the cinema manager's body. The genitals had been severed and inserted into the rectum. The head was never found, nor was the murderer brought to justice.

Life is not always long.

That night Raza made love to Bilquìs with a coarseness which she was willing to put down to his months in the wilderness. The name of Mengal was never mentioned between them, not even when the town was buzzing with the murder story, and soon afterwards Raza returned to Needle Valley. Bilquìs stopped going to the cinema, and although in this period she retained her queenly composure it seemed as though she were standing on a crumbling outcrop over an abyss, because she became prone to dizzy spells. Once, when she picked up her damaged daughter to play the traditional game of water-carrier, slinging Sufiya Zinobia on her back and pretending she was a water-skin, she collapsed to the floor beneath the delighted child before she had finished pouring her out. Soon afterwards she called Rani Harappa to announce that she was pregnant. While she was imparting this information, the lid of her left eye began, inexplicably, to nictate.

An itchy palm means money in the offing. Shoes crossed on the floor mean a journey; shoes turned upside-down warn of tragedy. Scissors cutting empty air mean a quarrel in the family. And a winking left eye means there will be bad news soon.

"On my next leave," Raza wrote to Bilquìs, "I shall be going to Karachi. There are family duties, and also Marshal Aurangzeb is giving a reception. One does not refuse one's Commander-in-Chief's invitation. In your condition, however, you will do better to rest. It would be thoughtless of me to ask you to accompany me on this non-compulsory and arduous trip."

Politeness can be a trap, and Bilquìs was caught in the web of her husband's courtesy. "As you wish," she wrote back, and what made her write this was not entirely guilt, but also something untranslatable, a law which obliged her to pretend that Raza's words meant no more than they said. This law is called *takallouf*. To unlock a society, look at its untranslatable words. *Takallouf* is a member of that opaque, world-wide sect of concepts which refuse to travel across linguistic frontiers: it refers to a form of tongue-tying formality, a social restraint so extreme as to make it impossible for the victim to express what he or she really means, a species of compulsory irony which insists, for the sake of good form, on being taken literally. When *takallouf* gets between a husband and a wife, look out.

Raza travelled alone to the capital . . . and now that an untranslatable word has brought Hyder and Harappa, unencumbered by spouses, very near to meeting once again, it is time to take stock of the situation, because our two duellists will shortly find themselves doing battle. Even now, the cause of their first altercation is allowing a servant girl to oil and braid her hair. She, Atiyah Aurangzeb, known to her intimates as "Pinkie," is contemplating, coolly, the soirée which she has decided to arrange in the name of her almost senile husband, the crumbling Marshal Aurangzeb, Joint Chief of Staff. Pinkie Aurangzeb is in her middle thirties, several years older than Raza and Iskander, but this does not diminish her allure; mature women have charms of their own, as is well known. Trapped in a marriage with a dotard, Pinkie finds her pleasures wherever she can.

Meanwhile, two wives are abandoned in their separate exiles, each with a daughter who should have been a son (more needs to be said about young Arjumand Harappa, more will certainly be written about poor, idiot Sufiya Zinobia). Two different approaches to the matter of revenge have been outlined. And while Iskander Harappa consorts with a fat pigmeat tub named Omar

Khayyam Shakil for purposes of debauchery etc., Raza Hyder would seem to have fallen under the influence of a grey eminence, who whispers austere secrets in the backs of Army limousines. Cinemas, sons of witches, bruises on foreheads, frogs, peacocks have all worked to create an atmosphere in which the stink of honour is all-pervasive.

Yes, it is high time the combatants took the field.

The fact is that Raza Hyder was smitten right between the eyes by Pinkie Aurangzeb. He desired her so badly that it made the bruise on his forehead ache, but he lost her to Iskander Harappa, right there at the Marshal's reception, while the old soldier slept in an armchair, relegated to a corner of the glittering throng, but even in that condition of somnolent cuckolded dotage never spilling a drop from the brimming tumbler of whisky-soda he clutched in his sleeping hand.

On that fateful occasion began a duel which was to continue at least until both protagonists were dead, if not longer. Its initial prize was the body of the Marshal's wife, but after that it moved on to higher things. First things first, however: and Pinkie's body, excitingly on display, in a green sari worn dangerously low upon the hips in the fashion of the women of the East Wing; with silver-and-diamond earrings in the form of crescent-and-star hanging brightly from pierced lobes; and bearing upon irresistibly vulnerable shoulders a light shawl whose miraculous work could only have been the product of the fabled embroiderers of Aansu, because amidst its minuscule arabesques a thousand and one stories had been portrayed in threads of gold, so vividly that it seemed the tiny horsemen were actually galloping along her collarbone, while minute birds appeared to be flying, actually flying, down the graceful meridian of her spine . . . this body is worth lingering over.

And lingering over it, when Raza had managed to fight his way through the whirlpools and eddies of young bucks and jealous women surrounding Pinkie Aurangzeb, was the half-drunk

Iskander Harappa, city playboy number one, at whom the vision of loveliness was smiling with a warmth that froze the thick perspiration of his arousal on to Raza's waxed moustache, while that notorious degenerate with his filthy tongue that put even his cousin Mir to shame told the goddess dirty jokes.

Raza Hyder stiff, at embarrassed attention, the garment of his lust rendered rigid by the starch of *takallouf* . . . but Isky hiccuped, "Look who's here! Our goddamn hero, the tilyar!" Pinkie tittered as Iskander adopted a professorial stance, adjusting invisible pince-nez: "The tilyar, madam, as you are possibly aware, is a skinny little migrating bird good for nothing but shooting out of the sky." Ripples of laughter spread outwards through the eddying bucks. Pinkie, annihilating Raza with a look, murmured, "Pleased to meet," and Raza found himself replying with a ruinously awkward and bombastic formality, "My honour, lady, and may I say that in my opinion and with the grace of God the new blood is going to be the making of our great new nation," but Pinkie Aurangzeb was pretending to stifle a laugh. "Fuck me in the mouth, tilyar," Iskander Harappa shouted gaily, "this is a party, yaar, no motherfucking speeches, for God's sake." The rage buried beneath Hyder's good manners was bubbling higher, but it was impotent against this sophistication that permitted obscenity and blasphemy and could murder a man's desire and his pride with clever laughter. "Cousin," he attempted catastrophically, "I am just a simple soldier," but now his hostess stopped pretending not to laugh at him, drew the shawl tighter around her shoulders, put a hand on Iskander Harappa's arm and said, "Take me into the garden, Isky. The air-conditioning is too cold in here, and outside it's nice and warm."

"Then into the warm, pronto!" Harappa cried gallantly, pressing his glass into Raza's hand for safe-keeping. "For you, Pinkie, I would enter the furnaces of hell, if you desire protection when you get there. My teetotal relative Raza is no less brave," he added over his departing shoulder, "only he goes to hell not for ladies, but for gas."

Watching from the sidelines as Iskander Harappa bore his prize away into the close, musky twilight of the garden was the flabby Himalayan figure of our peripheral hero, the doctor, Omar Khayyam Shakil.

Do not form too low an opinion of Atiyah Aurangzeb. She remained faithful to Iskander Harappa even after he turned serious and dispensed with her services, and retired without a word of complaint into the stoic tragedy of her private life, until the day of his death, when after setting fire to an old embroidered shawl she hacked out her own heart with a nine-inch kitchen knife. And Isky, too, was faithful to her in his fashion. From the time that she became his mistress he stopped sleeping with his wife Rani altogether, thus ensuring that she would have no more children, and that he would be the last of his line, an idea which, he told Omar Khayyam Shakil, was not without a certain appeal.

(Here I should explain the matter of daughters-who-should-have-been-sons. Sufiya Zinobia was the "wrong miracle" because her father had wanted a boy; but this was not Arjumand Harappa's problem. Arjumand, the famous "virgin Ironpants," regretted her female sex for wholly non-parental reasons. "This woman's body," she told her father on the day she became a grown woman, "it brings a person nothing but babies, pinches and shame.")

Iskander reappeared from the garden as Raza was preparing to leave, and attempted to make peace. With a formality the equal of Raza's own, he said: "Dear fellow, before you go back to Needle you must come up to Mohenjo, Rani would be so happy. Poor girl, I wish she enjoyed this city life . . . and I insist that you call your Billoo there also. Let the ladies have a good chat while we shoot tilyars all day long. What do you say?"

And *takallouf* obliged Raza Hyder to answer: "Thank you, yes."

The day before they passed the sentence of death Iskander Harappa would be permitted to telephone his daughter for one minute exactly. The last words he ever addressed to her in private were acrid with the hopeless nostalgia of those shrunken times: "Arjumand, my love, I should have gone out to fight this buffalo-fucker Hyder when he staked himself to the ground. I left that business unfinished; it was my biggest mistake."

Even in his playboy period Iskander occasionally felt bad about his sequestered wife. At such moments he rounded up a few cronies, bundled them into station-wagons and led a convoy of urban gaiety up to his country estate. Pinkie Aurangzeb was conspicuous by her absence; and Rani was queen for a day.

When Raza Hyder accepted Isky's invitation to Mohenjo, the two of them drove up together, followed by five other vehicles containing an ample supply of whisky, film starlets, sons of textile magnates, European diplomats, soda siphons and wives. Bilquìs, Sufiya Zinobia and the ayah were met at the private railway station Sir Mir Harappa had constructed on the mail line from the capital to Q. And, for one day, nothing bad happened at all.

After the death of Isky Harappa, Rani and Arjumand Harappa were kept locked up in Mohenjo for several years, and to fill the silences the mother told the daughter about the business of the shawl. "I had begun to embroider it before I heard that I was sharing my husband with Little Mir's woman, but it turned out to be a premonition of another woman entirely." By that time Arjumand Harappa had already reached the stage of refusing to hear anything bad about her father. She snapped back: "Allah, mother, all you can do is bitch about the Chairman. If he did not love you, you must have done something to deserve it." Rani Harappa shrugged. "Chairman Iskander Harappa, your father, whom I always loved," she replied, "was world champion of shamelessness; he was international rogue and bastard number one. You see, daughter, I remember those days, I remember Raza Hyder when he was not a devil with horns and a tail, and also Isky, before he became a saint."

The bad thing that happened at Mohenjo when the Hyders were there was started by a fat man who had had too much to drink. It happened on the second evening of that visit, on the very verandah on which Rani Harappa had gone on with her embroidery while Little Mir's men looted her home—an incursion whose effects could still be seen, in the empty picture-frames with fragments of canvas adhering to the corners, in the sofas whose stuffing stuck out through the ripped leather, in the odd assortment of cutlery at the dining table and the obscene slogans in the hall, which could still be made out beneath the coats of white-wash. The partial wreckage of the Mohenjo house gave the guests the feeling of holding a celebration in the midst of a disaster, and made them expect more trouble, so that the bright laughter of the film starlet Zehra acquired an edge of hysteria and the men all drank too fast. And all the time Rani Harappa sat in her rocking-chair and worked on her shawl, leaving the organization of Mohenjo to the ayah who was fawning over Iskander as if he were three years old, or a deity, or both. And finally the trouble did come, and because it was the fate of Omar Khayyam Shakil to affect, from his position on the periphery, the great events whose central figures were other people but which collectively made up his own life, it was he who said with a tongue made too loose by the neurotic drinking of the evening that Mrs. Bilquìs Hyder was a lucky woman, Iskander had done her a favour by pinching Pinkie Aurangzeb from under Raza's nose. "If Isky hadn't been there maybe our hero's Begum would have to console herself with children, because there would be no man to fill her bed." Shakil had spoken too loud, to gain the attention of the starlet Zehra, who was more interested in the over-bright looks she was getting from a certain Akbar Junejo, a well-known gambler and film producer; when Zehra moved away without bothering to make any excuses, Shakil was faced with the spectacle of a wife-eyed Bilquìs, who had just emerged on to the verandah after seeing her daughter into bed, and on whom the pregnancy was showing much too early . . . so who knows if that was the reason for Bilquìs's stand, if she was just trying to transfer her own guilt on to the shoulders of a husband whose probity was now also the subject of gossip?—Anyway, what happened was this: after it became clear to the guests that Omar Khayyam's words had been heard and understood by the woman who stood blazing on the evening verandah, a silence fell, and a stillness which reduced the party to a tableau of fear, and into that stillness Bilquìs Hyder shrieked her husband's name.

It must not be forgotten that she was a woman to whom the dupatta of womanly honour had clung even when the rest of her clothing had been torn off her body; not a woman to turn a deaf ear to public slanders. Raza Hyder and Iskander Harappa stared wordlessly at each other while Bilquìs pointed a long-nailed index finger at the heart of Omar Khayyam Shakil.

"You hear that man, husband? Hear what shame he is making for me."

O, the hush, the muteness, like a cloud that obscured the horizon! Even the owls forbore to screech.

Raza Hyder came to attention, because once the *afrit* of honour has been summoned from its sleep, it will not depart until satisfied. "Iskander," Raza said, "I will not fight inside your house." Then he did a strange and a wild thing. He marched off the verandah, entered the stables, returned with a wooden stake, a mallet and a length of good stout rope. The stake was driven into the rock-hard earth; and then Colonel Hyder, future President, tethered himself to it by the ankle and hurled the mallet away.

"Here I stand," he shouted. "Let the one who slanders my honour come out and find me." And there, all night long, he remained; because Omar Khayyam Shakil rushed indoors, to faint of alcohol and fright.

Hyder like a bull paced in circles, the rope a radius stretching taut from ankle to stake. The night thickened; the guests, embarrassed, drifted away to bed. But Isky Harappa stayed on the verandah, knowing that although the folly had been the fat man's, the true quarrel stood between the Colonel and himself. The

SHAME

starlet Zehra, on her way to a bed which it would be unforgivably loose-tongued of me to suggest was already occupied—so I shall say nothing at all on the subject—offered her host a warning. "Don't go getting any stupid ideas, Isky darling, you hear? Don't you dare go out there. He's a soldier, look at him, like a tank, he'll kill you for sure. Just let him cool off, O.K.?" But Rani Harappa gave her husband no advice. ("You see, Arjumand," she told her daughter, years later, "I recall your daddy when he was too mousy to take his medicine like a man.")

How it ended: badly, as it had to. Just before dawn. You can understand: Raza had been awake all night, stamping in the circle of his pride, his eyes red with rage and fatigue. Red eyes don't see clearly—and the light was poor—and who sees servants coming, anyway?—what I'm trying to say is that old Gulbaba woke early and walked across the yard with a brass lotah jug, on his way to ablute before saying his prayers; and, seeing Colonel Hyder tied to a stake, crept up behind him to ask, sir, what are you doing, will it not be better if you come . . . ? Old servants take liberties. It is the privilege of their years. But Raza, sleep-deafened, heard only steps, a voice; felt a tap on his shoulder; swung round; and with one terrible blow, felled Gulbaba like a twig. The violence loosened something inside the old man; let us call it life, because within a month old Gul was dead, with a confused expression on his face, like a man who knows he has mislaid an important possession and can't remember what it is.

In the aftermath of that murderous punch Bilquìs relented, emerging from the shadow of the house to persuade Raza to unhitch himself from his post. "The poor girl, Raza, don't make her see this thing." And when Raza came back to the verandah, Iskander Harappa, himself unslept and unshaven, offered his arms in embrace, and Raza, with considerable grace, hugged Isky, shoulder against shoulder, allowing their necks to meet, as the saying goes.

When Rani Harappa emerged from her boudoir the next day to say goodbye to her husband, Iskander went pale at the sight of the shawl she had wrapped around her shoulders, a completed

118

shawl as delicately worked as anything made by the craftswomen of Aansu, a masterpiece amidst whose minuscule arabesques a thousand and one stories had been portrayed, so artfully that it seemed as though horsemen were galloping along her collarbone, while tiny birds flew along the soft meridian of her spine. "Goodbye, Iskander," she told him, "and do not forget that the love of some women is not blind."

Well, well, friendship is a bad word for the thing between Raza and Iskander, but for a long time after the incident of the stake it was the word they both used. Sometimes the good words can't be found.

She has always wanted to be a queen, but now that Raza Hyder is at last a sort of prince the ambition has gone sour on her lips. A second baby has been born, six weeks early, but Raza has uttered no word of suspicion. Another daughter, but he hasn't complained about that either, saying only that it is quite proper that the first should be a boy and the second a girl, so one must not blame the new arrival for her elder sister's mistake. The girl has been named Naveed, that is Good News, and she is a model baby. But the mother has been damaged by this birth. Something has been torn inside, and the medical opinion is that she must have no more children. Raza Hyder will never have a son. He has spoken, just once, of the boy with fieldglasses at the window of the witches' house, but this subject, too, has been closed. He is withdrawing from her down the corridors of his mind, closing the doors behind him. Sindbad Mengal, Mohenjo, love: all these doors are closed. She sleeps alone, so that her old fears have her at their mercy, and it is in these days that she begins to be afraid of the hot afternoon wind that flows so fiercely out of her past.

Martial law has been declared. Raza has arrested Chief Minister Gichki and been appointed administrator of the region. He has moved into the Ministerial residence with his wife and children, abandoning to its memories that cracking hotel in which the last trained monkey has taken to wandering listlessly amidst the dying palms of the dining hall while ageing musicians scratch at their rotting fiddles for an audience of empty tables. She does not see much of Raza these days. He has work to do. The gas pipeline is progressing well, and now that Gichki is out of the way a programme of making examples of arrested tribals has been inaugurated. She fears that the bodies of hanged men will turn the citizens of Q. against her husband, but she does not say this to him. He is taking a firm line, and Maulana Dawood gives him all the advice he needs.

The last time I visited Pakistan, I was told this joke. God came down to Pakistan to see how things were going. He asked General Ayub Khan why the place was in such a mess. Ayub replied: "It's these no-good corrupt civilians, sir. Just get rid of them and leave the rest to me." So God eliminated the politicos. After a while, He returned; things were even worse than before. This time He asked Yahya Khan for an explanation. Yahya blamed Ayub, his sons and their hangers-on for the troubles. "Do the needful," Yahya begged, "and I'll clean the place up good and proper." So God's thunderbolts wiped out Ayub. On His third visit, He found a catastrophe, so He agreed with Zulfikar Ali Bhutto that democracy must return. He turned Yahya into a cockroach and swept him under a carpet; but, a few years later, He noticed the situation was still pretty awful. He went to General Zia and offered him supreme power: on one condition. "Anything, God," the General replied. "You name it." So God said, "Answer me one question and I'll flatten Bhutto for you like a chapati." Zia said: "Fire away." So God whispered in his ear: "Look, I do all these things for this country, but what I don't understand is: why don't people seem to love me any more?"

It seems clear that the President of Pakistan managed to give God a satisfactory answer. I wonder what it was.

III

SHAME,
GOOD NEWS
AND
THE VIRGIN

7

BLUSHING

Not so long ago, in the East End of London, a Pakistani father murdered his only child, a daughter, because by making love to a white boy she had brought such dishonour upon her family that only her blood could wash away the stain. The tragedy was intensified by the father's enormous and obvious love for his butchered child, and by the beleaguered reluctance of his friends and relatives (all "Asians," to use the confusing term of these trying days) to condemn his actions. Sorrowing, they told radio microphones and television cameras that they understood the man's point of view, and went on supporting him even when it turned out that the girl had never actually "gone all the way" with her boyfriend. The story appalled me when I heard it, appalled me in a fairly obvious way. I had recently become a father myself and was therefore newly capable of estimating how colossal a force would be required to make a man turn a knife-blade against his own flesh and blood. But even more appalling was my realization that, like the interviewed friends etc., I, too, found myself understanding the killer. The news did not seem alien to me. We who have grown up on a diet of honour and shame can still grasp what must seem unthinkable to peoples living in the aftermath of the death of God and of tragedy: that men will sacrifice their dearest love on the implacable altars of their pride. (And not only men. I have since heard of a case in which a woman committed the identical crime for identical reasons.) Between shame and shamelessness lies the axis upon which we turn; meteorological conditions at both these poles are of the most extreme, ferocious type. Shamelessness, shame: the roots of violence.

My Sufiya Zinobia grew out of the corpse of that murdered girl, although she will not (have no fear) be slaughtered by Raza Hyder. Wanting to write about shame, I was at first haunted by the imagined spectre of that dead body, its throat slit like a halal chicken, lying in a London night across a zebra crossing, slumped across black and white, black and white, while above her a Belisha beacon blinked, orange, not-orange, orange. I thought of the crime as having been committed right there, publicly, ritually, while at the windows eyes. And no mouth opened in protest. And when the police knocked on doors, what hope of assistance had they? Inscrutability of the "Asian" face under the eyes of the foe. It seems even the insomniacs at their windows closed their eyelids and saw nothing. And the father left with blood-cleansed name and grief.

I even went so far as to give the dead girl a name: Anahita Muhammad, known as Anna. In my imagination she spoke with an East London accent but wore jeans, blue brown pink, out of some atavistic reluctance to show her legs. She would certainly have understood the language her parents spoke at home, but would obstinately have refused to utter a word of it herself. Anna Muhammad: lively, no doubt attractive, a little too dangerously so at sixteen. Mecca meant ballrooms to her, rotating silver balls, strobe lighting, youth. She danced behind my eyes, her nature changing each time I glimpsed her: now innocent, now whore, then a third and a fourth thing. But finally she eluded me, she became a ghost, and I realized that to write about her, about shame, I would have to go back East, to let the idea breathe its favourite air. Anna, deported, repatriated to a country she had never seen, caught brain-fever and turned into a sort of idiot.

Why did I do that to her?—Or maybe the fever was a lie, a figment of Bilquìs Hyder's imagination, intended to cover up the damage done by repeated blows to the head: hate can turn a miracle-gone-wrong into a basket case. And that hakimi potion sounds pretty unconvincing. How hard to pin down the truth, especially when one is obliged to see the world in slices; snapshots conceal as much as they make plain.

All stories are haunted by the ghosts of the stories they might have been. Anna Muhammad haunts this book; I'll never write about her now. And other phantoms are here as well, earlier and now ectoplasmic images connecting shame and violence. These ghosts, like Anna, inhabit a country that is entirely unghostly: no spectral "Peccavistan," but Proper London. I'll mention two. A girl set upon in a late-night underground train by a group of teenage boys is the first. The girl "Asian" again, the boys predictably white. Afterwards, remembering her beating, she feels not angry but ashamed. She does not want to talk about what happened, she makes no official complaint, she hopes the story won't get out: it is a typical reaction, and the girl is not one girl but many. Looking at smoking cities on my television screen, I see groups of young people running through the streets, the shame burning on their brows and setting fire to shops, police shields, cars. They remind me of my anonymous girl. Humiliate people for long enough and a wildness bursts out of them. Afterwards, surveying the wreckage of their rage, they look bewildered, uncomprehending, young. Did we do such things? Us? But we're just ordinary kids, nice people, we didn't know we could . . . then, slowly, pride dawns on them, pride in their power, in having learned to hit back. And I imagine what would have happened if such a fury could have been released in that girl on her underground train—how she would have thrashed the white kids within an inch of their lives, breaking arms legs noses balls, without knowing whence the violence came, without seeing how she, so slight a figure, could command such awesome strength. And they, what would they have done? How to tell the police they were beaten up by a mere girl, just one weak female against the lot of them? How to look their comrades in the face? I feel gleeful about this notion: it's a seductive, silky thing, this violence, yes it is.

I never gave this second girl a name. But she, too, is inside my Sufiya Zinobia now, and you'll recognize her when she pops out.

The last ghost inside my heroine is male, a boy from a news clipping. You may have read about him, or at least his prototype: he was found blazing in a parking lot, his skin on fire. He burned to death, and the experts who examined his body and the scene of the incident were forced to accept what seemed impossible: namely that the boy had simply ignited of his own accord, without dousing himself in petrol or applying any external flame. We are energy; we are fire; we are light. Finding the key, stepping through into that truth, a boy began to burn.

Enough. Ten years have slipped by in my story while I've been seeing ghosts.—But one last word on the subject: the first time I sat down to think about Anahita Muhammad, I recalled the last sentence of *The Trial* by Franz Kafka, the sentence in which Joseph K. is stabbed to death. My Anna, like Kafka's Joseph, died under a knife. Not so Sufiya Zinobia Hyder; but that sentence, the ghost of an epigraphy, hangs over her story still:

" 'Like a dog!' he said: it was as if he meant the shame of it to outlive him.''

By the year of the Hyders' return from Q. the capital had grown, Karachi had become fat, so that people who had been there from the beginning could no longer recognize the slender girlish town of their youth in this obese harridan of a metropolis. The great fleshy folds of its endless expansion had swallowed up the primeval salt marshes, and all along the sandspit there erupted, like boils, the gaudily painted beach houses of the rich. The streets were full of the darkened faces of young men who had been drawn to the painted lady by her overblown charms, only to find that her price was too high for them to pay; something puritan and violent sat on their foreheads and it was frightening to walk amongst their disillusions in the heat. The night held smugglers who rode in scooter-rickshaws to the coast; and the Army, of course, was in power.

Raza Hyder got off the railway train from the West wreathed in rumours. This was the period shortly after the disappearance of the former Chief Minister Aladdin Gichki, who had finally been released from captivity for lack of hard evidence against him; he lived quietly with his wife and dog for several weeks until the day he went out to walk the Alsatian and never returned, even though his last words to Begum Gichki had been, "Tell the cook to make a dozen extra meatballs for dinner, I'm starving to death today." Meatballs, one to twelve, steamed expectantly in a dish, but something must have spoiled Gichki's appetite, because he never ate them. Possibly he was unable to resist the pangs of hunger and ate the Alsatian instead, because they never found the dog either, not so much as a hair of its tail. The Gichki mystery kept cropping up in conversations, and Hyder's name often got into these chats, perhaps because the mutual hatred between Gichki and the divine Maulana Dawood was well known, and Dawood's intimacy with Hyder was no secret either. Strange stories filtered back to Karachi from Q. and hung in the air-conditioned urban air.

The official version of Hyder's period of power in the West was that it had been an unmitigated success, and his career was continuing along its upward path. Dacoity had been eliminated, the mosques were full, the organs of state had been purged of Gichkism, of the corruption disease, and separatism was a dead duck. Old Razor Guts was now a Brigadier . . . but, as Iskander Harappa was fond of telling Omar Khayyam Shakil when the pair of them were in their cups, "Fuck me in the mouth, yaar, everybody knows those tribals are running wild out there because

Hyder kept hanging innocent people by the balls." There were also whispers about marital troubles in the Hyder household. Even Rani Harappa in exile heard the rumours of dissension, of the idiot child whose mother called her "Shame" and treated her like mud, of the internal injury which made sons impossible and which was leading Bilquìs down dark corridors towards a crack-up; but she, Rani, did not know how to talk to Bilquìs about these things, and the telephone receiver remained untouched on its hook.

Some things did not get talked about. Nobody mentioned a fat-mouthed boy called Sindbad Mengal, or speculated on the parentage of the younger Hyder girl . . . Brigadier Raza Hyder was driven directly from the station to the inner sanctum of the President, Field-Marshal Mohammad A., where according to some reports he was hugged affectionately and had his cheeks pulled in friendship, while others hinted that the blast of angry air issuing from the keyholes of that room was so intensely hot that Raza Hyder, standing to attention before his outraged President, must have been badly singed. What is certain is that he emerged from the Presidential presence as the national minister of education, information and tourism, while someone else climbed aboard a westbound train to assume the governorship of Q. And Raza Hyder's eyebrows remained intact.

Also intact: the alliance between Raza and Maulana Dawood, who had accompanied the Hyders to Karachi and who, once he was installed in the official residence of the new minister, at once distinguished himself by launching a vociferous public campaign against the consumption of prawns and blue-bellied crabs, which, being scavengers, were as unclean as any pig, and which, although understandably unavailable in far-off Q., were both plentiful and popular in the capital by the sea. The Maulana was deeply af-fronted to find these armoured monsters of the deep freely avail-able in the fishmarkets, and succeeded in enlisting the support of urban divines who did not know how to object. The city's fish-ermen found that the sales of shellfish began to drop alarmingly, and were therefore obliged to rely more than ever on the income they gained from the smuggling of contraband goods. Illicit booze and cigarettes replaced blue crabs in the holds of many dhows. No booze or cigarettes found their way into the Hyder residence, however. Dawood made unheralded raids on the servants' quarters to check that God was in charge. "Even a city of scuttling monstrosities," he assured Raza Hyder, "can be purified with the help of the Almighty."

Three years after Raza Hyder's return to Q., it became clear that his star had secretly been in decline, because the rumours from Q. (Mengal, Gichki, ball-hung tribals) never died down entirely; so that when the capital was shifted away from Karachi and taken up north into the clean mountain air and placed in hideous new buildings specially constructed for the purpose, Raza Hyder stayed put on the coast. The ministry of education, information and tourism went north along with the rest of the administration; but Raza Hyder (to be blunt) was sacked. He was returned to military duty, and given the futureless job of commanding the Military Training Academy. They permitted him to keep his house, but Maulana Dawood told him: "So what if you still have the marble walls? They have made you a crab in this marble shell. *Na-pak*: unclean."

We have leapt too far ahead: it is time to conclude our remarks about rumours and shellfish. Sufiya Zinobia, the idiot, is blushing.

I did it to her, I think, to make her pure. Couldn't think of another way of creating purity in what is supposed to be the Land of the Pure . . . and idiots are, by definition, innocent. Too romantic a use to make of mental disability? Perhaps; but it's too late for such doubts. Sufiya Zinobia has grown, her mind more slowly than her body, and owing to this slowness she remains, for me, somehow clean (*pak*) in the midst of a dirty world. See how, growing, she caresses a pebble in her hand, unable to say why goodness seems to lie within this smooth flat stone; how she glows with pleasure when she hears loving words, even though they are almost always meant for someone else . . . Bilquìs poured all her affection over her younger daughter, Naveed. "Good News"— the nickname had stuck, like a pulled face in the wind—was soaked in it, a monsoon of love, while Sufiya Zinobia, her parents' burden, her mother's shame, remained as dry as the desert. Groans, insults, even the wild blows of exasperation rained on her instead; but such rain yields no moisture. Her spirit parched for lack of affection, she nevertheless managed, when love was in her vicinity, to glow happily just to be near the precious thing.

She also blushed. You recall she blushed at birth. Ten years later, her parents were still perplexed by these reddenings, these blushes like petrol fires. The fearful incandescence of Sufiya Zinobia had been, it seemed, intensified by the desert years in Q. When the Hyders paid the obligatory courtesy call on Bariamma and her tribe, the ancient lady bent to kiss the girls and was alarmed to find that her lips had been mildly burned by a sudden rush of heat to Sufiya Zinobia's cheek; the burn was bad enough to necessitate twice-daily applications of lip salve for a week. This misbehaviour of the child's thermostatic mechanisms roused in her mother what looked like a practised wrath: "That moron," Bilquìs shouted beneath the amused gaze of Duniyad Begum and the rest, "just don't even look at her now! What is this? Anyone puts eyes on her or tells her two words and she goes red, red like a chilli! I swear. What normal child goes so beetroot hot that her clothes can smell of burning? But what to do, she went wrong and that's that, we must just grin and bear." The disappointment of the Hyders in their elder daughter had also been hardened in the noonday rays of the wilderness into a thing as pitiless as that shadow-frying sun.

The affliction was real enough. Miss Shahbanou, the Parsee ayah whom Bilquìs had employed on her return to Karachi, complained on her first day that when she gave Sufiya Zinobia a bath the water had scalded her hands, having been brought close to boiling point by a red flame of embarrassment that spread from the roots of the damaged girl's hair to the tips of her curling toes.

To speak plainly: Sufiya Zinobia Hyder blushed uncontrollably whenever her presence in the world was noticed by others. But she also, I believe, blushed for the world.

Let me voice my suspicion: the brain-fever that made Sufiya Zinobia preternaturally receptive to all sorts of things that float around in the ether enabled her to absorb, like a sponge, a host of unfelt feelings.

Where do you imagine they go?—I mean emotions that should have been felt, but were not—such as regret for a harsh word, guilt for a crime, embarrassment, propriety, shame?—Imagine shame as a liquid, let's say a sweet fizzy tooth-rotting drink, stored in a vending machine. Push the right button and a cup plops down under a pissing stream of the fluid. How to push the button? Nothing to it. Tell a lie, sleep with a white boy, get born the wrong sex. Out flows the bubbling emotion and you drink your fill . . . but how many human beings refuse to follow these simple instructions! Shameful things are done: lies, loose living, disrespect for one's elders, failure to love one's national flag, incorrect voting at elections, over-eating, extramarital sex, autobiographical novels, cheating at cards, maltreatment of womenfolk, examination failures, smuggling, throwing one's wicket away at the crucial point of a Test Match: and they are done *shamelessly*. Then what happens to all that unfelt shame? What of the unquaffed cups of pop? Think again of the vending machine. The button is pushed; but then in comes the shameless hand and jerks away the cup! The button-pusher does not drink what was ordered; and the fluid of shame spills, spreading in a frothy lake across the floor.

But we are discussing an abstract, an entirely ethereal vending machine; so into the ether goes the unfelt shame of the world. Whence, I submit, it is siphoned off by the misfortunate few, janitors of the unseen, their souls the buckets into which squeegees drip what-was-spilled. We keep such buckets in special cupboards. Nor do we think much of them, although they clean up our dirty waters.

Well then: Sufiya the moron blushed. Her mother said to the assembled relatives, "She does it to get attention. O, you don't know what it's like, the mess, the anguish, and for what? For no reward. For air. Thank God for my Good News." But goof or no goof, Sufiya Zinobia—by blushing furiously each time her mother looked sidelong at her father—revealed to watching family eyes that something was piling up between those two. Yes. Idiots can feel such things, that's all.

Blushing is slow burning. But it is also another thing: it is a *psychosomatic event*. I quote: "A sudden shut-down of the arteriovenous anastomoses of the face floods the capillaries with the blood that produces the characteristically heightened colour. People who do not believe in psychosomatic events and do not believe that the mind can influence the body by direct nervous pathways should reflect upon blushing, which in people of heightened sensibility can be brought on even by the recollection of an embarrassment of which they have been the subject—as clear an example of mind over matter as one could wish for."

Like the authors of the above words, our hero, Omar Khayyam Shakil, is a practitioner of medicine. He is, furthermore, interested in the action of mind over matter: in behaviour under hypnosis, for example; in the entranced self-mutilations of those fanatical Shias whom Iskander Harappa disparagingly calls "bedbugs"; in blushing. So it will not be long before Sufiya Zinobia and Omar Khayyam, patient and doctor, future wife and husband, come together. As they must; because what I have to tell is—cannot be described as anything but—a love story.

An account of what happened that year, the fortieth year in the life of Isky Harappa as well as Raza Hyder, probably ought to begin with the moment when Iskander heard that his cousin Little Mir had ingratiated himself with President A., and was about to be elevated to high office. He jumped clean out of bed when he heard the news, but Pinkie Aurangzeb, the owner of the bed and the source of the information, did not budge, even though she knew that a crisis had burst upon her, and that her forty-three-year-old body which Iskander had unveiled by jumping out of bed without letting go of the sheet no longer radiated the kind of light that could get men's minds off whatever was bugging them. "Shit on my mother's grave," Iskander Harappa yelled, "first Hyder becomes a minister and now him. Life gets serious when a man is pushing forty."

"Things are starting to fade," Pinkie Aurangzeb thought as she lay smoking eleven consecutive cigarettes while Iskander stalked the room wrapped in the bedsheet. She lit her twelfth cigarette as Isky absently let the sheet fall. Then she watched him in the nudity of his prime as he silently broke his ties with his present, and turned towards the future. Pinkie was a widow; old Marshal Aurangzeb had kicked the bucket at last, and nowadays her soirées were not quite such essential affairs, and the city gossip had begun to reach her late. "The ancient Greeks," Iskander said out of the blue, making Pinkie spill the ash off her cigarette-tip, "kept, in the Olympic games, no records of runners-up." Then he dressed quickly, but with the meticulous dandyism that she had always loved, and left her for good; that sentence was the only explanation she ever got. But in the years of her isolation she worked it out, she knew that History had been waiting for Iskander Harappa to notice Her, and a man who catches History's eye is thereafter bound to a mistress from whom he will never escape. History is natural selection. Mutant versions of the past struggle for dominance; new species of fact arise, and old, saurian truths go to the wall, blindfolded and smoking last cigarettes. Only the mutations of the strong survive. The weak, the anonymous, the defeated leave few marks: field-patterns, axe-heads, folk-tales, broken pitchers, burial mounds, the fading memory of their youthful beauty. History loves only those who dominate Her: it is a relationship of mutual enslavement. No room in it for Pinkies; or, in Isky's view, for the likes of Omar Khayyam Shakil.

Reborn Alexanders, would-be Olympic champions must conform to the most stringent of training routines. So after he left Pinkie Aurangzeb, Isky Harappa also vowed to eschew everything else that could eschew his spirit. His daughter Arjumand would always remember that that was when he gave up stud poker, chemin de fer, private roulette evenings, horse-race fixing, French food, opium and sleeping pills; when he broke his habit of seeking out beneath silver-heavy banqueting tables the excited ankles and compliant knees of society beauties, and when he stopped visiting the whores whom he had been fond of photographing with an eight millimetre Paillard Bolex movie camera while they performed, singly or in threes, upon his own person or that of Omar Khayyam, their musky languid rites. It was the beginning of that legendary political career which would culminate in his victory over death itself. These first triumphs, being merely victories over himself, were necessarily smaller. He expunged from his public, urban vocabulary his encyclopaedic repertoire of foul green village oaths, imprecations which could detach brim-full cut-glass tumblers from men's hands and shatter them before they reached the floor. (But when campaigning in the villages he allowed the air to turn green with obscenity once again, understanding the vote-getting powers of the filth.) He stifled for ever the high-pitched giggle of his unreliable playboy self and substituted a rich, full-throated, statesmanlike guffaw. He gave up fooling around with the women servants in his city home.

Did any man ever sacrifice more for his people? He gave up cock fights, bear fights, snake-and-mongoose duels; plus disco dancing, and his monthly evenings at the home of the chief film censor, where he had watched special compilations of the juiciest bits excised from incoming foreign films.

He also decided to give up Omar Khayyam Shakil. "When that degenerate comes to call," Iskander instructed the gatekeeper, "just throw the badmash out on his fat bottom and watch him bounce." Then he retired into the white-and-gilt rococo bedroom at the cool heart of his mansion in "Defence," an edifice of reinforced cement concrete and stone cladding that resembled a split-level Telefunken radiogram, and sank into meditation.

But, for a long time, surprisingly, Omar Khayyam neither visited nor telephoned his old friend. Forty days passed before the doctor was made aware of the change in his carefree, shame-free world . . .

Who sits at her father's feet while, elsewhere, Pinkie Aurangzeb grows old in an empty house? Arjumand Harappa: thirteen years old and wearing an expression of huge satisfaction, she sits cross-legged on the marble-chip floor of a rococo bedroom, watching Isky complete the process of remaking himself; Arjumand, who has not yet acquired the notorious nickname (the "virgin Ironpants") that will stick to her for most of her life. She has always known in the precocity of her years that there is a second man inside her father, growing, waiting, and now at last bursting out, while the old Iskander slips rustling and discarded to the floor, a shrivelled snakeskin in a hard diamond of sunlight. So what pleasure she takes in his transformation, in finally acquiring the father she deserves! "I did this," she tells Iskander, "my wanting it so badly finally made you see." Harappa smiles at his daughter, pats her hair. "That happens sometimes." "And no more Omar-uncle," Arjumand adds. "Good riddance to bad rubbish."

Arjumand Harappa, the virgin Ironpants, will always be ruled by extremes. Already, at thirteen, she has a gift for loathing; also for adulation. Whom she loathes: Shakil, the fat monkey who has been sitting on her father's shoulders, holding him down in the slime; and also her own mother, Rani in her Mohenjo of burrowing owls, the epitome of defeat. Arjumand has persuaded her father to let her live and go to school in the city; and for this father she bears a reverence bordering on idolatry. Now that her worship is at last acquiring an object worthy of itself, Arjumand cannot restrain her joy. "What things won't you do!" she cries. "Just wait and see!" Omar Khayyam's absent bulk carries with it the shadows of the past.

Iskander, supine in white-and-gold bed and sunk in frenzied reverie, states with sudden clarity: "It's a man's world, Arjumand. Rise above your gender as you grow. This is no place to be a woman in." The rueful nostalgia of these sentences marks the last death-throes of Iskander's love for Pinkie Aurangzeb, but his daughter takes him at his word, and when her breasts begin to swell she will bind them tightly in linen bandages, so fiercely that she blushes with pain. She will come to enjoy the war against her body, the slow provisional victory over the soft, despised flesh . . . but let us leave them there, father and daughter, she already building in her heart that Alexandrine god-myth of Harappa to which she will only be able to give free rein after his death, he devising in the councils of his new cleanness the strategies of his future triumph, of his wooing of the age.

Where is Omar Khayyam Shakil? What has become of our peripheral hero? He has aged, too; like Pinkie, he's in his middle forties now. Age has treated him well, silvering his hair and goatee beard. Let us remind ourselves that he was a brilliant student in his day, and that scholarly brightness remains undimmed; lecher and rakehell he may be, but he is also the top man at the city's leading hospital, and an immunologist of no small international renown. In the time since we last knew him well he has travelled to American seminars, published papers on the possibility of psychosomatic events occurring within the body's immune system, become an important chap. He is still fat and ugly, but he dresses now with some distinction; some of Isky's snappy sartorial ways have rubbed off on him. Omar Khayyam wears greys: grey

suits, hats, ties, grey suede shoes, grey silk underpants, as if he
hopes that the muteness of the colour will tone down the garish
effect of his physiognomy. He carries a present from his friend
Iskander: a silver-headed swordstick from the Aansu valley, twelve
inches of polished steel concealed in intricately carved walnut.

By this time he is sleeping for barely two and a half hours a
night, but the dream of falling off the world's end still troubles
him from time to time. Sometimes it comes to him when he is
awake, because people who sleep too little can find the boundaries
between the waking and sleeping worlds get difficult to police.
Things skip between the unguarded bollards, avoiding the customs post . . . at such times he is assailed by a terrible vertigo,
as if he were on top of a crumbling mountain, and then he leans
heavily on his sword-concealing cane to prevent himself from
falling. It should be said that his professional success, and his
friendship with Iskander Harappa, have had the effect of reducing
the frequency of these giddy spells, of keeping our hero's feet a
little more firmly on the ground. But still the dizziness comes,
now and then, to remind him how close he is, will always be,
to the edge.

But where has he got to? Why does he not telephone, visit,
get bounced out on his behind?—I discover him in Q., in the
fortress home of his three mothers, and at once I know that a
disaster has taken place, because nothing else could have lured
Omar Khayyam into the mother country once again. He has not
visited "Nishapur" since the day he left with his feet on a cooling
iceblock; bankers' drafts have been sent in his stead. His money
has paid for his absence . . . but there are other prices, too. And
no escape is final. His willed severance from his past mingles with
the chosen insomnia of his nights: their joint effect is to glaze his
moral sense, to transform him into a kind of ethical zombie, so
that his very act of distancing helps him to obey his mothers'
ancient injunction: the fellow feels no shame.

He retains his mesmeric eyes, his level hypnotist's voice. For
many years now Iskander Harappa has accompanied those eyes,

that voice to the Intercontinental Hotel and allowed them to go to work on his behalf. Omar Khayyam's outsize ugliness, combined with eyes-and-voice, makes him attractive to white women of a certain type. They succumb to his flirtatious offers of hypnosis, his unspoken promises of the mysteries of the East; he takes them to a rented hotel suite and puts them under. Released from admittedly scanty inhibitions they provide Isky and Omar with some highly charged sex. Shakil defends his behaviour: "Impossible to persuade a subject to do anything she is unwilling to do." Iskander Harappa, however, has never bothered with excuses . . . this, too, is a part of what Isky—as yet unbeknownst to Omar Khayyam—has forsaken. For History's sake.

Omar Khayyam is in "Nishapur" because his brother, Babar, is dead. The brother whom he has never seen, dead before his twenty-third birthday, and all that is left of him is a bundle of dirty notebooks, which Omar Khayyam will bring with him when he returns to Karachi after the forty days of mourning. A brother reduced to tattered, scribbled words. Babar has been shot, and the order to fire was given by . . . but no, the notebooks first:

When they brought his body down from the Impossible Mountains, smelling of corruption and goats, the notebooks they discovered in his pockets were returned to his family with many of their pages missing. Among the tattered remnants of these brutalized volumes it was possible to decipher a series of love-poems addressed to a famous playback singer whom he, Babar Shakil, could not possibly have met. And interspersed with the unevenly metrical expressions of this abstract love, in which hymns to the spirituality of her voice mingled uneasily with free verse of a distinctly pornographic sensuality, was to be found an account of his sojourn in an earlier hell, a record of the torment of having been the kid brother of Omar Khayyam.

The shade of his elder sibling had haunted every corner of

"Nishapur." Their three mothers, who now subsisted on the doctor's remittances and had no more dealings with the pawn-broker, had conspired in their gratitude to make Babar's child-hood a motionless journey through an unchanging shrine whose walls were impregnated by applause for the glorious, departed elder son. And because Omar Khayyam was so much his senior and had long since fled that provincial dustiness in whose streets, nowadays, drunken gas-field workers brawled desultorily with off-duty miners of coal, bauxite, onyx, copper and chrome, and over whose rooftops the cracked dome of Flashman's Hotel pre-sided with ever-increasing mournfulness, the younger child, Ba-bar, had the feeling of having been at once oppressed and abandoned by a second father; and in that household of women atrophied by yesterdays he celebrated his twentieth birthday by carrying examination certificates and gold medals and newspaper cuttings and old schoolbooks and files of letters and cricket bats and, in short, all the souvenirs of his illustrious sibling into the shadowed lightlessness of the central compound, and setting fire to the whole lot before his three mothers could stop him. Turning his back on the inglorious spectacle of old crones scrabbling amongst hot ashes for the charred corners of snapshots and for medallions which the fire had transmuted from gold into lead, Babar made his way via the dumb-waiter into the streets of Q., his anniversary thoughts slow with uncertainties about the future. He was wan-dering aimlessly, brooding upon the narrowness of his possibil-ities, when the earthquake began.

At first he mistook it for a shudder within his own body, but a blow to his cheek, inflicted by a tiny splinter of plunging sharp-ness, cleared the mists of self-absorption from the would-be poet's eyes. "It's raining glass," he thought in surprise, blinking rapidly at the lanes of the thieves' bazaar into which his feet had led him without knowing it, lanes of little shanty-stalls among which his supposed inner shudder was making a fine mess: melons burst at his feet, pointy slippers fell from trembling shelves, gemstones and brocades and earthenware and combs tumbled pell-mell into the glass-dusted alleys. He stood stupidly in that vitreous down-pour of broken windows, unable to shake off the feeling of having imposed his private turmoils on the world around him, resisting the insane compulsion to seize hold of someone, anyone, in the milling, panicky crowd of pickpockets, salesmen and shoppers, to apologize for the trouble he had caused.

"That earthquake," Babar Shakil wrote in his notebook, "shook something loose inside me. A minor tremor, but maybe it also shook something into place."

When the world was still again he made for a cheap brandy den, picking his way through fragments of glass and past the equally piercing howls of the proprietor; and as he entered (the notebooks stated) he caught sight through the corner of his left eye of a winged and golden-glowing man looking down on him from a rooftop; but when he twisted his head upwards the angel was no longer to be seen. Later, when he was in the mountains with the separatist tribal guerrillas, he was told the story of the angels and the earthquakes and the subterranean Paradise; their belief that the golden angels were on their side gave the guerrillas an unshakable certainty of the justice of their cause, and made it easy for them to die for it. "Separatism," Babar wrote, "is the belief that you are good enough to escape from the clutches of hell."

Babar Shakil spent his birthday getting drunk in that den of broken bottles, picking out, more than once, long splinters of glass from his mouth, so that by the evening's end his chin was streaked with blood; but the splashing liquor disinfected the cuts and minimized the risk of tetanus. In the brandy shop: tribals, a wall-eyed whore, travelling jokers with drums and horns. The jokes grew louder as the night wore on, and the mixture of humour and booze was a cocktail that gave Babar a hangover of such colossal proportions that he never recovered from it.

What jokes! Hee-hee-what-you-talking-man-someone-will-hear ribaldry:—Listen, yaar, you know when children get circumcised the circumciser speaks holy words?—Yah, man, I know.—Then what did he say when he did the cut on Old Razor Guts?—I don't know, what what?—Just one word only, yaar, one word and he got thrown out of the house!—God, must have been a bad word, man, come on, tell.—This was it, sir: "Oops."

Babar Shakil in a dangerous veil of brandy. Comedy enters his bloodstream, effects a permanent mutation.—Hey mister, you know what they say about us tribals, too little patriotism and too much sex-drive, well, it's all true, want to know why?—Yes.— So take patriotism. Number one, government takes our rice for Army troops, we should be proud, na, but we just complain there is none for us. Number two, government mines our minerals and economy gets a boost, but we just beef that nobody here sees the cash. Number three, gas from Needle now provides sixty per cent of national requirement, but still we are not happy, moaning all the time how the gas is not domestically available in these parts. Now how could people be less patriotic, you must agree. But fortunately our government loves us still, so much that it has made our sex-drive the top national priority.—How's that?— But it is obvious to see: this government is happy to go on screwing us from now till doomsday.

—O, too good, yaar, too good.

The next day Babar left home before dawn to join the guerrillas and his family never saw him alive again. From the bottomless chests of "Nishapur" he took an old rifle and its accompanying cartridge boxes, a few books and one of Omar Khayyam's academic medallions, which had been transmuted into base metal by a fire; no doubt to remind himself of the causes of his own act of separatism, of the origins of a hatred which had been powerful enough to cause an earthquake. In his hideout in the Impossible Mountains Babar grew a beard, studied the complex structure of the hill clans, wrote poetry, rested between raids on military outposts and railway lines and water reservoirs, and eventually, thanks to the exigencies of that dislocated existence, was able to discuss in his notebooks the relative merits of copulation with sheep and with goats. There were guerrillas who preferred the passivity of sheep; for others the goats' greater friskiness was impossible to resist. Many of Babar's companions went so far as to fall in love with four-legged mistresses, and although they were all wanted men they would risk their lives in the bazaars of Q. in order to purchase gifts for their loved ones: combs for fleeces were acquired, also ribbons and bells for darling nannies who never deigned to express their gratitude. Babar's spirit (if not his body) rose above such things; he poured his reservoir of unspent passion over the mental image of a popular singer of whose features he remained ignorant to his dying day, because he had only heard her sing on a crackling transistor radio.

The guerrillas gave Babar a nickname of which he was inordinately proud: they called him "the Emperor," in memory of that other Babar whose throne was usurped, who took to the hills with a ragged army and who at last founded that renowned dynasty of monarchs whose family name is still used as an honorific title bestowed on film tycoons. Babar, the Mogul of the Impossible Mountains . . . two days before the departure of Raza Hyder from Q., a sortie led for the last time by the great commander himself was responsible for firing the bullet which knocked Babar down.

But it didn't matter, because he had spent too long with the angels; up in the shifting, treacherous mountains he had watched them, golden-breasted and with gilded wings. Archangels flapped over his head as he sat doing sentry duty on a fierce outcrop of rock. Yes, perhaps Jibreel himself had hovered benignly over him like a golden helicopter while he violated a sheep. And shortly before his death the guerrillas noticed that their bearded comrade's skin had begun to give off a yellow light; the little buds of new wings were visible on his shoulders. It was a transformation familiar to the denizens of the Impossible Mountains. "You won't be here much longer," they told Babar with traces of envy in their voices, "Emperor, you're off; no more woolly fucks for you." The angeling of Babar must have been just about complete by the time of his death, when his guerrilla unit attacked a seemingly broken-down goods train and so fell into Raza Hyder's trap, because although eighteen bullets pierced his body, which made an easy target because it glowed yellow through his clothing in the night, it was easy for him to skip out of his skin and soar lucent and winged into the eternity of the mountains, where a great cloud of seraphs rose up as the world shook and roared, and where to the music of heavenly reed-flutes and celestial seven-stringed sarandas and three-stringed dumbirs he was received into the elysian bosom of the earth. His body, when they brought it down, was said to be as insubstantial and feathery as an abandoned snakeskin, such as cobras and playboys leave behind them when they change; and he was gone, gone for good, the fool.

Of course his death was not described in any notebook; it was enacted within the grieving imaginations of his three mothers, because, as they told Omar while recounting the tale of their son's transformation into an angel, "We have the right to present him with a good death, a death with which the living can live." Under the impact of the tragedy, Chhunni, Munnee and Bunny began to crumble inside, becoming mere façades, beings as insubstantial as the sloughed-off corpse of their son. (But they pulled themselves together at the end.)

The body was returned to them some weeks after eighteen bullets had entered it. They also received a letter on official note-paper. "Only the memory of the former prestige of your family name protects you from the consequences of your son's great infamy. It is our opinion that the families of these gangsters have much to answer for." The letter had been signed, before his departure, by the former governor, Raza Hyder himself; who must therefore have known that he had engineered the death of the boy whom he had seen, years previously, watching him through fieldglasses from the upper windows of the sealed mansion between the Cantt and the bazaar.

Out of pity for Omar Khayyam Shakil—to spare, let us say, his blushes—I shall not describe the scene at the gate of the Harappa town house that took place when the doctor finally turned up in a taxi-cab holding his brother's notebooks in his hand. He has been bounced in enough dirt for the moment; suffice to say that under the cold weight of Iskander's rejection, Omar Khayyam suffered an attack of vertigo so severe that he was sick in the back of the taxi. (Over that, too, I draw a fastidious veil.) Once again others had acted and by so doing had shaped the story of his life: Babar's flight, Hyder's bullets, the exaltation of Mir Harappa and the resulting alteration in Iskander added up, as far as our hero was concerned, to a kick in his personal teeth. Later, in his own home (we have not yet visited the Shakil residence: an unglamorous apartment in one of the city's older housing zones, four rooms notable for the complete absence of all but the most essential items of furniture, as though Shakil in his adulthood were rebelling against the fantasticated clutter of his mothers' home, and choosing, instead, the bare-walled asceticism of his selected father, the vanished, birdcaged schoolteacher Eduardo Rodrigues—a father is both a warning and a lure), which he had been obliged by the outraged taxi-driver to reach stinking and on foot, he retired to bed, heat-drained, his head still spinning; he placed a bundle of tattered notebooks on his bedside table and said as he drifted into sleep: "Babar, life is long."

The next day he returned to work; and the day after that he began to fall in love.

Once upon a time there was a plot of land. It was attractively situated in the heart of the First Phase of the Defence Services Officers' Co-operative Housing Society; to its right stood the official residence of the national minister for education, information and tourism, an imposing building whose walls were clad in green onyx marble streaked with red, and to its left was the home of the widow of the late Joint Chief of Staff, Marshal Aurangzeb. Despite location and neighbours, however, the plot of land remained empty; no foundations had been dug there, no shuttering raised to build walls of reinforced cement concrete. The plot of land lay, tragically for its owner, in a small hollow; so that when the two days of pouring rain which the city enjoyed each year arrived, the waters flooded into the empty plot and formed a muddy lake. This unusual phenomenon of a lake which came into being for two days a year and which was then boiled away by the sun, leaving behind a thin mulch of water-transported garbage and faeces, was enough to discourage all potential builders, even though the plot was, as stated above, congenially sited: the Aga Khan owned the lodge at the top of the nearby hill, and the eldest son of the President, Field-Marshal Mohammad A., also lived nearby. It was on this hapless patch of earth that Pinkie Aurangzeb decided to raise turkeys.

Deserted by living lover as well as dead husband, the Marshal's widow elected to turn her hand to business. Much taken by the success of the new shaver-chicken scheme which the national airline had recently begun to operate from batteries on the periphery of the airport, Pinkie decided to go for bigger birds. The officers of the housing society were incapable of resisting Mrs. Aurangzeb's allure (it might have been fading, but it was still too much for clerks), and turned blind eyes to the clouds of gobbling fowls which she released into the vacant, walled-in property. The arrival of the turkeys was treated by Mrs. Bilquìs Hyder as a personal insult. A highly strung lady, of whom it was said that troubles in her marriage were placing her brain under increasing stress, she took to leaning out of windows and abusing the noisy birds. "Shoo! Shut up, crazy fellows! Turkeys making God knows what-all racket right next to a minister's house! See if I don't slit your throats!"

When Bilquìs appealed to her husband to do something about the eternally gobbling birds who were destroying what remained of her peace of mind, Raza Hyder replied calmly, "She is the widow of our great Marshal, wife. Allowances must be made." The minister for education, information and tourism was tired at the end of a hard day's work in which he had approved measures which would legalize the piracy by the government of Western scientific text-books, personally supervised the smashing of one of the small portable presses on which anti-state propaganda was illicitly printed and which had been discovered in the basement of an England-returned arts graduate who had been corrupted by foreign ideas, and discussed with the city's leading art dealers the growing problem of pilferage of antiquities from the country's archaeological sites—discussed the issue, one should add, with such sensitivity that the dealers had been moved to present him, in recognition of his attitude, with a small stone head from Taxila, dating from the time of Alexander the Great's expedition into the north. In short, Raza Hyder was in no mood for turkeys.

Bilquìs had not forgotten what a fat man had hinted about her husband and Mrs. Aurangzeb on the verandah of Mohenjo years ago; she remembered the time when her husband had been willing to stake himself to the ground on her behalf; and she was also, in her thirty-second year, becoming increasingly shrill. That was the year in which the Loo blew more fiercely than ever before, and cases of fever and madness increased by four hundred and twenty per cent . . . Bilquìs placed her hands upon her hips and yelled at Raza in the presence of both her daughters: "O, a fine day for me! Now you humiliate me with birds." Her elder daughter, the mental case, began to blush, because it was evident that the gobbling turkeys did indeed represent one more victory for Pinkie Aurangzeb over the other men's wives, the last such victory, of which the victor was wholly unaware.

And once upon a time there was a retarded daughter, who for twelve years had been given to understand that she embodied her mother's shame. Yes, now I must come to you, Sufiya Zinobia, in your outsize cot with the rubber sheeting, in that ministerial residence of marble walls, in an upstairs bedroom through whose windows turkeys gobbled at you, while at a dressing table of onyx marble your sister screamed at the ayah to pull her hair.

Sufiya Zinobia at the age of twelve had formed the unattractive habit of tearing her hair. When her dark-brown locks were being washed by Shahbanou the Parsee ayah, she would continually kick and scream; the ayah was always forced to give up before the last of the soap had been rinsed out. The constant presence of sandalwood-scented detergent gave Sufiya Zinobia an appalling case of split ends, and she would sit in the enormous cot which her parents had constructed for her (and which they had brought all the way from Q., complete with expanses of rubber undersheets and large-size babies' comforters) and tear each damaged hair in two, all the way down to the root. This she did seriously, systematically, as if inflicting ritual injury upon herself like one of Iskander Harappa's bedbugs, the Shia dervishes in the processions of 14 Muharram. Her eyes, while she worked, acquired a dull glint, a gleam of distant ice or fire from far below their habitually opaque surface; and the torn cloud of hairs stood out around her face and formed in the sunlight a kind of halo of destruction.

It was the day after the turkey outburst of Bilquìs Hyder. Sufiya Zinobia tore her hair in her cot; but Good News, plain-faced as a chapati, was determined to prove that her great thick mane had grown long enough to sit upon. Straining her head backwards she shouted at pale Shahbanou: "Pull down! Hard as you can! What're you waiting for, stupid? *Yank!*"—and the ayah, hollow-eyed, frail, tried to tuck hair-tips under Good News's bony rump. Tears of pain stood in the girl's determined eyes: "A woman's beauty," Good News gasped, "grows down from the top of her head. It is well known that men go crazy for shiny hair that you can put under your bums." Shahbanou in flat tones stated: "No good, bibi, won't go." Good News pummelling the ayah turned on her sister in her wrath: "You. Thing. Look at you. Who would marry you with that hair, even if you had a brain? Turnip. Beetroot. Angrez radish. See how you make trouble for me with your tearing. Elder sister should marry first but who will come for her, ayah? I swear, my tragedy, what do you know. Come on now, pull again, this time don't pretend it won't reach—no, never mind that fool now, leave her with her stinky blushes and her wetting. She doesn't understand, what could she understand, zero." And Shahbanou, shrugging, impervious to Naveed Hyder's blows: "You shouldn't talk so bad to your sister, bibi, one day your tongue will go black and fall off."

Two sisters in a room while outside the hot wind begins to blow. Shutters are put up against the wildness of the blast, and over the garden wall turkeys panic in the feverish clutches of the gale. As the Loo increases in fury, the house subsides into sleep. Shahbanou on a mat on the floor beside Sufiya Zinobia's cot; Good News, exhausted by hair-pullery, sprawled on her ten-year-old's bed.

Two sisters asleep: in repose, the younger girl's face revealed its plainness, stripped of its waking determination to be attractive; while the simpleton lost, in sleep, the bland vacuity of her expression, and the severe classicism of her features would have pleased any watching eye. What contrasts in these girls! Sufiya Zinobia, embarrassingly small (no, we shall avoid, at all costs, comparing her to an Oriental miniature), and Good News rangy, elongated. Sufiya and Naveed, shame and good news: the one slow and silent, the other quick with her noise. Good News would stare brazenly at her elders; Sufiya averted her eyes. But Naveed Hyder was her mother's little angel, she got away with everything. "Imagine," Omar Khayyam would think in later years, "if that marriage scandal had happened to Sufiya Zinobia! They'd have cut her skin off and sent it to the dhobi."

Listen: you could have taken the whole quantity of sisterly love inside Good News Hyder, sealed it in an envelope and posted it anywhere in the world for one rupee airmail, that's how much it weighed . . . where was I? Oh, yes, the hot wind blew, its howl a maw of sound that swallowed all other noise, that dry gale bearing disease and madness upon its sand-sharp wings, the worst Loo in living memory, releasing demons into the world, forcing its way through shutters to plague Bilquìs with the insupportable phantoms of her past, so that although she buried her head under a pillow she still saw before her eyes a golden equestrian figure carrying a pennant on which there flamed the terrifyingly cryptic word *Excelsior*. Not even the gobbling of the turkeys could be heard above the gale, as the world took shelter; then the searing fingers of the wind penetrated a bedroom in which two sisters slept, and one of them began to stir.

It's easy to blame trouble on a wind. Maybe that pestilential blast did have something to do with it—maybe, when it touched Sufiya Zinobia, she reddened under its awful hand, she burned, and maybe that's why she got up, eyes blank as milk, and left the room—but I prefer to believe that the wind was no more than a coincidence, an excuse; that what happened happened because twelve years of unloved humiliation take their toll, even on an idiot, and there is always a point at which something breaks, even though the last straw cannot be identified with any certainty: was it Good News's marriage worries? Or Raza's calmness in the face of shrieking Bilquìs? Impossible to say.

She must have been sleepwalking, because when they found her she looked rested, as if she'd had a good deep sleep. When the wind died and the household awoke from its turbulent afternoon slumber Shahbanou noticed the empty cot at once and raised the alarm. Afterwards nobody could work out how the girl had escaped, how she managed to sleepwalk through an entire houseful of government furniture and sentries. Shahbanou would always say that it must have been quite a wind, it sent soldiers to sleep at the gate and wrought a somnambulist miracle of such potency that Sufiya Zinobia's passage through the house, into the garden and over the wall acquired the power of infecting anyone she passed, who must have fallen instantly into a wind-sick trance. But it is my opinion that the source of the power, the worker of the miracle, was Sufiya Zinobia herself; there would be other such occasions, when one could not blame the wind . . .

They found her in the aftermath of the Loo, sitting fast asleep under the sun's ferocity in the turkey-yard of the widow Aurangzeb, a little huddled figure snoring gently amidst the corpses of the birds. Yes, they were all dead, every one of the two hundred and eighteen turkeys of Pinkie's loneliness, and people were so shocked that they forgot to clear away the corpses for a whole day, leaving the dead birds to rot in the heat and in the crepuscular gloom of the evening and beneath the ice-hot stars, two hundred and eighteen that would never find their way into ovens or onto dining tables. Sufiya Zinobia had torn off their heads and then reached down into their bodies to draw their guts up through their necks with her tiny and weaponless hands. Shahbanou, who found her first, did not dare to approach her; then Raza and Bilquìs arrived, and soon everybody, sister, servants, neighbours, was standing and gaping at the spectacle of the bloodied girl and the decapitated creatures with intestines instead of heads. Pinkie Aurangzeb looked hollowly upon the carnage, and was struck by the meaningless hatred in Bilquìs's eyes; the two women remained silent, each in the grip of a different horror, so that it was Raza Hyder, his watery black-rimmed eyes riveted upon the face of his daughter with her bloodied lips, who spoke first in a voice echoing with admiration as well as revulsion: "With her bare hands," the new government minister trembled, "what gave the child such strength?"

Now that the iron hoops of the silence had been snapped Shahbanou the ayah began wailing at the top of her voice: "Ullu-ullu-ullu!" a gibberish lament of such high pitch that it dragged Sufiya Zinobia out of her lethal sleep; she opened those eyes of watered milk and on seeing the devastation around her she fainted, echoing her own mother on that far-off day when Bilquìs found herself naked in a crowd and passed out cold for shame.

What forces moved that sleeping three-year-old mind in its twelve-year-old body to order an all-out assault upon feathered turkey-cocks and hens? One can only speculate: Was Sufiya Zinobia trying, like a good daughter, to rid her mother of the gobbler plague? Or did the anger, the proud outrage which Raza Hyder ought to have felt, but refused to do so, preferring to make allowances for Pinkie, find its way into his daughter instead?— What seems certain is that Sufiya Zinobia, for so long burdened with being a miracle-gone-wrong, a family's shame made flesh, had discovered in the labyrinths of her unconscious self the hidden path that links *sharam* to violence; and that, awakening, she was as surprised as anyone by the force of what had been unleashed.

The beast inside the beauty. Opposing elements of a fairy-tale combined in a single character . . . Bilquìs did not, on this occasion, faint. The embarrassment of her daughter's deed, the ice of this latest shame lent a frozen rigidity to her bearing. "Be quiet," she ordered the ululating ayah. "Go in and bring out scissors." Until the ayah had completed her enigmatic errand Bilquìs would let nobody touch the girl; she circled her in a manner so forbidding that not even Raza Hyder dared go near. While Shahbanou ran for scissors Bilquìs spoke softly, under her breath, so that only a few words wafted as far as the watching husband, widow, younger daughter, servants, anonymous passers-by. ". . . Tear your hair . . . birthright . . . woman's pride . . . all fuzzy-wuzzy like a *hubshee* female . . . cheapness . . . loose . . . crazy," and then the scissors came, and still nobody dared intervene, as Bilquìs grabbed hold of great clumps of her daughter's savaged tresses, and cut, and cut, and cut. At last she stood up, out of breath, and working the scissors absently with her fingers she turned away. Sufiya Zinobia's head looked like a cornfield after a fire: sad, black stubble, a catastrophic desolation wrought by maternal rage. Raza Hyder picked his daughter up with a gentleness born of his infinite puzzlement and carried her indoors, away from the scissors that were still snipping at air in Bilquìs's uncontrollable hand.

Scissors cutting air mean trouble in the family.

"O, Mummy!" Good News giggled with fear. "What did you do? She looks like . . ."

"We always wanted a boy," Bilquìs replied, "but God knows best."

In spite of being shaken, timidly by Shahbanou and more roughly by Good News, Sufiya Zinobia did not awaken from her faint.

By the next evening a fever had mounted in her, a hot flush spread from her scalp to the soles of her feet. The fragile-looking Parsee ayah, whose sunken eyes made her seem forty-three years old but who turned out to be only nineteen, never moved from the side of the great barred cot except to fetch fresh cold compresses for Sufiya's brow. "You Parsees," Good News told Shahbanou, "you've got a soft spot for mental cases, seems to me. Must be all your experience." Bilquìs showed no interest in the application of compresses. She sat in her room with the scissors that seemed to be stuck to her fingers, snipping at empty air. "Wind fever," Shahbanou called her charge's nameless affliction, which had made that shorn head blaze; but on the second night it cooled, she opened her eyes, it was thought that she had recovered. The next morning, however, Shahbanou noticed that something frightful had begun to happen to the girl's tiny body. It had started to come out in huge blotchy rashes, red and purple with small hard pimples in the middle; boils were forming between her toes, and her back was bubbling up into extraordinary vermilion lumps. Sufiya Zinobia was over-salivating; great jets of spittle flew out through her lips. Appalling black buboes were forming in her armpits. It was as though the dark violence which had been engendered within that small physique had turned inwards, had forsaken turkeys and gone for the girl herself; as if, like her grandfather Mahmoud the Woman who sat in an empty cinema and waited to pay for his double bill, or like a soldier falling on his sword, Sufiya Zinobia had chosen the form of her own end. The plague of shame—in which I insist on including the unfelt shame of those around her, for instance what had not been felt by Raza Hyder when he gunned down Babar Shakil—as well as the unceasing shame of her own existence, and of her hacked-off hair— the plague, I say, spread rapidly through that tragic being whose chief defining characteristic was her excessive sensitivity to the bacilli of humiliation. She was taken to hospital with pus bursting from her sores, dribbling, incontinent, with the rough, cropped proof of her mother's loathing on her head.

What is a saint? A saint is a person who suffers in our stead.

On the night when all this happened, Omar Khayyam Shakil had been beset, during his brief sleep, by vivid dreams of the past, in all of which the white-clothed figure of the disgraced teacher Eduardo Rodrigues played a leading role. In the dreams Omar Khayyam was a boy again. He kept trying to follow Eduardo everywhere, to the toilet, into bed, convinced that if he could just catch up with the teacher he would be able to jump inside him and be happy at long last; but Eduardo kept shooing him away with his white fedora, slapping at him and motioning to him to go, get lost, buzz off. This mystified the doctor until many days later, when he realized that the dreams had been prescient warnings against the dangers of falling in love with underage females and then following them to the ends of the earth, where they inevitably cast you aside, the blast of their rejection picking you up and hurling you out into the great starry nothingness beyond gravity and sense. He recalled the end of the dream, in which Eduardo, his white garments now blackened and tattered and singed, seemed to be flying away from him, floating above a bursting cloud of fire, with one hand raised above his head, as if in farewell . . . a father is a warning; but he is also a lure, a precedent impossible to resist, and so by the time that Omar Khayyam deciphered his dreams it was already far too late to take their advice, because he had fallen for his destiny, Sufiya Zinobia Hyder, a twelve-year-old girl with a three-year-old mind, the daughter of the man who killed his brother.

You can imagine how depressed I am by the behaviour of Omar Khayyam Shakil. I ask for the second time: what kind of hero is this? Last seen slipping into unconsciousness, stinking of vomit and swearing revenge; and now, going crazy for Hyder's daughter. How is one to account for such a character? Is consistency too much to ask? I accuse this so-called hero of giving me the most godawful headache.

Certainly (let's take this slowly; no sudden moves, please) he was in a disturbed state of mind. A dead brother, rejection by his best friend. These are extenuating circumstances. We shall take them into account. It is also fair to assume that the vertigo which assailed him in the taxi returned, over the next few days, to knock him even further off balance. So there is some sort of flimsy case for the defence.

Step by step, now. He wakes up, engulfed in the emptiness of his life, alone in the insomnia of the dawn. He washes, dresses, goes to work; and finds that by burying himself in his duties he can manage to keep going; even the vertigo attacks are kept at bay.

What is his area of expertise? We know this: he is an immunologist. So he cannot be blamed for the arrival at his hospital of Hyder's daughter; suffering an immunological crisis, Sufiya Zinobia is brought to the country's leading expert in the field.

Carefully, now. Avoid loud noises. To an immunologist in search of the calm that comes of challenging, absorbing work, Sufiya Zinobia seems like a godsend. Delegating as many of his responsibilities as possible, Omar Khayyam devotes himself more or less full-time to the case of the simpleton girl whose body's defence mechanisms have declared war against the very life they are supposed to be protecting. His devotion is perfectly genuine (the defence refuses to rest): in the succeeding weeks, he makes himself fully acquainted with her medical background, and afterwards he will set down in his treatise *The Case of Miss H.* the important new evidence he has unearthed of the power of the mind to affect, "via direct nervous pathways," the workings of the body. The case becomes famous in medical circles; doctor and patient are for ever linked in the history of science. Does this make other, more personal links more palatable? I reserve judgment. Go on one step:

He becomes convinced that Sufiya Zinobia is willing the damage to herself. This is the significance of her case: it shows that even a broken mind is capable of marshalling macrophages and polymorphs; even a stunted intelligence can lead a palace revolution, a suicidal rebellion of the janissaries of the human body against the castle itself.

"Total breakdown of the immune system," he notes after his first examination of the patient, "most terrible uprising I ever saw."

Now let us put this as kindly as possible for the moment. (I have more accusations, but they will wait.) Afterwards, no matter how furiously he concentrates, trying to summon up every last detail of those days from the poisoned wells of memory, he is unable to pinpoint the moment at which professional excitement turned into tragic love. He does not claim that Sufiya Zinobia has given him the least encouragement; that would, in the circumstances, be patently absurd. But at some point, perhaps during his night-long bedside vigils, spent monitoring the effects of his prescribed course of immunosuppressive drugs, vigils in which he is joined by the ayah Shahbanou, who consents to wear sterile cap, coat, gloves and mask, but who absolutely refuses to leave the girl alone with the male doctor—yes, perhaps during those preposterously chaperoned nights, or possibly later, when it is clear that he has triumphed, that the praetorian revolt has been quelled, the mutiny suppressed by pharmaceutical mercenaries, so that the hideous outcrops of Sufiya Zinobia's affliction fade from her body and the colour returns to her cheeks—somewhere along the line, it happens. Omar Khayyam falls stupidly, and irretrievably, in love.

"It's not rational," he reproaches himself, but his emotions, unscientifically, ignore him. He finds himself behaving awkwardly in her presence, and in his dreams he pursues her to the ends of the earth, while the mournful remnant of Eduardo Rodrigues looks down pityingly at his obsession from the sky. He, too, thinks of the extenuating circumstances, tells himself that in his distressed psychological condition he has become the victim of a mental disorder, but he is too ashamed even to think of taking advice . . . No, damn it! Headache or no headache, I will not let him get off as lightly as this. I accuse him of being ugly inside as well as out, a Beast, just as Farah Zoroaster had divined all those years ago. I accuse him of playing God or at least Pygmalion, of feeling he had rights of ownership over the innocent whose life he had saved. I accuse that fat pigmeat tub of working out that the only chance he had of getting a beautiful wife was to marry a nitwit, sacrificing wifely brains for the beauty of the flesh.

Omar Khayyam claims his obsession with Sufiya Zinobia has cured his vertigo. Poppycock! Flim-flam! I accuse the villain of attempting a shameless piece of social climbing (he never felt giddy when he did that!)—ditched by one great figure of the period, Omar Khayyam seeks to hitch himself to another star. So unscrupulous is he, so shameless, that he will court an idiot in order to woo her father. Even a father who gave the order which sent eighteen bullets into the body of Babar Shakil.

But we have heard him mumble: "Babar, life is long."—O, I'm not fooled by that. You conceive of a revenge plot?—Omar Khayyam, by marrying the unmarriageable child, is enabled to stay close to Hyder for years, before, during and after his Presidency, biding his time, because revenge is patient, it awaits its perfect moment?—Piffle! Wind! Those sick (and no doubt whisky-soaked) words of a fainting whale were no more than a fading, hollow echo of the favourite threat of Mr. Iskander Harappa, our hero's erstwhile patron, fellow-debauchee and chum. Of course he never meant them; he is not the avenging type. Did he feel anything at all for that dead brother whom he never knew? I doubt it; his three mothers, as we shall see, doubted it. This is not a possibility one can take seriously. Revenge? Pah! Huh! Phooey!

If Omar Khayyam thought about his brother's demise, it is more likely that he thought this: "Fool, terrorist, gangster. What did he expect?"

I have one last, and most damning, accusation. Men who deny their pasts become incapable of thinking them real. Absorbed into the great whore-city, having left the frontier universe of Q. far behind him once again, Omar Khayyam Shakil's home-town now seems to him like a sort of bad dream, a fantasy, a ghost. The city and the frontier are incompatible worlds; choosing Karachi, Shakil rejects the other. It becomes, for him, a feathery insubstantial thing, a discarded skin. He is no longer affected by what happens there, by its logic and demands. He is homeless: that is to say, a metropolitan through and through. A city is a camp for refugees.

God damn him! I'm stuck with him; and with his poxy love.

Very well; let's get on. I've lost another seven years of my story while the headache banged and thumped. Seven years, and now there are marriages to attend. How time flies!

I dislike arranged marriages. There are some mistakes for which one should not be able to blame one's poor parents.

8

BEAUTY
AND
THE BEAST

J ust imagine having a fish up your fundament, an eel that
spits at your insides," Bilquìs said, "and you won't need me
to tell you what happens on a woman's wedding night." Her
daughter Good News submitted to this teasing and to the tracing
of henna patterns upon the ticklish soles of her feet with the
demure obstinacy of one who is guarding a terrible secret. She
was seventeen years old and it was the eve of her wedding. The
womenfolk of Bariamma's family had assembled to prepare her;
while Bilquìs applied henna, mother and daughter were surrounded by eager relatives bearing oils for the skin, hairbrushes,
kohl, silver polish, flatirons. The mummified figure of Bariamma
herself supervised everything blindly from her vantage point of
a takht over which a Shirazi rug had been spread in her honour;
gaotakia bolsters prevented her from toppling over on to the floor
when she guffawed at the horrifically off-putting descriptions of
married life with which the matrons were persecuting Good News.

"Think of a sikh kabab that leaks hot cooking fat," Duniyazad Begum suggested, old quarrels bright in her eyes. But the virgins offered more optimistic images. "It's like sitting on a rocket that sends you to the moon," one maiden conjectured, earning a rocket from Bariamma for her blasphemy, because the faith clearly stated that lunar expeditions were impossible. The women sang songs insulting Good News's fiancé, young Haroun, the eldest son of Little Mir Harappa: "Face like a potato! Skin like a tomato! Walks like an elephant! Tiny plantain in his pant." But when Good News spoke up for the first and last time that evening, nobody could think of a single word to say.

"Mummy dear," Naveed said firmly into the scandalized silence, "I won't marry that stupid potato, you just see if I do."

Haroun Harappa at twenty-six was already accustomed to notoriety, because during the one year he had spent at an Angrez university he had published an article in the student paper in which he had described the private dungeons at the vast Daro estate into which his father would fling people for years on end. He had also written about the punitive expedition which Mir Harappa once led against the household of his cousin Iskander, and of the foreign bank account (he gave the number) into which his father was transferring large quantities of public money. The article was reprinted in *Newsweek*, so that the authorities back home had to intercept the entire shipment of that subversive issue and rip out the offending pages from every copy; but still the contents became common knowledge. When Haroun Harappa was expelled from his college at the end of that year, on the grounds that after three terms studying economics he had failed to master the concepts of supply and demand, it was generally supposed that he had written his article out of a genuine and innocent stupidity, hoping, no doubt, to impress the foreigners with his family's acumen and power. It was known that he had spent his university career almost exclusively in the gaming clubs and whorehouses of London, and the story went that when he entered the examination hall that summer he had glanced at the question paper without sitting down, shrugged, announced cheerfully, "No, there's nothing here for me," and strolled out to his Mercedes-Benz coupé without more ado. "The boy's a dope, I'm afraid," Little Mir told President A., "no need to take steps against him, I hope. He'll come home and settle down."

Little Mir made one attempt to persuade Haroun's college to keep him on. A large filigree-silver cigar box was presented to the Senior Common Room. The fellows of the college refused, however, to believe that a man as distinguished as Mir Harappa would try to bribe them, so they accepted the gift and chucked his son out on his ear. Haroun Harappa came home with numerous squash rackets, addresses of Arab princes, whisky decanters, bespoke suits, silk shirts and erotic photographs, but without a foreign degree.

But the seditious *Newsweek* article had not been the product of Haroun's stupidity. It had been born of the profound and undying hatred the son felt for his father, a hatred which would even survive Mir Harappa's terrible death. Little Mir had been a sternly authoritarian parent, but that in itself was not unusual and might even have engendered love and respect if it had not been for the matter of the dog. On Haroun's tenth birthday, at Daro, his father had presented him with a large parcel, done up in green ribbon, from which a muffled barking could clearly be heard. Haroun was an inward and only child who had grown fond of solitude; he did not really want the long-haired collie puppy who emerged from the package, and thanked his father with a perfunctory surliness that irritated Little Mir intensely. In the next few days it became obvious that Haroun intended to leave the dog to be cared for by the servants; whereupon Mir with the foolhardy stubbornness of his irritation issued orders that nobody was to lay a finger on the animal. "The damn hound is yours," Mir told the boy, "so you look after it." But Haroun was as obstinate as his father, and did not so much as give the puppy a name, so that

in the bitter heat of the Daro sunshine the puppy had to forage
for its own food and drink, contracted mange, distemper and
curious green spots on the tongue, was driven mad by its long
hair and finally died in front of the main door to the house,
emitting piteous yelps and leaking a thick yellow porridge from
its behind. "Bury it," Mir told Haroun, but the boy set his jaw
and walked away, and the slowly decomposing corpse of the
unnamed pooch mirrored the growth of the boy's loathing for
his father, who was thereafter forever associated in his mind with
the stench of the rotting dog.

After that Mir Harappa understood his mistake and went to
great lengths to regain his son's affection. He was a widower
(Haroun's mother had died in childbirth) and the boy was genuinely important to him. Haroun was outrageously spoiled, because although he refused to ask his father for so much as a new
vest Mir was always trying to guess what was in the boy's heart,
so that Haroun was showered with gifts, including a complete
set of cricket equipment comprising six stumps, four bails, twelve
sets of pads, twenty-two white flannel shirts and trousers, eleven
bats of varying weight and enough red balls to last a lifetime.
There were even umpires' white coats and score-books, but
Haroun was uninterested in cricket and the lavish present languished, unused, in a forgotten corner of Daro, along with the
polo gear, the tent pegs, the imported gramophones and the home-
movie camera, projector and screen. When he was twelve the
boy learned to ride and after that was to be found gazing longingly
at the horizon beyond which lay the Mohenjo estate of his uncle
Iskander. Whenever he heard that Isky was visiting his ancestral
home Haroun would ride without stopping to sit at the feet of
the man who ought by rights, he believed, to have been his father.
Mir Harappa did not protest when Haroun expressed a wish to
move to Karachi; and as he grew up in that mushrooming city
Haroun's infatuation with his uncle mushroomed too, so that he
began to affect the same dandyism and bad language and admiration for European culture that were Isky's trademarks before

his great conversion. This was why the young man insisted on being sent to study abroad, and why he passed his time in London engaged in whoring and gambling. After his return he went on in the same way; it had become a habit by then and he was unable to give it up even when his idolized uncle renounced such un-statesmanlike activities, so that the gossip in the town was that a little Isky had taken over where the big one left off. Mir Harappa continued to foot the bill for his son's outrageous behaviour, still hoping to win back the love of his only progeny; to no avail. Haroun in his habitually intoxicated state began to talk too much, and in loose-mouthed company. He spouted, drunkenly, the rev-olutionary political notions that had been current among Euro-pean students during his year abroad. He castigated Army rule and the power of oligarchies with all the enthusiastic garrulity of one who despises every word he is saying, but hopes that it will wound his even more detested parent. When he went so far as to mention the possibility of mass-producing Molotov cocktails, none of his cronies took him seriously, because he said it at a beach party while astride the shell of a weeping Galapagos turtle which was dragging itself up the sand to lay its infertile eggs; but the state informant in the gathering made his or her report, and President A., whose administration had become somewhat rocky, flew into a rage so terrible that Little Mir had to prostrate himself on the floor and beg for mercy for his wayward son. This incident would have forced Mir into a confrontation with Haroun, which he greatly feared, but he was spared the trouble by his cousin Iskander, who had also heard about Haroun's latest outrage. Haroun, summoned to Isky's split-level radiogram of a house, shifted from foot to foot under the brilliantly scornful eyes of Arjumand Harappa while her father spoke in gentle, implacable tones. Iskander Harappa had taken to dressing in green outfits styled by Pierre Cardin to resemble the uniforms of the Chinese Red Guards, because as the Foreign Minister in the government of President A. he had become famous as the architect of a friend-ship treaty with Chairman Mao. A photograph of Isky embracing the great Zedong hung on the wall of the room in which the uncle informed his nephew: "Your activities are becoming an embarrassment to me. Time you settled down. Take a wife." Arjumand Harappa stared furiously at Haroun and obliged him to do as Iskander asked. "But who?" he inquired lamely, and Isky waved a dismissive hand. "Some decent girl," he said, "plenty to choose from."

Haroun, realizing that the interview was at an end, turned to go. Iskander Harappa called after him: "And if you're interested in politics you better stop riding sea-turtles and start working for me."

The transformation of Iskander Harappa into the most powerful new force on the political scene was by this time complete. He had set about engineering his rise with all the calculated brilliance of which Arjumand had always known him to be capable. Concentrating on the high-profile world of international affairs, he had written a series of articles analysing his country's requirements from the great powers, the Islamic world and the rest of Asia, following these up with an arduous programme of speeches whose arguments proved impossible to resist. When his notion of "Islamic socialism" and of a close alliance with China had gained such wide public support that he was effectively running the nation's foreign policy without even being a member of the cabinet, President A. had had no option but to invite him into the government. His enormous personal charm, his way of making the plain, bolster-chested wives of visiting world leaders feel like Greta Garbo and his oratorical genius made him an instant hit. "The thing that satisfies me most," he told his daughter, "is that now we've given the go-ahead to the Karakoram road to China, I can have fun kicking around the minister for public works." The works minister was Little Mir Harappa, his old friendship with the President having failed to outweigh Iskander's public appeal. "That bastard," Iskander said to Arjumand with glee, "is finally under my thumb."

When the A. regime started losing popularity, Iskander Harappa resigned and formed the Popular Front, the political party which he funded out of his bottomless wealth and whose first Chairman he became. "For an ex-foreign minister," Little Mir told the President sourly, "your protégé seems to be concentrating pretty heavily on the home front." The President shrugged. "He knows what he's doing," said Field-Marshal A., "unfortunately."

Rumours of the government's corruption provided the fuel, but Isky's campaign for a return to democracy was perhaps unstoppable anyway. He toured the villages and promised every peasant one acre of land and a new water-well. He was put in jail; huge demonstrations secured his release. He screamed in regional dialects about the rape of the country by fat cats and tilyars, and such was the power of his tongue, or perhaps of the sartorial talents of Monsieur Cardin, that nobody seemed to recall Isky's own status as a landlord of a distinctly obese chunk of Sind . . . Iskander Harappa offered Haroun political work in his home district. "You have anti-corruption credentials," he told the youth. "Tell them about the *Newsweek* article." Haroun Harappa, offered this golden opportunity of running down his father on their home turf, took the job at once.

"Well, Abba," he thought happily, "life is long."

Two days after Haroun lectured an egg-laying turtle about revolution, Rani Harappa at Mohenjo was telephoned by a male voice so muted, so crippled by apologies and embarrassment that it was a few moments before she recognized it as belonging to Little Mir, with whom she had had no contact since his looting of her home, although his son Haroun had been a regular visitor. "God damn it, Rani," Little Mir finally admitted through the spittle-heavy clouds of his humiliation, "I need a favour."

Rani Harappa at forty had defeated Iskander's formidable ayah by the simple method of outliving her. The days of irreverently giggling village girls rummaging through her underwear were long past; she had become the true mistress of Mohenjo by dint of the unassailable calm with which she embroidered shawl after shawl on the verandah of the house, persuading the villagers that she was composing the tapestry of their fate, and that if she wished to she could foul up their lives by choosing to sew a bad future into the magical shawls. Having earned respect, Rani was strangely content with her life, and maintained cordial relations with her husband in spite of his long absences from her side and his permanent absence from her bed. She knew all about the end of the Pinkie affair and knew in the secret chambers of her heart that a man embarking on a political career must sooner or later ask his wife to stand beside him on the podium; secure in a future which would bring her Isky without her having to do a thing, she discovered without surprise that her love for him had refused to die, but had become, instead, a thing of quietness and strength. This was a great difference between her and Bilquìs Hyder: both women had husbands who retreated from them into the enigmatic palaces of their destinies, but while Bilquìs sank into eccentricity, not to say craziness, Rani subsided into a sanity which made her a powerful, and later on a dangerous, human being.

When Little Mir rang, Rani had been looking towards the village where the white concubines were playing badminton in the twilight. In those days many of the villagers had gone West to work for a while, and those who returned had brought with them white women for whom the prospect of life in a village as a number-two wife seemed to hold an inexhaustibly erotic appeal. The number-one wives treated these white girls as dolls or pets and those husbands who failed to bring home a guddi, a white doll, were soundly berated by their women. The village of the white dolls had become famous in the region. Villagers came from miles around to watch the girls in their neat, clean whites giggling and squealing as they leapt for shuttlecocks and displayed their frilly panties. The number-one wives cheered for their number-twos, taking pride in their victories as in the successes of children, and offering them consolation in defeat. Rani Harappa was deriving such gentle pleasure from observing the

SHAME

dolls at play that she forgot to listen to what Mir was saying. "Fuck me in the mouth, Rani," he shouted at last with the fury of his suppressed pride, "forget our differences. This business is too important. I need a wife, most urgently."

"I see."

"Ya Allah. Rani, don't be difficult, for God's sake. Not for me, what do you think, would I ask? For Haroun. It's the only way."

The desperation with which Little Mir stammered out the need for a good woman to stabilize his wayward son overcame any initial reluctance Rani might have felt, and she said at once, "Good News." "Already?" Little Mir asked, misunderstanding her. "You women don't waste any time!"

How a marriage is made: Rani suggested Naveed Hyder, thinking that a wedding in the family would do Bilquìs good. By that time the telephone link between the two women was no longer a means by which Rani found out what was going on in the city, no longer an excuse for Bilquìs to gossip and condescend while Rani humbly snatched from her friend's conversation whatever crumbs of life it offered. Now it was Rani who was strong, and Bilquìs, her old regal dreams in ruins since Raza's sacking from the government, who needed support, and who found in the unchanging solidity of Rani Harappa the strength to sustain her through her increasingly bewildered days. "Just what she needs," Rani thought with satisfaction, "trousseau, marquees, sweet-meats, too much to think about. And that daughter of hers can't wait to get hitched."

Little Mir consulted the President before agreeing to the match. The Hyder family had become accident-prone of late: the old rumours from Q. still circulated, and it had not been easy to keep the incident of the dead turkeys out of the papers. But now, in the mountainous coolness of the new northern capital, the President had begun to feel the chilly winds of his unpopularity, and agreed to the marriage, because, he decided, it was time to draw the hero of Aansu close to him again, like a warm blanket or

166

shawl. "No problem," A. told Little Mir, "my congrats to the happy pair."

Mir Harappa visited Rani at Mohenjo to discuss the details. He rode up stiff with embarrassment and behaved with bad-tempered humility throughout. "What a father will do for a son!" he burst out at Rani as she sat on the verandah working on the interminable shawl of her solitude. "When my boy is a daddy himself he will know how a daddy feels. I hope this Good News of yours is a fertile girl."

"Proper sowing ensures a good harvest," Rani replied serenely. "Please take some tea."

Raza Hyder did not object to the betrothal. In those years when his only responsibility was to oversee the intake and training of raw recruits, when the fact of his decline stared him in the face every day, multiplied, replicated in the gawky figures of youths who didn't know which end of a bayonet meant business, he had been observing the rise of Iskander Harappa with barely suppressed envy. "The time will come," he prophesied to himself, "when I'll have to go begging that guy for an extra pip." In the turbulent climate of the government's instability Raza Hyder had been wondering which way to jump, whether to come out in support of the Popular Front's demand for elections, or to put what remained of his reputation behind the government in the hope of preferment. The offer of Haroun Harappa for a son-in-law gave him the chance of having it both ways. The match would please the President: that much had been made clear. But Raza also knew of Haroun's hatred for his father, which had placed the boy firmly in Isky Harappa's pocket. "A foot in both camps," Raza thought, "that's the ticket."

And it is possible that Raza was delighted to be able to get rid of Good News, because she had developed, as she grew, something of the full-mouthed insouciance of the late Sindbad Mengal. Haroun's mouth was also thick and wide, a part of his family inheritance. "Two fat-lip types," Raza Hyder told his wife in tones more jovial than he normally used when addressing her, "made for each other, na? The babies will look like fishes." Bilquìs said, "Never mind."

How a marriage is made: I see that I have somehow omitted to mention the views of the young persons concerned. Photographs were exchanged. Haroun Harappa took his brown envelope to his uncle's house and opened it in the presence of Iskander and Arjumand: there are times when young men turn to their families for support. The monochrome photograph had been artistically retouched to give Good News skin as pink as blotting-paper and eyes as green as ink.

"You can see how he's made her pigtail longer," Arjumand pointed out.

"Let the boy make up his own mind," Iskander reproved her, but Arjumand at twenty had conceived a strange dislike of the picture. "Plain as a plate," she announced, "and not so fair-skinned as all that."

"It's got to be somebody," Haroun stated, "and there's nothing wrong with her." Arjumand cried, "How can you just say that? Got eyes in your head or ping-pong balls?" At this point Iskander ordered his daughter to be quiet and told the bearer to bring sweetmeats and celebratory glasses of lime juice. Haroun went on staring at that photograph of Naveed Hyder, and because nothing, not even the paintbrush of a zealous photographer, could mask Good News's unquenchable determination to be beautiful, her fiancé was quickly overpowered by the iron will of her celluloid eyes, and began to think her the loveliest bride on earth. This illusion, which was entirely the product of Good News's imagination, entirely the result of the action of mind over matter, would survive everything, even the wedding scandal; but it would not survive Iskander Harappa's death.

"What a girl," said Haroun Harappa, driving Arjumand from the room in disgust.

As for Good News: "I don't need to look at any stupid photograph," she told Bilquìs, "he's famous, he's rich, he's a husband, let's catch him quick." "His reputation is bad," Bilquìs said, as a mother should, offering her daughter the chance to withdraw, "and he is bad to his daddy."

"I'll fix him," Good News replied.

Later, alone with Shahbanou as the ayah brushed her hair, Good News added some further thoughts. "Hey, you with the eyes at the bottom of a well," she said, "you know what marriage is for a woman?"

"I am a virgin," Shahbanou replied.

"Marriage is power," Naveed Hyder said. "It is freedom. You stop being someone's daughter and become someone's mother instead, ek dum, fut-a-fut, pronto. Then who can tell you what to do?—What do you mean," a terrible notion occurred to her, "do you think I'm not a virgin also? You shut your dirtyfilthy mouth, with one word I could put you on the street."

"What are you talking, bibi, I only said."

"I tell you, how great to be away from this house. Haroun Harappa, I swear. Too good, yaar. Too good."

"We are modern people," Bilquìs told her daughter. "Now that you have accepted you must get to know the boy. It will be a love match."

Miss Arjumand Harappa, the "virgin Ironpants," had rejected so many suitors that although she was barely twenty years old the city's matchmakers had already begun to think of her as being on the shelf. The flood of proposals was not entirely, or even primarily, the result of her extreme eligibility as the only child of Chairman Iskander Harappa; it had its true source in that extraordinary, defiant beauty with which, or so it seemed to her, her body taunted her mind. I must say that of all the beautiful women in that country packed full of improbable lovelies, there is no doubt who took the prize. In spite of bound and still-apple-sized breasts, Arjumand carried off the palm.

Loathing her sex, Arjumand went to great lengths to disguise her looks. She cut her hair short, wore no cosmetics or perfume, dressed in her father's old shirts and the baggiest trousers she could find, developed a stooped and slouching walk. But the harder she tried, the more insistently her blossoming body outshone her disguises. The short hair was luminous, the unadorned face learned expressions of infinite sensuality which she could do nothing to control, and the more she stooped, the taller and more desirable she grew. By the age of sixteen she had been obliged to become expert in the arts of self-defence. Iskander Harappa had never tried to keep her away from men. She accompanied him on his diplomatic rounds, and at many embassy receptions elderly ambassadors were found clutching their groins and throwing up in the toilet after their groping hands had been answered by a well-aimed knee. By her eighteenth birthday the throng of the city's most coveted bachelors outside the gate of the Harappa house had become so swollen as to constitute an impediment to traffic, and at her own request she was sent away to Lahore to a Christian boarding college for ladies, whose anti-male rules were so severe that even her father could see her only by appointment in a tattered garden of dying roses and balding lawns. But she found no respite in that prison populated exclusively by females, all of whom she scorned for their gender; the girls fell for her just as hard as the men, and final-year students would clutch at her behind when she passed. One lovelorn nineteen-year-old, despairing of catching Ironpants's eye, pretended to sleepwalk into the empty swimming pool and was removed to hospital with multiple fractures of the skull. Another, crazed by love, climbed out of the college compound and went to sit at a café in the famous red-light district of Heeramandi, having decided to become a whore if she could not have Arjumand's heart. This distressed girl was abducted from the café by the local pimps, who forced her father, a textile magnate, to pay a ransom of one lakh of rupees for her safe return. She never married, because although the pimps insisted that they had their honour, too, nobody believed she had not been touched, and after a medical inspection the college's devoutly Catholic headmistress absolutely refused to concede that the wretch might have been deflowered upon her antiseptic premises. Arjumand Harappa wrote to her father and asked him to take her away from the college. "It's no relief," the letter said. "I should have known girls would be worse than boys."

The return from London of Haroun Harappa unleashed a civil war inside the virgin Ironpants. His remarkable physical resemblance to photographs of her father at twenty-six unnerved Arjumand, and his fondness for whoring, gambling and other forms of debauchery convinced her that reincarnation was not simply a crazy notion imported by the Hyders from the country of the idolaters. She attempted to suppress the idea that beneath Haroun's dissolute exterior a second great man, almost the equal of her father, lay concealed, and that, with her help, he could discover his true nature, just as the Chairman had . . . refusing even to whisper such things to herself in the privacy of her room, she cultivated in Haroun's presence that attitude of scornful condescension which quickly persuaded him that there was no point in his trying where so many others had failed. He was not insensible to her fatal beauty, but the reputation of the virgin Ironpants, when combined with that terrible and uninterruptedly disgusted gaze, was enough to send him elsewhere; and then the photograph of Naveed Hyder bewitched him, and it was too late for Arjumand to change her approach. Haroun Harappa was the only man, other than her father, whom Arjumand ever loved, and her rage in the days after his betrothal was awful to behold. But Iskander was preoccupied in those days, and failed to pay any attention to the war inside his child.

"God damn," Arjumand said to her mirror, unconsciously reflecting the former habit of her mother alone in Mohenjo, "life is shit."

It was once explained to me by one of the world's Greatest Living Poets—we mere prose scribblers must turn to poets for wisdom, which is why this book is littered with them; there was my friend who hung upside-down and had the poetry shaken out of him, and Babar Shakil, who wanted to be a poet, and I suppose Omar Khayyam, who was named for one but never was—that the classic fable *Beauty and the Beast* is simply the story of an arranged marriage.

"A merchant is down on his luck, so he promises his daughter to a wealthy but reclusive landowner, Beast Sahib, and receives a lavish dowry in exchange—a great chest, I believe, of broad pieces of gold. Beauty Bibi dutifully marries the zamindar, thus restoring her father's fortunes, and naturally at first her husband, a total stranger, seems horrible to her, monstrous even. But eventually, under the benign influence of her obedient love, he turns into a Prince."

"Do you mean," I ventured, "that he inherits a title?" The Great Living Poet looked tolerant and tossed back his silvery shoulder-length hair.

"That is a bourgeois remark," he chided me. "No, of course the transformation would have taken place neither in his social status nor in his actual, corporeal self, but in her perception of him. Picture them as they grow closer to each other, as they move inwards over the years from the opposed poles of Beautyness and Beastdom, and become at last, and happily, just plain Mr. Husband and Mrs. Wife."

The Great Living Poet was well-known for his radical ideas and for the chaotic complexity of his extramarital love life, so I thought I would please him by commenting slyly: "Why is it that fairy-tales always treat marriage as an ending? And always such a perfectly happy one?"

But instead of the man-to-man wink or guffaw for which I'd been hoping (I was very young), the Great Living Poet adopted a grave expression. "That is a masculine question," he replied, "no woman would be so puzzled. The proposition of the fable is clear. Woman must make the best of her fate; for if she does not love Man, why then he dies, the Beast perishes, and Woman is left a widow, that is to say less than a daughter, less than a wife, worthless." Mildly, he sipped his Scotch.

"Whatif, whatif," I stammered, "I mean, uncle, whatif the girl really couldn't bear the husband chosen for her?" The Poet, who had begun to hum Persian verses under his breath, frowned in distant disappointment.

"You have become too Westernized," he said. "You should spend some time, maybe seven years or so, not too long, with our village people. Then you will understand that this is a completely Eastern story, and stop this whatif foolishness."

The Great Poet is unfortunately no longer living, so I cannot ask him whatif the story of Good News Hyder were true; nor can I hope for the benefit of his advice on an even more ticklish subject: whatif, whatif a Beastji somehow lurked *inside* Beauty Bibi? Whatif the beauty were herself the beast? But I think he might have said I was confusing matters: "As Mr. Stevenson has shown in his *Dr. Jekyll and Mr. Hyde*, such saint-and-monster conjunctions are conceivable in the case of men; alas! such is our nature. But the whole essence of Woman denies such a possibility."

The reader may have divined from my last whatifs that I have two marriages to describe; and the second, waiting in the peripheries of the first, is of course the long-hinted-at Nikah of Sufiya Zinobia Hyder and Omar Khayyam Shakil.

Omar Khayyam finally screwed up the courage to ask for Sufiya Zinobia's hand when he heard about the betrothal of her younger sister. When he arrived, grey respectable fifty, at her marble home and made his extraordinary request, the impossibly old and decrepit divine Maulana Dawood let out a scream that made Raza Hyder look around for demons. "Spawn of obscene hags," Dawood addressed Shakil, "from the day you descended to earth in the machine of your mothers' iniquity I knew you. Such filthy suggestions you come to make in this house of lovers of God!

May your time in Hell be longer than a thousand lifetimes." The rage of Maulana Dawood created, in Bilquìs, a mood of perverse obstinacy. In these days she was still prone to lock doors furiously, to defend herself against the incursions of the afternoon wind; the light in her eyes was a little too bright. But the engagement of Good News had given her a new purpose, just as Rani had hoped; so it was with a fair approximation of her old arrogance that she spoke to Omar Khayyam: "We understand that you have been obliged to bring your own proposal because of the absence of your family members from Town. The irregularity is forgiven, but we must now consider in private. Our decision will be communicated to you in due course." Raza Hyder, struck dumb by this reappearance of the old Bilquìs, was unable to disagree until Shakil had left; Omar Khayyam, arising, placing grey hat on grey hair, was betrayed by a sudden reddening beneath the pallor of his skin. "Blushing," Maulana Dawood screeched, extending a sharp-nailed finger, "that is only a trick. Such persons have no shame."

After Sufiya Zinobia recovered from the immunological catastrophe that followed the turkey massacre, Raza Hyder had discovered that he could no longer see her through the veil of his disappointment in her sex. The memory of the tenderness with which he had lifted her out of the scene of her somnambulist violence refused to leave him, as did the realization that while she was ill he had been beset by emotions that could only be described as arising out of fatherly love. In short, Hyder had changed his opinion of his retarded child, and had begun to play with her, to take pride in her tiny advances. Together with the ayah Shahbanou the great war hero would play at being a train or steamroller or crane, and would lift the girl and throw her in the air as if she really were still the small child whose brain she had been forced to retain. This new pattern of behaviour had perplexed Bilquìs, whose affections remained concentrated on the younger girl . . . at any rate, Sufiya Zinobia's condition had improved. She had grown two and a half inches, put on a little weight, and her mental age had risen to about six and a half. She was nineteen years old, and had conceived for her newly loving father a child's version of that same devotion which Arjumand Harappa felt for her father the Chairman.

"Men," Bilquìs told Rani on the telephone, "you can't depend on them."

As for Omar Khayyam: the complexity of his motives has already been discussed. He had spent seven years failing to cure himself of that obsession which relieved him of vertigo attacks, but during those years of struggle he had also arranged to examine Sufiya Zinobia at regular intervals, and had ingratiated himself with her father, building on the gratitude Raza felt towards him for having saved his daughter's life. But a proposal of marriage was something else again, and once he was safely out of the house Raza Hyder began to voice his doubts.

"The man is fat," Raza reasoned. "Ugly also. And we must not forget his debauched past."

"A debauched life led by the child of debauched persons," Dawood added, "and a brother shot for politics."

But Bilquìs did not mention her memory of Shakil drunk at Mohenjo. Instead she said, "Where are we going to find the girl a better match?"

Now Raza understood that his wife was as anxious to be rid of this troublesome child as he was to see the back of her beloved Good News. The realization that there was a kind of symmetry here, a sort of fair exchange, weakened his resolve, so that Bilquìs detected the uncertainty in his voice when he asked, "But a damaged child: should we look for husbands at all? Should we not accept the responsibility, wife? What is this marriage business where such a girl is concerned?"

"She is not so stupid now," Bilquìs argued, "she can dress herself, go to the pot, and she does not wet her bed."

"For God's sake," Raza shouted, "does that qualify her to be a wife?"

"That frogspawn slime," Dawood exclaimed, "that messenger

of Shaitan. He has come here with his proposal to divide this holy house."

"Her vocabulary is improving," Bilquìs added, "she sits with Shahbanou and tells the dhobi what to wash. She can count the garments and handle money."

"But she is a child," Raza said hopelessly.

Bilquìs grew stronger as he weakened. "In a woman's body," she replied, "the child is nowhere to be seen. A woman does not have to be a brainbox. In many opinions brains are a positive disadvantage to a woman in marriage. She likes to go to the kitchen and help the khansama with his work. At the bazaar she can tell good vegetables from bad. You yourself have praised her chutneys. She can tell when the servants have not polished the furniture properly. She wears a brassière and in other ways also her body has become that of an adult woman. And she even does not blush."

This was true. The alarming reddenings of Sufiya Zinobia were, it seemed, things of the past; nor had the turkey-assassinated violence recurred. It was as if the girl had been cleansed by her single, all-consuming explosion of shame.

"Maybe," Raza Hyder slowly said, "I am worrying too much."

"Besides," Bilquìs said with finality, "he is her doctor, this man. He saved her life. Into whose hands could we more safely place her? Into nobody's, I say. This proposal has come to us from God."

"Catch your ears," Dawood shrieked, "tobah, tobah! But your God is great, great in his greatness, and so he may forgive such blasphemy."

Raza Hyder looked old and sad. "We must send Shahbanou with her," he insisted. "And a quiet wedding. Too much hullabaloo would frighten her."

"Just let me finish with Good News," Bilquìs said in delight, "and we will have a wedding so quiet that only the birds will sing."

Maulana Dawood withdrew from the scene of his defeat. "Girls married in the wrong order," he said as he departed; "what began with a necklace of shoes cannot end well."

On the day of the polo match between the Army and Police teams Bilquìs shook Good News awake early. The match was not scheduled to begin until five o'clock in the afternoon, but Bilquìs said, "Eleven hours dolling yourself up to meet your future husband is like money in the bank." By the time mother and daughter arrived at the polo ground Good News was in such tip-top condition that people thought a bride had abandoned her wedding feast to come and watch the game. Haroun Harappa met them by the little table at which the match commentator sat surrounded by microphones and led them to the chairs he had saved for them; the spectacle of Good News's get-up was so overpowering that he came away with a clearer impression of the design of her nose-jewellery than of the fortunes of the game. Every so often during that afternoon he ran off and returned bearing paper plates heaped with samosas or jalebis, with cups of fizzing cola balanced along his forearms. During his absences Bilquìs watched her daughter like a hawk, to make sure she tried no funny business like catching the eyes of other boys; but when Haroun returned Bilquìs became unaccountably absorbed in the game. The great star of the Police team was a certain Captain Talvar Ulhaq, and in that time of the Army's unpopularity his annihilation of their polo squad that afternoon turned him into something of a national hero, especially as he conformed to all the usual heroic requirements, being tall, dashing, mustachioed, with a tiny scar on his neck that looked exactly like a love-bite. This Captain Talvar was to be the cause of the wedding scandal out of which, it could be argued with some plausibility, the whole of the future grew.

From the stammering and awkward conversation she had with Haroun that day Good News discovered to her consternation that her future husband had no ambitions and a tiny appetite. Nor was he in any hurry to have children. The confidence with which

Naveed Hyder had stated, "I'll fix him," ebbed out of her in the physical presence of this pudding of a young man, so it was perhaps inevitable that her eyes should become glued to the up-right, capering, mythological figure of Talvar Ulhaq on his whirl-ing horse. And maybe it was also inevitable that her excessive dressiness should attract the interest of the young police captain who was famous for being the most successful stud in the city—so maybe the whole thing was Bilquìs's fault for dressing up her daughter—at any rate, Bilquìs for all her vigilance missed the moment when their eyes met. Good News and Talvar stared at each other through the dust and hooves and polo-sticks, and at that moment the girl felt a pain shoot up her insides. She managed to turn the shuddering moan which escaped her lips into a violent sneeze and cough before anyone noticed, and was assisted in her subterfuge by the commotion on the polo field, where Captain Talvar's horse had inexplicably reared and thrown him down into the perils of the flying hooves and sticks. "I just went stiff all over," Talvar told Naveed later, "and the horse lost its temper with me."

The game ended shortly afterwards, and Good News went home with Bilquìs, knowing that she would never marry Haroun Harappa, no, not in a million years. That night she heard pebbles rattling on her bedroom window, tied her bedsheets together and climbed down into the arms of the polo star, who drove her in a police car to his beach hut at Fisherman's Cove. When they had finished making love she asked the most modest question of her life: "I'm not so great looking," she said, "why me?" Talvar Ulhaq sat up in bed and looked as serious as a schoolboy. "On account of the hunger of your womb," he told her. "You are appetite and I am food." Now she perceived that Talvar had a pretty high opinion of himself and began to wonder whether she might have bitten off more than she could chew.

It turned out that Talvar Ulhaq had had the gift of clairvoyancy from childhood, a talent which assisted him greatly in his police work, because he could divine where crimes were going to be committed before the thieves had worked it out themselves, so that his record of arrests was unbeatable. He had foreseen in Naveed Hyder the children who had always been his greatest dream, the profusion of children who would make him puff up with pride while she disintegrated under the awesome chaos of their numbers. This vision had made him willing to undertake the extremely dangerous course of action to which he was now committed, because he knew that Raza Hyder's daughter was engaged to be married to the favourite nephew of Chairman Iskander Harappa, that the invitations to the wedding had already gone out, and that by any normal standards his situation was hopeless. "Nothing is impossible," he told Naveed, got dressed and went outside into the salty night to find a sea-turtle to ride. Naveed emerged a little later to find him whooping with joy as he stood on a turtle's back, and while she was enjoying his simple pleasure the fishermen came and grinned at them. Afterwards Naveed Hyder was never sure whether this had been a part of Talvar's plan, whether he had signalled to the fishermen from the back of the weeping turtle, or if he had visited the Cove in advance to plan the whole thing, because after all it was well known that the fishermen and the police force were great allies, being regularly in cahoots for smuggling purposes . . . Talvar, however, never admitted any responsibility for what happened.

What happened was that the fishermen's leader, a patriarch with an honest and open face in which an unblemished set of white teeth gleamed improbably in the moonlight, informed the couple pleasantly that he and his fellows intended to blackmail them. "Such ungodly goings-on," the old fisherman said sadly, "it is bad for our peace of mind. Some compensation, some comfort must be given."

Talvar Ulhaq paid up without arguing and drove Good News home. With his help, she managed to climb up the rope of bed-sheets without being discovered. "I won't see you again," he said at their parting, "until you break your engagement and allow what must be to be."

His second sight informed him that she would do as he had asked, so he went home to prepare for marriage and for the storm which would surely break.

Good News (let us remind ourselves) was her mother's favourite daughter. Her fear of forfeiting this position fought inside her with the equal and opposite fear that the fishermen would continue their blackmail; the insane love she had conceived for Talvar Ulhaq wrestled with the duty she owed to the boy her parents had selected; the loss of her virginity drove her wild with worry. But until the last evening before her wedding she remained silent. Talvar Ulhaq told her afterwards that her inaction had brought him close to the point of insanity, and that he had resolved to turn up at the wedding and shoot Haroun Harappa, whatever the consequences, if she had decided to go through with the match. But at the eleventh hour Good News told her mother, "I won't marry that stupid potato," and all hell broke loose, because love was the last thing anyone had been expecting to foul up the arrangements.

O glee of female relatives in the face of unconcealable scandal! O crocodile tears and insincere pummelling of breasts! O delighted crowing of Duniyazad Begum as she dances upon the corpse of Bilquìs's honour! And the forktongued offers of hope: Who knows, talk to her, many girls panic on their wedding eve, yes, she'll see sense, just try only, time to be firm, time to be gentle, beat her up a little, give her a loving hug, O God, but how terrible, how can you cancel the guests?

And when it is clear that the girl cannot be moved, when the delicious horror of it all is out in the open, when Good News admits that there is Someone Else—then Bariamma stirs on her bolsters and the room falls silent to hear her judgment.

"This is your failure as a mother," Bariamma wheezes, "so now the father must be called. Go now and bring him, my Raza, run and fetch."

.   .   .

Two tableaux. In the bridal chamber Naveed Hyder sits immovable and mulish while all around her are women frozen by their delight into living statues, women holding combs, brushes, silver-polish, antimony, staring at Naveed, disaster's source, with petrified joy. Bariamma's lips are the only moving features in the scene. Time-honoured words are dripping out of them: floozy, hussy, whore. And in Raza's bedroom Bilquìs is clinging to her husband's legs as he struggles into his pants.

Raza Hyder awoke to catastrophe from a dream in which he saw himself standing on the parade-ground of his failure before a phalanx of recruits all of whom were exact replicas of himself, except that they were incompetent, they could not march in step or dress to the left or polish their belt buckles properly. He had been screaming his despair at these shades of his own ineptitude, and the rage of the dream infected his waking mood. His first reaction to the news which Bilquìs forced past lips that did not want to let it through was that he had no option but to kill the girl. "Such shame," he said, "such havoc wrought to the plans of parents." He decided to shoot her in the head in front of his family members. Bilquìs clung to his thighs, slipped down as he began to move, and was dragged from the bedroom, her nails digging into his ankles. The cold sweat of her fear made her pencilled eyebrows run down her face. The ghost of Sindbad Mengal was not mentioned, but O, he was there all right. Army pistol in hand, Raza Hyder entered Good News's room; the screams of women greeted him as he came.

But this is not the story of my discarded Anna M.; Raza, raising his gun, found himself unable to use it. "Throw her into the street," he said, and left the room.

Now the night is full of negotiations. Raza in his quarters stares at an unused pistol. Deputations are sent; he remains unbending.

Then the ayah Shahbanou, rubbing sleep from black-rimmed eyes, so like Hyder's own, is dispatched by Bilquìs to plead Good News's cause. "He likes you because you are good with Sufiya Zinobia. He'll listen maybe to you when he won't to me." Bilquìs is crumbling visibly, has been reduced to pleading with servants. Shahbanou holds Good News's future in her hands—Good News, who has kicked, abused, hit—"I'll go, Begum Sahib," Shahbanou says. Ayah and father confer behind closed doors: "Forgive my saying, sir, but don't pile shame on shame."

At three a.m. Raza Hyder relents. There must be a wedding, the girl must be handed over to a husband, any husband. That will get rid of her and cause less of a stir than kicking her out. "A whore with a home," Raza summons Bilquìs to announce, "is better than a whore in the gutter." Naveed tells her mother the name: not without pride, she says clearly to one and all: "It must be Captain Talvar Ulhaq. Nobody else will do."

Telephone calls. Mir Harappa awoken to be informed of the change of plan. "Your bastard family. Fuck me in the mouth if I don't get even." Iskander Harappa receives the news calmly, relays it to Arjumand who is in her nightgown beside the telephone. Something flickers in her eyes.

It is Iskander who tells Haroun.

And one more call, to a police captain who has not slept a wink, who like Raza has spent part of the night fingering a pistol. "I will not tell you what I think of you," Raza Hyder roars into the mouthpiece, "but get your hide here tomorrow and take this no-good female off my hands. Not one paisa of dowry and keep out of my sight for ever after."

"Ji, I shall be honoured to marry your daughter," Talvar politely replies. And in the Hyder household, women who can scarcely believe their luck begin once again to make preparations for the great day. Naveed Hyder goes to bed and falls sound asleep with an innocent expression on her face. Dark henna on her soles turns orange while she rests.

"Shame and scandal in the family," Shahbanou tells Sufiya Zinobia in the morning. "Bibi, you don't know what you missed."

Something else was happening that night. On university campuses, in the bazaars of the cities, under cover of darkness, the people were assembling. By the time the sun rose it was clear that the government was going to fall. That morning the people took to the streets and set fire to motor cars, school buses, Army trucks and the libraries of the British Council and United States Information Service to express their displeasure. Field-Marshal A. ordered troops into the streets to restore peace. At eleven-fifteen he was visited by a General known to everyone by the nickname "Shaggy Dog," an alleged associate of Chairman Iskander Harappa. General Shaggy Dog informed the distraught President that the armed forces were absolutely refusing to fire on civilians, and soldiers would shoot their officers rather than their fellow-countrymen. This statement convinced President A. that his time was up, and by lunchtime he had been replaced by General Shaggy, who placed A. under house arrest and appeared on the brand-new television service to announce that his sole purpose in assuming power was to lead the nation back towards democracy; elections would take place within eighteen months. The afternoon was spent by the people in joyful celebration; Datsuns, taxi-cabs, the Alliance Française building and the Goethe Institute provided the fuel for their incandescent happiness.

Mir Harappa heard about the bloodless coup of President Dog within eight minutes of Marshal A.'s resignation. This second major blow to his prestige drained all the fight out of Little Mir. Leaving a letter of resignation on his desk he fled to his Daro estate without bothering to await developments, and immured himself there in a mood of such desolation that the servants could hear him muttering under his breath that his days were numbered. "Two things have happened," he would say, "but the third is yet to come."

Iskander and Arjumand spent the day with Haroun in Karachi. Iskander on the telephone all day, Arjumand so aroused by the news that she forgot to sympathize with Haroun about his cancelled wedding. "Stop looking so fish-faced," she told him, "the future has begun." Rani Harappa arrived by train from Mohenjo, thinking she was about to spend a carefree day at Good News's Nikah celebrations, but Isky's chauffeur Jokio told her at the station that the world had changed. He drove her to the town house, where Iskander embraced her warmly and said, "Good you came. Now we must stand together before the people; our moment has come." At once Rani forgot all about weddings and began to look, at forty, as young as her only daughter. "I knew it," she exulted inwardly. "Good old Shaggy Dog."

So great was the excitement of that day that the news of the events in the Hyder household was blotted out completely, whereas on any other day the scandal would have been impossible to cover up. Captain Talvar Ulhaq came alone to the wedding, having chosen to involve neither friends nor family members in the shameful circumstances of his nuptials. He had to struggle through streets that were hot with burning cars in a police jeep that mercifully escaped the ministrations of the crowds, and was received by Raza Hyder with glacial formality and scorn. "It is my earnest intention," Talvar told Raza, "to be the finest son-in-law that you could wish for, so that in time you may reconsider your decision to cut your daughter out of your life." Raza gave the briefest of replies to this courageous speech. "I don't care for polo players," he said.

Those guests who had managed to reach the Hyder residence through the unstable euphoria of the streets had taken the precaution of dressing in their oldest, most tattered clothes; nor did they wear any jewellery. They had put on these unfestive rags to avoid attracting the attention of the people, who usually put up with rich folk but might just have elected in their elation to add the city's elite to their collection of burning symbols. The dilapidated condition of the guests was one of the strangest features of that day of strangenesses; Good News Hyder, oiled hennaed bejewelled, looked in that gathering of frightened celebrants even more out of place than she had appeared at the polo match of her inescapable destiny. "It's like being married in a palace full of beggars," she whispered to Talvar, who sat flower-garlanded beside her on a little podium beneath the glittering, mirrorworked marquee. The sweetmeats and delicacies of Bilquìs's motherly pride languished uneaten on long whiteclothed tables in the bizarre atmosphere of that horrified and dislocated time.

Why the guests refused to eat: already unbalanced by the dangers of the streets, they had been almost completely deranged by the information, which was conveyed to them on little handwritten erratum slips which Bilquìs had been writing out for hours, that while the bride was indeed the expected Good News Hyder there had been a last-minute change of groom. "Owing to circumstances beyond our control," read the little white chitties of humiliation, "the part of husband will be taken by Police Capt. Talvar Ulhaq." Bilquìs had had to write this line five hundred and fifty-five times over, and each successive inscription drove the nails of her shame deeper into her heart, so that by the time the guests arrived and the servants handed out the erratum slips she was as stiff with dishonour as if she had been impaled on a tree. As the shock of the coup was replaced on the guests' faces by the awareness of the size of the catastrophe that had befallen the Hyders, Raza, too, became numb all over, anaesthetized by his public disgrace. The presence of the Himalaya of uneaten food struck the chill of shame into the soul of Shahbanou the ayah, who was standing by Sufiya Zinobia in a condition of such extreme despondency that she forgot to greet Omar Khayyam Shakil. The doctor had lumbered into that gathering of millionaires disguised as gardeners; his thoughts were so full of the ambiguities of his own engagement to the halfwit of his obsessions that he utterly failed to notice that he had walked into a mirage from the past, a ghost-image of the legendary party given by the three Shakil sisters in their old house in Q. The erratum slip rested unread in his plump tight fist until, belatedly, the meaning of the uneaten food dawned on him.

It was not an exact replica of that longago party. No food was eaten, but still a wedding took place. Can there ever have been a Nikah at which nobody flirted with anybody else, at which the hired musicians were so overwhelmed by the occasion that they neglected to play a single note? Certainly there could not have been many nuptial feasts at which the last-minute groom was all but murdered on his podium by his newly acquired sister-in-law.

O dear, yes. I regret to have to inform you that (setting the seal, as it were, on that perfect disaster of a day) the somnolent demon of shame that had possessed Sufiya Zinobia on the day she slew the turkeys emerged once more beneath the mirror-shiny shamiana of disgrace.

A glazing-over of her eyes, which acquired the milky opacity of somnambulism. A pouring-in to her too-sensitive spirit of the great abundance of shame in that tormented tent. A fire beneath the skin, so that she began to flame all over, a golden blaze that dimmed the rouge on her cheeks and the paint on her fingers and toes . . . Omar Khayyam Shakil spotted what was going on, but too late, so that by the time he shouted "Look out!" across that catatonic gathering the demon had already hurled Sufiya Zinobia across the party, and before anyone moved she had grabbed Captain Talvar Ulhaq by the head and begun to twist, to twist so hard that he screamed at the top of his voice, because his neck was on the point of snapping like a straw.

Good News Hyder grabbed her sister by the hair and pulled with all her might, feeling the burning heat of that supernatural passion scorch her fingers; then Omar Khayyam and Shahbanou and Raza Hyder and even Bilquìs joined in, as the guests sank further into their speechless stupor, aghast at this last expression of the impossible fantasy of the day. The combined efforts of the five desperate people succeeded in detaching Sufiya Zinobia's hands before Talvar Ulhaq's head was ripped off like a turkey's; but then she buried her teeth in his neck, giving him a second scar to balance that famous love-bite, and sending his blood spurting long distances across the gathering, so that all her family and many of the camouflaged guests began to resemble workers in a halal slaughterhouse. Talvar was squealing like a pig, and when they finally dragged Sufiya Zinobia off him she had a morsel of his skin and flesh in her teeth. Afterwards, when he recovered, he was never able to move his head to the left. Sufiya Zinobia Hyder, the incarnation of her family's shame and also, once again, its chief cause, fell limply into her fiancé's arms, and Omar Khayyam had assailant and victim taken immediately to hospital, where Talvar Ulhaq remained on the critical list for one hundred and one hours, while Sufiya Zinobia had to be brought out of her self-induced trance by the exercise of more hypnotic skill than Omar had ever been required to display. Good News Hyder spent her wedding night weeping inconsolably on her mother's shoulder in a hospital waiting-room. "That monster," she sobbed bitterly, "you should have had her drowned at birth."

A short inventory of the effects of the wedding scandal: the stiff neck of Talvar Ulhaq, which terminated his career as a polo star; the birth of a spirit of forgiveness and reconciliation within Raza Hyder, who found it hard to ostracize a man whom his daughter had almost killed, so that Talvar and Good News were not, after all, cast out of the bosom of that accursed family; also the accelerated disintegration of Bilquìs Hyder, whose breakdown could no longer be concealed, even though she became, in the following years, little more than a whisper or rumour, because Raza Hyder kept her away from society, under a kind of unofficial house arrest.

What else?—When it became clear that Iskander Harappa's Popular Front would do extremely well in the elections, Raza paid a call on Isky. Bilquìs stayed at home with her hair hanging loose, railing at the heavens because her husband, her Raza, had gone to abase himself before that blubber-lips who always got everything he wanted. Hyder tried to force himself to apologize for the wedding fiasco, but Iskander said merrily, "For God's sake, Raza, Haroun can take care of himself, and as for your Talvar Ulhaq, I'm pretty impressed by the coup that fellow engineered. I tell you, he's the man for me!" Not long after this meeting, once the insanity of the elections had passed and President Shaggy Dog had retired into private life, Prime Minister Iskander Harappa made Talvar Ulhaq the youngest police chief in the country's history, and also promoted Raza Hyder to the rank of General and placed him in command of the Army. Hyders and Harappas moved north to the new capital in the hills; Isky told Rani, "From now on Raza has no option but to be my man. With the amount of scandal sitting on his head, he knows he'd have been lucky to keep his commission if I hadn't come along."

Haroun Harappa, his heart broken by Good News, flung himself into the party work given him by Iskander, becoming an important figure in the Popular Front; and when, one day, Arjumand declared her love, he told her bluntly, "Nothing I can do. I have decided never to marry." The rejection of the virgin Ironpants by Good News's jilted fiancé engendered in that formidable young woman a hatred of all Hyders which she would never lose; she took the love she had intended to give Haroun and poured it like a votive offering over her father instead. Chairman and daughter, Iskander and Arjumand: "There are times," Rani thought, "when she seems more like his wife than I do." And another unspoken tension in the Harappa camp was that between Haroun Harappa and Talvar Ulhaq, who were obliged to work together, which they did for many years without ever finding it necessary to exchange a single spoken word.

The quiet marriage of Omar Khayyam Shakil and Sufiya Zinobia went off, incidentally, without further incident. But what of Sufiya Zinobia?—Let me just say for the moment that what had reawoken in her did not go back to sleep for good. Her transformation from Miss Hyder into Mrs. Shakil will not be (as we shall see) the last permanent change . . .

And along with Iskander, Rani, Arjumand, Haroun, Raza, Bilquìs, Dawood, Naveed, Talvar, Shahbanou, Sufiya Zinobia and Omar Khayyam, our story now moves north, to the new capital and the ancient mountains of its climactic phase.

Once upon a time there were two families, their destinies inseparable even by death. I had thought, before I began, that what I had on my hands was an almost excessively masculine tale, a saga of sexual rivalry, ambition, power, patronage, betrayal, death, revenge. But the women seem to have taken over; they marched in from the peripheries of the story to demand the inclusion of their own tragedies, histories and comedies, obliging me to couch my narrative in all manner of sinuous complexities, to see my "male" plot refracted, so to speak, through the prisms of its reverse and "female" side. It occurs to me that the women knew precisely what they were up to—that their stories explain, and even subsume, the men's. Repression is a seamless garment; a society which is authoritarian in its social and sexual codes, which crushes its women beneath the intolerable burdens of honour and propriety, breeds repressions of other kinds as well. Contrariwise: dictators are always—or at least in public, on other people's behalf—puritanical. So it turns out that my "male" and "female" plots are the same story, after all.

I hope that it goes without saying that not all women are crushed by any system, no matter how oppressive. It is commonly and, I believe, accurately said of Pakistan that her women are much more impressive than her men . . . their chains, nevertheless, are no fictions. They exist. And they are getting heavier.

If you hold down one thing you hold down the adjoining.

In the end, though, it all blows up in your face.

IV

IN THE FIFTEENTH CENTURY

9

ALEXANDER
THE
GREAT

*I*skander Harappa stands in the foreground, finger pointing towards the future, silhouetted against the dawn. Above his patrician profile the message curls; from right to left the flowing golden shapes. A NEW MAN FOR A NEW CENTURY. The fifteenth century (Hegiran calendar) peeps over the horizon, extending long fingers of radiance into the early sky. The sun rises rapidly in the tropics. And glinting on Isky's finger is a ring of power, echoing the sun . . . the poster is omnipresent, stamping itself on the walls of mosques, graveyards, whorehouses, staining the mind: Isky the sorcerer, conjuring the sun from the black depths of the sea.

What is being born?—A legend. Isky Harappa rising, falling; Isky condemned to death, the world horrified, his executioner drowned in telegrams, but rising above them, shrugging them off, a compassionless hangman, desperate, afraid. Then Isky dead and buried; blind men regain their sight beside his martyr's grave.

And in the desert a thousand flowers bloom. Six years in power, two in jail, an eternity underground . . . the sun sets quickly, too. You can stand on the coastal sandspits and watch it dive into the sea.

Chairman Iskander Harappa, dead, stripped of Pierre Cardin and of history, continues to cast his shadow. His voice murmurs in his enemies' secret ears, a melodious, relentless monologue gnawing their brains like a worm. A ring finger points across the grave, glinting its accusations. Iskander haunts the living; the beautiful voice, golden, a voice holding rays of dawn, whispers on, unsilenced, unstoppable. Arjumand is sure of this. Afterwards, when the posters have been torn down, in the aftermath of the noose which, winding round him like a baby's umbilical cord, maintained such respect for his person that it left no mark upon his neck; when she, Arjumand, has been shut away in once-more-looted Mohenjo, along with a mother who looks like a grandmother and who will not accept her dead husband's divinity; then the daughter remembers, concentrating on details, telling herself the time will come for Iskander to be restored to history. His legend is in her care. Arjumand stalks the brutalized passages of the house, reads cheap love-fiction, eats like a bird and takes laxatives, empties herself of everything to make room for the memories. They fill her up, her bowels, her lungs, her nostrils; she is her father's epitaph, and she knows.

From the beginning, then. The elections which brought Iskander Harappa to power were not (it must be said) as straight-forward as I have made them sound. As how could they be, in that country divided into two Wings a thousand miles apart, that fantastic bird of a place, two Wings without a body, sundered by the land-mass of its greatest foe, joined by nothing but God . . . she remembers that first day, the thunderous crowds around the polling stations. O confusion of people who have lived too long under military rule, who have forgotten the simplest things about democracy! Large numbers of men and women were swept away by the oceans of bewilderment, unable to locate ballot-boxes or even ballots, and failed to cast their votes. Others, stronger swimmers in those seas, succeeded in expressing their preferences twelve or thirteen times. Popular Front workers, distressed by the general lack of electoral decorum, made heroic attempts to save the day. Those few urban constituencies making returns incompatible with the West-Wing-wide polling pattern were visited at night by groups of enthusiastic party members, who helped the returning officers to make a recount. Matters were much clarified in this way. Outside the errant polling stations large numbers of democrats assembled, many holding burning brands above their heads in the hope of shedding new light on the count. Dawn light flamed in the streets, while the crowds chanted loudly, rhythmically, spurring on the returning officers in their labours. And by morning the people's will had been expressed, and Chairman Isky had won a huge and absolute majority of the West Wing's seats in the new National Assembly. *Rough justice*, Arjumand remembers, *but justice all the same.*

The real trouble, however, started over in the East Wing, that festering swamp. Populated by whom?—O, savages, breeding endlessly, jungle-bunnies good for nothing but growing jute and rice, knifing each other, cultivating traitors in their paddies. Perfidy of the East: proved by the Popular Front's failure to win a single seat there, while the riff-raff of the People's League, a regional party of bourgeois malcontents led by the well-known incompetent Sheikh Bismillah, gained so overwhelming a victory that they ended up with more Assembly seats than Harappa had won in the West. *Give people democracy and look what they do with it.* The West in a state of shock, the sound of one Wing flapping, beset by the appalling notion of surrendering the government to a party of swamp aborigines, little dark men with their unpronounceable language of distorted vowels and slurred consonants; perhaps not foreigners exactly, but aliens without a doubt. President Shaggy Dog, sorrowing, dispatched an enormous army to restore a sense of proper proportion in the East.

Her thoughts, Arjumand's, do not dwell on the war that followed, except to note that of course the idolatrous nation positioned between the Wings backed the Eastern bastards to the hilt, for obvious, divide-and-rule reasons. A fearful war. In the West, oil-refineries, airports, the homes of God-fearing civilians bombarded by heathen explosives. The final defeat of the Western forces, which led to the reconstitution of the East Wing as an autonomous (*that's a laugh*) nation and international basket case, was obviously engineered by outsiders: stone-washers and damn-yankees, yes. The Chairman visited the United Nations and bawled those eunuchs out: "You won't destroy us while I'm alive." He stormed out of the General Assembly, handsome, intemperate, great: "My country hearkens for me! Why should I stay in this harem of transvestite whores?"—and returned home to take up the reins of government in what was left of the land of God. Sheikh Bismillah, the architect of division, became chief of the junglees. Later, inevitably, they swarmed into his palace and shot him and his family full of holes. Sort of behaviour one expects from types like that.

The catastrophe: throughout the war, hourly radio bulletins described the glorious triumphs of the Western regiments in the East. On that last day, at eleven a.m., the radio announced the last and most spectacular of these feats of arms; at noon, it curtly informed its audience of the impossible: unconditional surrender, humiliation, defeat. The traffic stood still in city streets. The nation's lunch remained uncooked. In the villages, the cattle went unfed and the crops unwatered despite the heat. Chairman Iskander Harappa, on becoming Prime Minister, correctly identified the national reaction to the astounding capitulation as one of just rage, fuelled by shame. What calamity could have befallen an army so rapidly? What reversal could have been so sudden and so total as to turn victory into disaster in a mere sixty minutes? "Responsibility for that fatal hour," Iskander pronounced, "lies, as it must, at the top." Policemen, also dogs, surrounded the home of ex-President Shaggy within fifteen minutes of this decree. He was taken to jail, to be tried for war crimes; but then the Chairman, reflecting, once again, the mood of a people sickened by defeat and yearning for reconciliation, for an end to analyses of shame, offered Shaggy a pardon in return for his acceptance of house arrest. "You are our dirty laundry," Iskander told the incompetent old man, "but, lucky for you, the people don't want to see you beaten clean upon a stone."

There were cynical people who sneered at this pardon; that is needless-to-say, since all nations have their nihilists. These elements pointed out that Iskander Harappa had been the principal beneficiary of the civil war that ripped his country in half; they spread rumours of his complicity in the whole sad affair. "Shaggy Dog," they muttered in their shabby dens, "was always Harappa's pet; ate out of Isky's hand." Such negativistic elements are an ugly fact of life. The Chairman treated them with contempt. At a rally attended by two million people, Iskander Harappa unbuttoned his shirt. "What have I to hide?" he shouted. "They say I have benefitted; but I have lost fully half my beloved country. Then tell me, is this gain? Is this advantage? Is this luck? My people, your hearts are scarred by grief; behold, my heart bears the same wounds as yours." Iskander Harappa tore off his shirt and ripped it in half; he bared his hairless breast to the cheering, weeping crowd. (The young Richard Burton once did the same thing, in the film *Alexander the Great*. The soldiers loved Alexander because he showed them his battle scars.)

Some men are so great that they can be unmade only by themselves. The defeated Army needed new leadership; Isky packed off the discredited old guard into early retirement, and put Raza Hyder in control. "He will be my man. And with such a compromised leader the Army can't get too strong." This single error proved to be the undoing of the ablest statesman who ever ruled that country which had been so tragically misfortunate, so accursed, in its heads of state.

They could never forgive him for his power of inspiring love. Arjumand at Mohenjo, replete with memories, allows her remembering mind to transmute the preserved fragments of the past into the gold of myth. During the election campaign it had been common for women to come up to him, in full view of his wife and daughter, and declare their love. Grandmothers in villages perched on trees and called down as he passed: "O, you, if I were thirty years younger!" Men felt no shame when they kissed his feet. Why did they love him? "I am hope," Iskander told his daughter . . . and love is an emotion that recognizes itself in others. People could see it in Isky, he was plainly full of the stuff, up to the brim, it spilled out of him and washed them clean.—Where did it come from?—Arjumand knows; so does her mother. It was a diverted torrent. He had built a dam between the river and its destination. Between himself and Pinkie Aurangzeb.

In the beginning Arjumand had hired photographers to snap Pinkie secretly, Pinkie in the bazaar with a plucked chicken, Pinkie in the garden leaning on a stick, Pinkie naked in the shower like a long dried date. She left these pictures for the Chairman to see. "Look, Allah, she's fifty years old, looks a hundred, or seventy anyway, what is kept in her?" In the photographs the face was puffy, the legs vein-scarred, the hair careless, thin, white. "Stop showing me these pictures," Iskander shouted at his daughter (she remembers because he almost never lost his temper with her), "don't you think I know what I did to her?"

If a great man touches you, you age too quickly, you live too much and are used up. Iskander Harappa possessed the power of accelerating the ageing processes of the women in his life. Pinkie at fifty was beyond turkeys, beyond even the memory of her beauty. And Rani had suffered, too, not so badly because she had seen less of him. She had been hoping, of course; but when it became clear that he only wanted her to stand on election platforms, that her time was past and would not return, then she went back to Mohenjo without any argument, becoming once more the mistress of peacocks and game-birds and badminton-playing concubines and empty beds, not so much a person as an aspect of the estate, the benign familiar spirit of the place, cracked and cobwebby just like the ageing house. And Arjumand herself has always been accelerated, mature too young, precocious, quick as needles. "Your love is too much for us," she told the Chairman, "we'll all be dead before you. You feed on us."

But they all outlived him, as it turned out. His diverted love (because he never saw Pinkie again, never lifted a telephone or wrote a letter, her name never passed his lips; he saw the photographs and after that nothing) splashed over the people, until one day Hyder choked off the spring.

It splashed, too, over Arjumand; for whom it was more than enough. She moved in with him to the Prime Minister's residence in the new northern capital, and for a while Rani kept writing to her, suggesting boys, even sending photographs; but Arjumand would return the letters and the photographs to her mother after ripping them to shreds. After several years of tearing potential husbands in half the virgin Ironpants finally defeated Rani's hopes, and was allowed to continue down her chosen road. She was twenty-three when Isky became Prime Minister, she looked older, and although she was still far too beautiful for her own good the passage of time eroded her prospects, and at last she ran out of suitors. Between Arjumand and Haroun nothing more was said. *He tore me in half long ago.*

Arjumand Harappa qualified in the law, became active in the green revolution, threw zamindars out of their palaces, opened dungeons, led raids on the homes of film stars and slit open their mattresses with a long two-edged knife, laughing as the black money poured out from between the pocketed springs. In court she prosecuted the enemies of the state with a scrupulous ferocity that gave her nickname a new and less ribald meaning; once she arrived at her chambers to find that some joker had broken in during the night and had left, standing in the centre of the room, a mocking gift: the lower half of an antique and rusty suit of armour, a pair of satirical metal legs placed at attention, heels together, on the rug. And laid neatly across the hollow waist, a padlocked metal belt. Arjumand Harappa, the virgin Ironpants.

That night she cried, sitting on the floor of her father's study, her head resting on his knee. "They hate me." Iskander grabbed her and shook her until the astonishment dried the tears. "Who hates you?" he demanded. "Just ask that. It is my enemies who are yours, and our enemies are the enemies of the people. Where's the shame in being hated by those bastards?" She understood then how love engenders hate. "I am making this country," Iskander told her quietly, "making it as a man would build a marriage. With strength as well as caring. No time for tears if you're going to help." She wiped her eyes and grinned. "Polygamist," she punched his leg, "what an old-fashioned backward type at heart! It's just marriages and concubines you want. Modern man, my foot."

"Mr. Harappa," the Angrez television interviewer is asking, "many commentators would say, there is a widely held view, some sectors of opinion maintain, your opponents allege, what would you say to the suggestion, that by some standards, from certain points of view, in a way, your style of government might be described as being perhaps, to some extent . . ."

"I see they are sending children to interview me now," Isky interposes. The interviewer has begun to sweat. Off-camera, but Arjumand remembers.

". . . patrician," he finishes, "autocratic, intolerant, repressive?"

Iskander Harappa smiles, sits back in his Louis Quinze chair, sips roohafza from a cut-glass tumbler. "You could say," he replies, "that I do not suffer fools gladly. But, as you see, I suffer them."

Arjumand at Mohenjo replays her father's videotapes. Played in the room where it was made, this conversation overwhelms her, this electronic resurrection by remote control. Yes, he suffered them. His name was etched on history in letters of burning gold; why should he go for brassy types? Here they are on the tape, trust a Western journalist to go digging in the cess-tank and come up holding handfuls of scum. He tortured me, they whine, he fired me, he put me in jail, I ran for my life. Good television: make our leaders look like primitives, wild men, even when they have foreign educations and fancy suits. Yes, always the malcontents, that's all they care about.

He never liked arguments. Do as he ordered and do it now, fut-a-fut, or out on your ear you go. This was as it should be. Look what he had to work with—even his ministers. Turncoats, nest-featherers, quislings, timeservers, the lot of them. He trusted none of these characters, so he set up the Federal Security Force with Talvar Ulhaq at its head. "Information is light," Chairman Iskander Harappa said.

The clairvoyancy of Talvar Ulhaq enabled him to compile exhaustive dossiers on who-was-bribing-whom, on conspiracies, tax evasion, dangerous talk at dinner parties, student sects, homosexuality, the roots of treason. Clairvoyancy made it possible for him to arrest a future traitor before he committed his act of treason, and thus save the fellow's life. The negativist elements attacked the FSF, they would have put out that great cleansing light, so off to jail they went, best place for malcontents. No time for such types during a period of national regeneration. "As a nation we have a positive genius for self-destruction," Iskander told Arjumand once, "we nibble away at ourselves, we eat our children, we pull down anyone who climbs up. But I insist that we shall survive."

"Nobody can topple me," Isky's ghost tells the electronic shade of the Angrez journalist, "not the fat cats, not the Americans, not even you. Who am I? I am the incarnation of the people's love."

Masses versus classes, the age-old opposition. Who loved him? "The people," who are no mere romantic abstractions: who are sensible, and smart enough to know what serves them best. Who loved him? Pinkie Aurangzeb, Rani Harappa, Arjumand, Talvar, Haroun. What dissensions among this quintet!—Between wife and mistress, mother and daughter, jilted Arjumand and jilting Haroun, jilted Haroun and usurping Talvar . . . perhaps, Arjumand muses, his fall was our fault. Through our divided ranks they drove the regiments of his defeat.

They. Fat cats, smugglers, priests. City socialites who remembered his carefree youth and could not tolerate the thought that a great man had sprung out of that debauched cocoon. Factory bosses who had never paid as much attention to the maintenance of their workers as they lavished on the servicing of their imported looms, and whom he, the Chairman, forced to accept the unthinkable, that is, unionization. Usurers, swindlers, banks. The American Ambassador.

Ambassadors: he got through nine of them in his six years. Also five English and three Russian heads of mission. Arjumand and Iskander would place bets on how long each new arrival would survive; then, happy as a boy with a new stick and hoop, he would set about giving them hell. He made them wait weeks for audiences, interrupted their sentences, denied them hunting licences. He invited them to banquets at which the Russian Ambassador was served birds'-nest soup and Peking Duck, while the American got borscht and blinis. He refused to flirt with their wives. With the British Ambassador he would pretend to be a hick just down from the villages, and speak only in an obscure regional dialect; in the case of the United States, however, he took the opposite tack and addressed their legate in incomprehensibly florid French. Embassies would constantly be subjected to power cuts. Isky would open their diplomatic bags and personally add outrageous remarks to the Ambassadors' reports, so that one Russian was summoned home to explain certain unusual theories of his about the parentage of various leading Politburo chiefs; he never returned. The Jack Anderson column in America carried a leaked document in which the U.S. delegate to Iskander's court had apparently confessed that he had long felt a strong sexual attraction towards Secretary Kissinger. That was the end of that Ambassador. "It took time to get into my stride," Iskander admitted to Arjumand, "but once I got the hang of it, those guys never got any sleep."

He had two-way bugs placed in their telephones and after that the Soviet Ambassador was plagued by interminable recordings of *Hail to the Chief* whenever he picked up his receiver, while the American got the complete thoughts of Chairman Mao. He smuggled a series of beautiful young boys into the British Ambassador's bed, much to the consternation, not to say delight, of his wife, who developed thereafter the habit of retiring to her room very early, just in case. He expelled cultural attachés and agricultural attachés. He summoned the Ambassadors to his office at three in the morning and screamed at them until dawn, accusing them of conspiring with religious fanatics and disaffected textile tycoons. He blocked their drains and censored their incoming mail, depriving the English of their subscription copies of horse-racing journals, the Russians of *Playboy* and the Americans of everything else. The last of the nine Americans lasted only eight weeks, dying of a heart attack two days before the coup which dethroned Isky and ended the game. "If I last long enough," the Chairman mused, "maybe I can destroy the whole international diplomatic network. They'll run out of Ambassadors before I run out of steam."

In the fifteenth century a great man came to power. Yes, he seemed omnipotent, he could trifle with the emissaries of the mighty, *Look at me*, he was saying, *you can't catch me*. Immortal, invulnerable Harappa. He gave people pride . . . the tenth American Ambassador arrived after Iskander's arrest, an expression of blessed relief on his face. When he presented his credentials to Raza Hyder he murmured quietly, "Forgive me, sir, but I hope you lack your predecessor's sense of humour."

"The question of national stability," Hyder replied, "is no joke."

Once, when Arjumand visited her father in his hell-hole of a jail, Iskander, bruised, wasted, sick with dysentery, forced a grin to his lips. "This tenth bastard sounds like a real shit," he said painfully. "I wish I could have made it into double figures."

In the fifteenth century . . . but the century did not, despite posters, turn in the year of his accession. That happened later. But such was the impact of his coming that the actual change, thirteen hundred into fourteen hundred, felt like an anticlimax when it finally occurred. *His greatness overpowered Time itself.* A NEW MAN FOR A NEW CENTURY . . . yes, he ushered it in, ahead of Time. But it did the dirty on him. Time's revenge: it hung him out to dry.

They hanged him in the middle of the night, cut him down, wrapped him up and gave him to Talvar Ulhaq, who put him into a plane and flew him to Mohenjo, where two women waited, under guard. When the body had been unloaded the pilot and crew of the Fokker Friendship refused to leave the aircraft. The plane waited for Talvar at the top of Mohenjo's runway, giving off a nervous haze, as if it could not bear to stay in that place an instant longer than necessary. Rani and Arjumand were driven by staff car to Sikandra, that outlying zone of Mohenjo where Harappas had always been buried. And saw amid the marble umbrellas of the tombs a fresh, deep hole. Talvar Ulhaq at attention beside the white-swathed body. Rani Harappa, white-haired now, like the phantom of Pinkie Aurangzeb, refused to cry. "So it's him," she said. Talvar bowed, stiff-necked, from the waist. "Prove it," said Rani Harappa. "Show me my husband's face."

"You should spare yourself," Talvar replied. "He was hanged."

"Be quiet," Rani said. "Pull back the sheet."

"I greatly regret," Talvar Ulhaq bowed again, "but I have orders."

"What orders?" Rani did not raise her voice. "Who can deny me such a thing?" But Talvar said again, "Sincerely. I regret,"